The Horse-Lover's Wife

Julie Bowen Kearney

SILKHAY
PRESS

The Horse-Lover's Wife
First published in Australia by Silkhay Press 2025
www.juliekearney.com.au

A catalogue record for this
book is available from the
National Library of Australia

ISBN: 978-1-7637866-0-8 (pbk)
ISBN: 978-1-7637866-1-5 (ebk)

Typesetting and cover design by Publicious Book Publishing
Published in collaboration with Publicious Book Publishing
www.publicious.com.au

Teachers' notes and reading group notes for
The Horse-Lover's Wife available at
juliekearney.com.au

For Peter

No one knows I have a story. I don't write it down. That is only vanity. Ink will fade and stories writ on paper turn to dust. I tell this story for myself only.

PART 1

Free Agents For Hire
(25 November 1875)

WE CAME down the gangway into an inferno. Zinc roofs blazing and the very shadows on the ground like half-lit withered ghosts. A wind out of an oven bothering our skirts that we must hold tight to on account of the great class of loafers crowded around, whistling and bellowing songs whose words were best forgot.

Hey, Sheila! the men yelled. What's your name, Sheila?

Shut your gobs, Polly shouted back. She was red in the face, we all were from the heat, but hers from temper as well.

The men crowded in, grabbing and pinching, squeezing any parts they could reach. A foul-smelling brute charged at Kitty and yanked her bonnet off her head.

Have you lost your hat, Sheila? he roared through his filthy matted beard, and others took it up.

Have you lost your hat, Sheila, or the other feckin' thing?

It was all the wardsman from the Immigration Depot could do to get us away in good order. He was a big burly man, which was all to the good.

Keep together, girls, he called, swinging his heavy stick. Follow me, he ordered. Quick march now. We'll have you out of here in no time.

Girls around me were sobbing. What the feck? hissed Orla.

The colonial men pursued us, shoving and catcalling, but they weren't so wild when the wardsman halted outside a timber building on a steep street. They fell back muttering when the door opened and a woman appeared, dressed from head to toe in black widow's weeds. A small, skinny woman with a ramrod straight back, she had a level gaze that pierced you through and could stop anyone in their tracks.

As soon as we were safe inside we swarmed around her, clamouring and wailing while we wiped the sweat off our faces and shook dust from our hopsack skirts. The noise coming from seventy-seven mouths was enough to deafen anyone. Girls collapsing and crying in huddles, it was bedlam for a time. Till the heat got the better of us and we quietened down under our new Matron's direction.

Mrs Morphy, her name was. A strict woman who didn't like to hear talk of complaints.

And what is the matter with Townsville anyway? she said quite sharp to Polly who was complaining the loudest, about how we'd been carried past Brisbane. And told her she was to blame for not making proper inquiries in the first place, as to which port our ship was bound for.

One at a time, she ordered, and said tea was on the boil in the kitchen and drinking water on the bench for those that needed it. For girls were groaning and fanning themselves with their skirt hems, and Lizzie Doyle had quietly fainted and lay stretched out on the floor.

Stop! Mrs Morphy cried when Bridget bent over a barrel in the corner.

Bridget pointed at the queue waiting to get at the water pails. The look on her perspiring face said it all.

That's washing water and don't you forget it, Mrs Morphy scolded. Remember that, girls. On no account drink from the barrel if you want to be on your feet tomorrow. You'll be no use to your employer or anyone else. The Queensland government don't give you free passage to have you die on them.

There weren't enough stretcher-beds to go round—they hadn't expected so many, Mrs Morphy said—and Ellen and I were among the ones counted off to sleep on the floor. Which was no bother to us as we were used to that article at home. I gave Ellen the benefit of an older sister's advice while we were on our knees, stuffing straw in the sacks the wardsman had lugged in to be made into pallets.

It's God's will, Ellie, I said. You'd better forget any schemes you're hatching. If Dev jumps ship they'll catch him for sure and put him in irons. You don't want that for him, do you?

I'd lie down in nettles for him, Ellen said, sending red sparks from her eyes. But don't fret yourself, I'm not planning on doing a bolt with him. That dream has gone to smash.

True for you, I thought. Or maybe not. Maybe it was a scalding lie. I couldn't guess which. She was determined to marry her sailor friend, that much I did know.

We must have made a sorry if comical sight at midday, as the Townsville men would have known, since they were pressed up at the curtainless windows, watching us struggle to fry the great lumps of flesh-meat we had never cooked before. The pots and pans in the kitchen proved wobbly or missing their handles, and caused more than a few burnt fingers and cries of pain. And as many loud guffaws from the watchers outside the windows.

Mrs Morphy was quick to disclaim any fault on Townsville's part.

These pans have nothing to do with us, she declared. They were sent up by steamer from Brisbane.

But no one, not even Polly, got cranky the once. We were that glad to be off the *Kapunda* and walking about on dry land.

The Captain must have let the single men off the ship next, for they turned up in the afternoon and straightaway made a mighty nuisance of themselves. Singing rude songs outside the windows like the Townsville lads, and getting into fights with the latter, owing to some joke that was played on them at the waterfront. The wardsman refused to tell us what.

No prize for knowing the Cavan and Leitrim boys wouldn't take being made fools of like meek lambs. Meek lambs the Irish have never been, and after three months' enforced abstinence on board the *Kapunda* they were fighting drunk besides, and up for all games. One passerby fell off his pennyfarthing bicycle from the single men's attentions, which brought an Inspector of Nuisances along on another one, to haul the wrongdoers to jail.

We had a ringside seat to watch the sparring going on between the single men and colonial men. Any number of drunken carousers facing off up and down the steep street. The men might stare at us through the windows, but we could look too, and found them uncouth and wild. Girls gathered in knots, sharing their alarm at the brawls breaking out on the street, with only a thin timber wall separating us from the fists.

Making an unholy spectacle of themselves, Polly said. You'd think we were watching a Punch and Judy show.

Without the Judy, said Kitty wonderingly.

Ain't no woman fool enough to walk out there, Lizzie Doyle said.

I'm scared, whispered Bridget. I want to go home.

We were in a dusty class of habitation. An abandoned printery, judging by the sign on the door, but better than the single men's quarters any rate. All they had were tents along the seashore, so Mrs Morphy told.

And some of them rotten I believe, she said. And others only flys without ropes.

A small smile flitted across her lips. Oh yes, the mozzies will feast on the Irish lads tonight, but you girls are fortunate. The Townsville ladies have rallied on your behalf and donated their spare muskito-nets.

She paused to let this sink in, and said abruptly, I only tell you so you can be properly grateful.

But when it came time to disrobe and let down the muslin nets, many proved sadly dilapidated. Mrs Morphy surveyed the rents and gaping holes and looked pained.

Immigrants cannot expect luxuries, she said, though I do believe the muskito-nets are quite disgraceful.

Stripped down to our chemises, and drawers if we wore them, we had no choice but to crawl under the holey nets onto the stretcher-beds and pallets.

Wha's that? Ellen mumbled in the darkness. I lifted my head, heard something heavy falling. A man's voice cursing.

We are attacked! a girl cried.

A sudden smell of alcohol. Dimly lit figures were crawling through the windows. Girls were screaming, flailing and twisting in the arms of grunting men. Polly screeching in the darkness, *Get your maulies off me, you depraved maggot!*

And still more figures climbing through the windows. Impossible to know if they were friend or foe till I heard Irish voices and knew it was the single men. Come to our rescue.

The single men and local men closed in battle, and a great fight erupted among the stretcher-beds and pallets. Sickening crunches of bone on bone, guttural yells from those on the receiving end. Fearful sounds to hear in the dark and no way of knowing when a fist or elbow or boot would land on you instead.

Being at the back of the room Ellen and I were so far untouched, but now the men were almost upon us. Our only hope lay in finding a place of safety.

But where was safe? The door was locked. Under the stretcher-beds? The walls?

I felt for and found Ellen in the darkness, tugged her chemise to alert her to my plan. Making myself small as possible I squeezed between the grappling bodies, guessing from the looming shapes when to duck and weave. Heading for the nearest wall. Getting knocked sideways, staggering on.

Ellen followed close behind, clutching the back of my chemise.

A hand grabbed my breast and I poked a finger in the owner's eye, screaming, *Get away off of me!*

Other girls fell to their knees and crawled under the stretcher-beds. I heard their gasps and frantic slithering and almost trod on a girl in front of me. Someone was shrieking at the top of her voice.

Bridget was it?

Whistles shrilled and the door flew open that forceful it knocked Orla to the floor. She was giving out the spake, and Polly adding choice words of her own as to the celery sauce she would make of their gizzards. Though not such choice words, for it was police constables the girls were scolding, come to join in the fray. And by the oaths and cries the colonial police let out subsequent they must have been sadly used for their pains.

Ellen and I reached the wall at the moment a great roar of a bellow resounded in the room. Sure, the man's mother must have heard his cry in Ireland, it was that loud.

You bastard! he screamed. You bit my ear off!

It was on for young and old till the wardsman and Mrs Morphy in a white nightdress with her hair wrapped in curling-papers came running with lanterns. And what a spectacle then. All the hairy-faced men lepping out the windows and skiddering through the door like so many rabbits.

In the upshot and shouting and weeping and wailing the wardsman lost his temper and gave Polly and Orla notice they were discharged from the Depot.

For using language, he said when they screamed at him, wanting to know why. Girls your age! he scolded. To even know such words. You'll be turned out of doors in the morning.

Half naked girls sobbed in each other's arms. Bridget and Sheila had to have smelling salts held under their noses by Mrs Morphy to stop their shrieks. Blood ran down Orla's neck and her right eye was swelling up. Meg Byrne was crouched in a corner, white-faced and gasping. She was hiding under a stretcher-bed when two men crashed onto it.

The muskito-nets lay torn and trampled on the floor. If not for Mrs Morphy offering her precious vial of Ceylonese citronella, to smear the fierce-smelling oil on our limbs, none of us would have slept that night owing to the whining little devils. Though later I woke up, covered in sweat, and heard shudders and groans and stifled sobs coming from the stretcher-beds and pallets around me. It seemed not too many of us could sleep anyway.

Next morning, at breakfast, Mrs Morphy announced the ear-chewing cannibal had been arrested and would be sentenced by the magistrate that very morning. We weren't to worry on that score because larrikins got short shrift in Townsville, it being a respectable town or trying to be.

What about us? Polly demanded, laying down her porridge spoon. Will the men be charged for breaking into our quarters? Not forgetting the way we were knocked to the floor and trampled underfoot by their hobnailed boots. Aren't we to get justice too?

Mrs Morphy drew herself up. You still have your two ears, I see.

Polly gaped at her. They were planning to rape us, you know yourself.

But they didn't, countered Mrs Morphy. You need to toughen up, miss, if you want to get any kind of foothold in this town. Only mawkish women make the mistake of expecting justice here. If it's justice you're after you must arrange that yourself.

She turned away. Don't dilly-dally, girls. Eat up quick. We have to set the place tidy before the hiring starts. You got a big day ahead of you. Say goodbye to your friends now for likely you won't see them tonight.

After breakfast Polly and Orla put on their shawls and took up their swags. Their plan was to obtain shelter at an inn if they could find one with locks on the bedroom doors.

Mrs Morphy reckoned that was highly unlikely.

Townsville has only six pubs, she said, and every one of them on the waterfront, an area shunned by decent woman. And I have it on good account they're all crawling with cockroaches, and the walls and ceilings are permanently blackened by flies.

She gave Polly and Orla the name of a 'halfway tolerable' boarding house in a quieter part of town, for which they were grateful and thanked her. Polly went so far as to put aside her rebel airs and give our Matron a hug. I had to smother my laughter at the look of astonishment and confusion on Mrs Morphy's face.

Armed with her valuable information, Polly and Orla went out to the footpath where a couple of single men were waiting to escort them. The single men were much in favour now, regarded as heroes owing to their gallant defence of our maidenhood, and unbeknown to anyone, amid last night's uproar, Polly had contrived to meet up with these two. The colonial police had left the front door wide open wouldn't you know, and a girl could slip out unnoticed if she had a mind to.

Well done, I congratulated Polly silently. The single men she had found and chatted with on the pavement looked to be a sturdy class of lad and respectful in their manners, just as their mammies in Ireland would want them to be. Polly and Orla stood a better chance of surviving now.

Polly's friends crowded outside to wave goodbye.

Good luck to yous! she called. This is a mad old place right enough. Take care will yez.

I watched the little party of four walk down the street and disappear round a corner. What chance would I ever see Polly or Orla again?

Come inside, girls, ordered Mrs Morphy. You have thirty minutes to tidy yourselves before the wardsman opens the door for the hiring.

A mad rush then, frantic jostling around the cracked mirror that hung on a nail on the kitchen wall. Much shouting and shoving till we were all thoroughly flustered and over-heated. Then we squeezed together on forms pushed up against the walls, in a room the wardsman had cleared for the purpose.

Mrs Morphy marched up and down, inspecting us in our rows. Feet together, no crossed ankles, she barked.

When she was satisfied with our appearance she stood before us, straight as a stick, and told us the going rates for general servants and nursemaids, and the higher amounts if we went to the bush.

You'll do well to keep your wits sharp, she said. Girls have been tricked often enough by low wages, or paid less than agreed. Or not paid at all.

She glanced at the window through which we could see a portly red-faced gentleman in white mopping his brow with a white handkerchief. Pressed up behind him, a crowd of women also wearing white, and a number of gentlemen the same, were staring at us through the glass panes.

I see the Immigration Doctor has arrived, come to give you the benefit of his advice, Mrs Morphy said. But first I'll give you mine.

She lowered her voice and we leaned in to listen.

Australia is a new country, she said, which some reckon is a great one, as I myself believe. It has no wild beasts to speak of, nor wolves neither, except those in sheep's clothing if you take my meaning.

We looked at one another, whispering.

You're to mingle with the ladies and gents, that is required, but if you've got any sense you'll steer clear of the single men wanting housekeepers. Likely they have other duties in mind.

While we were digesting this information the wardsman unlocked the door to let in the Immigration Doctor, closing it quick to stop the women in white from following. The Immigration Doctor turned out to be none other than Dr Salmond, the man who came on board our ship in Keppel Bay and wrote down our complaints. A ripple of nudges and murmurs ran through the girls. He must have travelled up with us on the ship.

He stood in the middle of the room, thumbs stuck in the armholes of his white waist-coat, and talked about the fine new Immigration Depot that was being built in Townsville, which would be open for business in the new year.

In the meantime, he huffed, you must make do with Mr Hanran's printing-house and think yourselves lucky to do so. You may leave if you wish. You're free agents of course, but you risk being tricked by any sharper in town. You'll find yourselves fair game outside these walls. Dogs may be set on you. You may be hunted down with pleasure. But inside these premises you're safe—

Girls tittered at this and Ellen gave her snort, which made Dr Salmond stop speaking and frown at her.

In my experience, he said, blowing out his moustaches, immigrant girls are credulous and easily impressed, so it's in your interest to have government protection until you find yourselves situations. But I must warn you, the wardsman has been instructed to dismiss any girl who refuses fair wages. You'll be sent away just like those two troublemakers this morning.

He jutted out his chin and took himself off, and when he was safely departed through the back door, the wardsman opened the street door to let in the servant-hungry townsfolk.

In they pushed in their finery, the colonial ladies in white gowns and hats and gloves the same. Most of the men likewise in white shirts and trousers, and white waistcoats if they wore them. The unwashed dun-coloured mob that had shoved us on the wharf and broken into our sleeping quarters was nowhere to be seen. Lying low probably, to escape the attentions of the colonial police.

Most of us hung back on giving answers to the lonesome men who wanted housekeepers, though I noticed Caity disappear discreetly to pack her swag and depart with her new master. We were the lionesses of the day you might think. Sheep corralled for auction more like, but either way, everyone wanted a piece of us. You could hardly hear yourself speak from all the haggling going on with the Townsville ladies.

For Mrs Morphy's words made us want to try our luck with the women, even the beady-eyed ones who drove hard bargains.

Can you cook? one lady asked me. She seemed almost to count my teeth like a farmer on horse market day.

Yes, ma'am, I said. I cooked at home.

Can you scrub, wash and do the ironing?

Sure I can, ma'am, I said, though I lied about the ironing.

So you're able to do the work of a general servant?

Yes, ma'am.

But when I told her twelve shillings a week same as Mrs Morphy advised, the lady almost dropped her fancy reticule in astonishment.

What? Twelve shillings a week! she said. Why, I can get servants thoroughly acquainted with the ways of the colony for less.

Well, ma'am, I said, I hope you can but it won't be me.

She wagged a white-gloved finger at me. You must realise you'll be no use to your mistress to begin with. A government pauper like yourself!

She bustled her way through the crowd.

Such ladies, Ellen said under her breath. Sure, they never had a shite like the rest of us.

Shush, Ellie, I said. Let me do the talking.

I could see she was in a dangerous mood and tried to keep by her if I could. I had it fixed in my heart we wouldn't be parted, but find situations under the same roof. But the one time I settled on an arrangement with a stout lady that had Ellen or myself acting as cook, my sister provoked her.

I've not come all this way to slave over an oven for nothing, she said, staring the lady down. I want sixteen shillings a week and full board.

But that's absurd, the lady replied. I can get the best cook in town for fourteen.

And how do you know I ain't a good cook? Ellen said. It's a wonder you come to the Depot if you can get one for less.

So off went the lady in a huff, and when I tried to reason with my sister she only tossed her head, and gave as her opinion we would have to be very low on offers and certifiable mentally to get stuck with an old sourpuss like that.

But while she was gabbing her nonsense I noticed a gentleman on the other side of the room. He was turning a woven-leaf hat in his hands and staring at me.

The force of his gaze had me wondering if he was some sort of crank or lady's man, yet I didn't look away. He was attractive enough with his piercing gaze and unruly moustache. The body on him limber under a creased blue shirt and moleskin trousers.

He kept up his stare till the heat mounting my cheeks obliged me to turn away.

Oh Ellen, you would drive a saint in Heaven wild! was all I could think to say in my confusion.

What with her carry-on we signed no papers that day, as most of the girls did, and after dinner Ellen brushed out her hair and twisted it up in front of the cracked mirror in the kitchen.

I'm just off to the jacks, she said. Be back soon.

On my own, she said when I told her I would come too. And was gone out the door in a flash.

I knew she was going to Dev and tried to follow, but Mrs Morphy stopped me, saying I must apply for a key same as my sister had done. And no surprise to find the backyard empty when I got outside.

A dog was howling in the darkness when I saw her coming home—if Mr Hanran's abandoned printery could be called home. I had sat at the window for hours, and now, in the yellow glare of the street-lamp, I saw my sister returning on unwilling feet, handcuffed between two police constables. Her hair hanging down in dishevelled locks and tears falling from her like a mountain stream.

The constables delivered her into Mrs Morphy's sleepy care.

Bit of a she-cat, this one, the older man grumbled.

I didn't know whether to hug or slap Ellen. But my body did. My arms went out, wrapping her in a fierce hug, while Mrs Morphy watched on like a wise woman.

Ellen pulled out of my arms, a raving lunatic from the pain of love.

They've taken him, she cried. Oh Annie, what will I do?

She went on sobbing and wouldn't be stopped. I'm twenty-two and ever so healthy, she raved. How can I live the long years without him? I'll *kill* myself so I will! I'll kill myself!

No one slept much that night from her keening, and from wondering what the next day would bring.

Alone Among Strangers

YOU ARE still here, said the gentleman, taking off his cabbage-tree hat. I thought you might be gone by now. I saw you yesterday with your friend, talking with a lady.

We are still here, I said. My friend, my sister, is resting from the heat.

I'm sorry to hear it.

He was not a tall man but not short neither, and by his voice a gentleman. An Irish one at that.

Well now, he said, fingering his hat, I'm looking for a housekeeper. I have a property south of here and require the services of one. Would that suit you?

I didn't answer. I was tired from all the devilry and mayhem of the last two nights, and not so quick on the uptake as might be, or I would have walked away at once.

Would you be interested at all?

I must stay with my sister, I said. She is unwell.

Oh the heat is very bad, he agreed. The new chums feel it mightily at first.

I'm not fitted for housekeeping duties, sir. Only cleaning and wash-day work if required.

Now tell me, he said, you're not a Westmeath girl are you, by any chance? I fancy I recognise that accent. I've not heard it in a while.

I'm from Cavan.

Ah, next door then. The Cavan lads are a wild lot, I hear. He smiled when he said that, to show he was jesting.

The lively eyes of him. Looking at me. And myself in a fine moil under my brown hopsack gown, though I looked back at him steady enough. But a housekeeper! His *hoor*? That wasn't for me, not ever. I wasn't that class of obliging woman.

I'm sorry, sir. I don't think I shall suit, I said, and walked away.

He followed me even so. Miss Callahan, he said, that is your name I know, Mrs Morphy has told me. Perhaps you would consider another arrangement. Marriage perhaps. That is what I meant to say.

Then why didn't you? I thought.

The two of us facing on the dusty floorboards. Taking each other's measure.

I have a farmstead close to the amenities of town, he said, matter of fact. A hundred acres of good grazing land on permanent water. A horse-farm breeding bloodstock horses, with pedigree bulls as a sideline. Freehold you understand. No landlord to pay rent to. What do you say?

I was giving him the full stare by now. Was he a lord to be paying no rent? There was no smell of drink on him, only the smell of soap which pleased me. Men that wash are better than men that stink of their own sweat, and there was plenty of that commodity in Australia for the smelling of, whether you wished to or not.

Well now, he said. Are you with me, lass? I don't propose every day so I'm waiting on your answer.

No words would come to me, I was that taken aback.

A kind of craziness took over me, to have the thing I lacked. A husband the likes of him, and land as well. A hundred acres of it if he was to be believed. Dada and Uncle Michael made do with twenty-two between them and owned not a single one. This was a very strange nation I had come to, I realised, where gentlemen ask servant-girls to wed. Though I didn't forget that gentlemen are no different to ordinary men and no more to be trusted.

A cold feeling came in my stomach like water rising up.

She is always married too soon that gets a bad husband. She is never married too late that gets a good one. Mam used to say that.

It seemed to me everything was back to front and upside down in Australia. I was twenty-four and alone in a wild-mannered country, and must go careful with what I said. If I agreed to marry this man I would be safe from the brawlers with their roaming hands. And Ellen too, I would make sure of that. I could write to my father and tell him to fret no more, because an Irishman had given me the protection of his name. And I remembered the men in the Corcashel townland I used to swoon in the arms of in my dreams, who were not so fine as the one before me.

Which church would that be, sir? I asked. Would it be Catholic or Protestant?

Whatever you wish, Miss Callahan, he said back, quick as you like. One church is as good as another to me, for there are none in the bush and I've spent the last seven years wandering that wilderness without the benefit of sermons.

But what do folk do on Sunday?

He laughed. Sleep in if they choose, or take a swim in a creek. There's no one to say otherwise.

I suppose it's no sin if there's no priest, I said, doubtful all the same. And I inquired was there a church near his dwelling-place.

As to that, you can rest easy. You can have the buggy on Sundays and a man at the reins for your safety.

And for my sister? I asked, holding his gaze. If I agree to marry you, she must come too.

She must of course, he said. There can be no other arrangement. She shall stay with us at Serpentine Water and make herself useful to you in the house while she's about it.

I wouldn't want my sister to be treated as a servant.

Useful to you as a companion I mean. I have a very good cook and general servant who take care of house duties.

Where is your farmstead, sir? I asked, thinking it could be anywhere in this sprawling country.

Back came his answer, pat. We're only three miles from town. An easy drive, it wouldn't inconvenience you.

Excuse me, Mr Wilson, said Mrs Morphy, appearing beside him in her black bombazine gown.

Certainly, ma'am, he replied, inclining his head.

Allow me to introduce you, she said briskly, and turned to me. Miss Callahan, this is Mr Wilson. Mr Wilson, may I present Miss Callahan.

She bustled away through the dwindling crowd.

Wilson? What kind of name was that? So not the true Irish after all. Anglo-Irish for sure, and almost certainly Protestant. Which gave me a reason to dislike him.

I saw the amusement in his eyes. We're respectable now, he said. Officially introduced.

I didn't smile back.

Is it the sunstroke afflicts your sister? he asked. For that could take a while to get over, and I was hoping to put you on a steamer going south tomorrow. That is, if you're willing. I've finished my business here and must be back in Rockhampton as quick as I can.

Not sunstroke exactly, I said, thinking fast. Just the prickly heat troubling my sister, and not so bad as would prevent her from travelling.

Thinking in my heart tomorrow was a very speedy business and too sudden altogether. For myself as well as Ellen. I was beginning to consider more carefully what I was getting into and whether I should get into it at all.

I must go to my sister, I said.

Mr Wilson wafted his hat to cool his brow and said he would return in the afternoon for my answer.

Don't disappear till I get back, he said.

The way he smiled it wasn't an order. More like a wry request. A joke we might share if the risk of my accepting a better offer in his absence wasn't so real.

I watched him cross the room at an easy pace, nodding polite to Mrs Morphy along the way. In a very great dither I hurried off to find Ellen, wondering what to say.

My sister was lying on a stretcher-bed, her eyes shut fast, but she sat up quick enough when I rushed into the room. Not having the time to be choosing my words I told her straight about Mr Wilson, and she flew into a temper at once. Which comforted me, to see her no longer prostrate, but back in her old fighting form.

Is it led on by blarney you are to think of marrying a stranger? she shouted. And a Proddy at that. You'd be mad if you did. Why, you don't even love him!

Love has done you no great service, I thought, but said, He's a clean man with mannerly ways, and it's my life will be spent with him and I shall do so if I choose.

But to agree at the outset! Ellen cried. No man will respect a girl who gives herself up at the first shot. He'll think you're a soft daft slut and why wouldn't he if you don't make inquiries as to his character?

She went on with a lot more that was true, as I knew in my heart it was. Any girl, she scolded, even one with a humped back or broken character, could get herself married in this country bereft of females. A blind lass couldn't fail to notice the scarcity.

You can pick and choose, you eejit, she said, so why would you want to fall prey to the first Proddy that presents himself?

She ran out of breath and slumped down on the stretcher-bed. Looked at me with mournful eyes.

Oh Annie, she said. We're alone among strangers.

We clung to each other then, Ellen crying and myself thinking about Mr Wilson. About his wavy brown hair and his eyes with the twinkle at the back of them, and the voice of him issuing forth from under his moustache. Deep as bog water and dark as Dada's pipe tobacco. Hearing it in my head again.

Ah, there you are, Miss Callahan, said Mrs Morphy, rustling into the room in her black widow's cap and buttoned-up black gown. Your sister is at it again I see. Well, what's done can't be undone I always say.

What would you know about it? Ellen said between sobs.

You must bear up and be resigned to your situation, Mrs Morphy told her. Don't begin any of your nonsense with me for no one cares or will listen if you do.

Sure, you're making all the row yourself.

Mrs Morphy quelled Ellen with one of her death stares.

Of all the impudent females who come out here to be servants. You'll hold your tongue, miss, if you know what's good for you. I've not come here to speak to you any rate.

She turned to me. I'd like a word with you in the front parlour, Miss Callahan, if I may.

And out the door she swished, myself following like a rowboat trailing in a ship's wake.

But when we were sitting in the little office-room she used as her parlour, Mrs Morphy put aside her law-di-daw manner and permitted herself a smile.

You have made a conquest, she said. A respectable gent too. Mr Wilson has asked me to have a word with you as to his character.

My heart started jumping about. Do you know him? I asked.

Oh I do, I do indeed, she said, fanning herself. Not personally of course, but my late husband had dealings with him about the cattle. Mr Wilson has been coming up this way for years with his livestock, and Mr Morphy often helped him with the yarding and such. Your gentleman is in the way of droving breeding bulls and thoroughbred horses up north, him and his offsider Harry Roche. They go all the way up past the Kennedy River I believe, through some very wild country. Though he's never had any trouble with the natives. Knows how to get on with them he told Mr Morphy. Well that don't surprise me. Mr Wilson gets on with everyone it seems.

She swiped her fan at a persistent fly. Oh yes, you've done well, girl, to nab him with them big soulful eyes of yours. You was in the right place at the right time.

I tucked Mrs Morphy's words away like a squirrel hides its nuts.

There's no need to return to the levee room, she said. You might like to go shopping instead, for the articles you will require. A proper straw hat perhaps, you'll need one in this climate. The English bonnet is useless here. And a puggaree to keep off the flies that I know Mr Wilmett has in stock, owing to a shipment has just arrived from down south.

This seemed to me an excellent plan as I had at that moment a great wish to appear presentable in Mr Wilson's eyes. And not only in a new straw hat but in a white gown same as the colonial ladies wore.

I thanked Mrs Morphy and hurried out to the backyard. Trembling at my daring, I locked myself in the jacks and unstitched one of Dada's pound notes from my skirt hem. Then ventured forth into the blistering streets to find Mr Wilmett's store.

The metal roofs shimmered in the heat and I was much in fear of the rough men, so kept my eyes about me. But there were none to be seen and might have been only a nightmare I had dreamed for all their whereabouts. Not a man or woman or dog stirred in the dusty street. All that moved was a billy goat in the shadow of an alleyway, chewing on something I thought it better not to look at too close. Though it might be it was only newspapers the animal was eating, that were on top of that thing. Flies swarmed over it, that was all I knew, and a smell coming off it that made me hurry past holding my nose. Stenches were everywhere in this town. The wonder was the citizens were still alive and not wiped out by plague.

I looked about very curious at the weatherboard shops with their verandahs and iron awnings. How flimsy they were, nothing like the buildings at home. Though the one called Vincent's Dance Hall wasn't so different from the Palace of Dance in Ballyconnell, that is only a shed itself. Then I found Wilmett's Store and bought two straw hats and two puggarees of green muslin to wind around them, and had a long bit of a yarn with the woman of the shop, till I chose a length of white voile and the makings to go with it.

Heart beating fast, I carried the parcel back to the Depot and showed Ellen her new hat. She refused to look at it but for once I took no notice of her sulks. So strong was my desire to have the new gown the billowy fabric was pinned and cut before a girl came to the door to say I was wanted in Mrs Morphy's parlour.

Which made my heart break into a gallop to think it might be Mr Wilson. Come back as promised.

It was himself right enough. As soon as I entered the room he stepped forward and held out a parcel.

I have taken the liberty of purchasing a few items, he said in his deep voice. It occurred to me that you and your sister could do with a cooler style of dress.

Oh no, sir, I said. I cannot accept gifts from a gentleman.

If we are to be wed there can be no impropriety, he said. And I very much hope we are.

He searched my face. Are we to marry, Miss Callahan?

We are, yes, Mr Wilson.

You are quite certain? he asked.

I am, yes, quite certain, I said.

At that he put the parcel in my hands and seemed pleased, and nothing was said for a moment.

He looked at me and I gazed back.

I'll not be travelling with you on the steamer, he said. Have to return the way I came.

On horseback did he mean? Right, so, I said.

Which will take longer, so I'll send a telegraph message to arrange for your lodging on arrival.

And for my sister, I reminded him.

For you both. Parts' Boarding House it's called. A respectable family hotel with no alcohol allowed. You'll find it in East-street in the centre of town.

East-street, I repeated, looking at his eyes. Bluish brown with little flecks of gold. Hazel, you'd call the colour.

I must leave you now, he said. Have to get down to the wharf to sort out your tickets. Which reminds me. How do you spell your name? With a *g*?

Without the *g*.

And your first name? He hesitated. The initial will do, if you prefer.

It's Annie, I said. My sister's name is Ellen.

Annie, he repeated, staring at me. Well ... goodbye then, Miss Callahan. We will meet again in Rockhampton. I hope your voyage is a comfortable one.

I watched him leave the room and stride across the hall to the front door. Then he was gone.

When I opened the parcel Ellen and I gasped in delight. Two ladies' gowns with lace at the neck and little bustles at the back. Made of fine Indian muslin in the latest style, according to Mrs Morphy. The handful of girls still at the Depot crowded round just to touch the gossamer folds.

Mrs Morphy watched on in silence.

One gown was pale blue and the other dazzling white, and I knew at once I must have the white one to be my wedding gown. Which pleased Ellen for she had a hankering for the blue. But that wasn't all. We found two pair of ladies' shoes in good thin leather, though misfortunately they didn't fit. Neither of us had small feet, being barefoot girls who grew up without the constriction of shoes.

Mrs Morphy picked up a shoe and examined the sole.

These boots were bought at Trimball's store, she declared. If you're quick about it you can take them back and change them.

So we did that, and carried our new shoes out of the shop, very pleased with ourselves.

I think a horse couldn't carry all the money your man has, Ellen said as we walked back to the Depot. The Protestant English always do well for themselves.

Mr Wilson's not English, I said

Ellen snorted. I'll go bail he is if he's rich and has a name like that. English or Scottish for sure.

That night I dreamed a vivid dream. I'm back in Ballyconnell at the Palace of Dance, watching the dancers dip and twirl. Their shoes make no sound on the floor and the dust flies up around them in showers of gold motes. It is eerie watching the couples circle the floor in their silence, as if they are unreal: a picture of people who no longer exist, seen through the lens of a Magic Lantern. But now the dance is over and I leave the dance hall and find myself in the night-dark streets of Townsville. I must get to the wharf for I am to travel by sea to meet Mr Wilson astride a white stallion, riding by land to meet me. I go up one alleyway and down another, searching for the wharf, while all around me in the darkness the dancers are making their way home. They know where they're going but I do not. I pass wooden cottages with a stern billy-goat standing guard at each gate, bleating *Beware! Beware!* and find I can't walk at the proper pace. My steps become slower and slower until my feet stop in mid air and cannot continue.

Then the fear of not reaching the ship wakes me, and I find myself under the shawls of the mended muskito-net, and hear Ellen's slow breathing in my ear.

Servantalism

MRS MORPHY came down to the wharf to see us off, which she didn't do as a rule she said, but since four girls were leaving she considered it proper. There were Ellen and myself of course, and Bridget and Isabelle returning to Brisbane as they had good reason to do. Bridget had a situation waiting for her in that town, and Isabelle a fiancé, affianced to her by mail.

I shan't forget Mrs Morphy's kindness, the way she hustled the dock men to make sure our luggage was put on board the SS *Boomerang*, for our ship boxes still lay in a shed on the wharf and had to be dragged out of its darkness under her supervision.

She spoke to each of us in turn and wished us good fortune in our new lives, and waited on the wharf to wave goodbye. An upright black-clad figure, fluttering a white, lace-edged handkerchief.

I stood at the ship rail, returning her waves until she became a blur.

Ellen and I never saw Bridget and Isabelle after that. They were travelling in steerage while we were very grand on the poop deck with the first-class passengers, and had a cabin to ourselves, and other comforts like pillows and hooks for our clothes. At night we put on our lightsome muslin gowns and calfskin shoes, and went upstairs to the dining room.

In the doorway we hesitated, startled by the sight of so many well-dressed people. A sea of white tablecloths stretched into the distance, glittering with stemmed glasses and silverware.

Just remember, I told Ellen from the side of my mouth, we don't have to drink from those glasses if they put intoxicating liquor in them.

We had both sworn a solemn vow to our parish priest never to touch alcohol.

So many nobs, Ellen muttered.

The men at table wore cream suits and had brightly coloured sashes wound round their waists. The women were very elegant in pale evening gowns, with scented flowers in their hair or in their bodices where the bosoms begin. They were bold, the women, flirting with the men, tapping their starched shirt fronts with painted fans. A delicate swooning scent from their nosegays floated across to us in the doorway.

A man—a servant?—approached. He had a cloth folded over one arm, though otherwise he looked as dapper as the gentlemen diners.

What's he coming over here for? Ellen said. Is he going to kick us out?

The same thought had occurred to me but I took heart from our store-bought gowns, and from knowing we had gone to some trouble with our hair. Twisting it up in imitation of the ladies at the Depot, and allowing curls to fall down the back in a style we had seen on a girl on the poop deck. No flowers in our hair though—our one mistake. We hadn't known about the Indian fashion of wearing scented flowers in the evening, and couldn't have laid hands on any if we had.

We have first-class tickets, I reminded Ellen. If this fellow says anything we shall tell him so. If necessary we can go back to our cabin and get the tickets to prove it.

The man arrived and stood before us. Swept a bow.

Good evening, ladies, he said. May I escort you to your table?

Ellen giggled and I gave her a sharp nudge.

You may, I said.

He led us across the room to a table, where he pulled out two chairs and we sat down with the ladies and gentlemen. Very law-di-daw.

Isn't that the Captain there, at the head of the table? Ellen asked in a low voice. I didn't answer, being occupied checking what the others were doing with their squares of starched white cloth.

The gentleman seated between us inclined his head to each of us in turn. Allow me to introduce myself, he said. Rawson's the name.

Mine is Annie, I told him.

And I'm Ellen, said Ellen. Pleased to meet you, Rawson. I like your waist sash, sir.

The sepoy style, he said, smiling at her. All the rage this season. And if I may return the compliment, it's a pleasure finding myself seated next to two such fashionable young ladies as yourselves.

Hearing this exchange, the lady sitting across from us frowned. Will you be staying for the concert after dinner, Lancelot? she asked.

Ellen and I exchanged glances. Didn't he just say his name was Rawson? Whatever it was, the lady started a conversation with him and never once included us in her line of sight.

Another gentleman further along the table was holding forth. A dour, shaggy-browed fellow, not one any woman would dare to tap with her fan.

Separation from New South Wales had been the making of Brisbane, all the benefits go to its pockets, he was giving out in a gravelly voice.

Darn right they do, said another man, and went on a rant about the Darling Downs squatters. Silvertails he called them.

Hear hear! said a gentleman with a large moustache. The sweat of our brows goes to paying for Brisbane's roads. We must draw a line south of Rockhampton and form our own state.

By that reckoning, remarked Lancelot, the new colony to the north will soon be sending Rockhampton the sweat of theirs. But tell me, I'm interested, how does that help us poor mugs who've taken up land in the far north?

The other gentlemen and ladies laughed at this question. It tickled their fancy, or they pretended it did. When they had enough of laughing, the men discussed the native people.

The Brisbane men sleep safe in their beds, said the shaggy-browed man. They think nothing of hanging us poor chaps for protecting our families.

The ladies at table nodded their approval while Ellen and I stole glances at each other. Not knowing what the men were talking about, but beginning to get an idea. Another man agreed, and said the trouble with the Blacks was they knew they weren't allowed to be shot anymore.

The niggers have been pinching our corn, he said, and not a darn thing we can do about it except have a word with Captain Brown. But he's agreed to take the Native Police over next week and do a dispersal.

This pleased everyone at the table, the Captain included, for much harrumphing and chuckling followed.

You've got to keep your word and deliver what you promise, the second man said. Whether it's sugar or a shot up the backside.

The gentlemen laughed, and the ladies simpered and looked sideways at each other behind their fans.

When the waiters removed the plates from the table, the gentlemen pushed back their chairs and strolled off to the smoking-room. And no sooner were they out the door than the small lady on my right turned to me.

You're new to the colony, I can tell, she said. Are you married or are you a single lady?

I'm single though soon to be married, I said, copying her voice.

Ellen shot me a dark look.

Just as I thought, said the lady, smiling. Then let me give you a piece of advice which I hope will prove useful. I'm certain marital harmony in the tropics is disrupted by wash-day dinners more than anything else. I hope you won't fall into that awful practice, Miss er…

Callahan, I said. But I'm afraid I know nothing about wash-day dinners.

She shrugged her beribboned shoulders. Some women make the mistake of helping the wash-girl on Mondays, so what can they expect? In this climate they are quite prostrate by dinner time and haven't the strength to supervise their cooks.

Is that right? Ellen asked.

Oh indeed, the lady said. I mean, what do we pay servants for if not to do the weekly wash?

The Irish biddies that come off the boats have no idea of humility, said the lady on my left. They care not one jot that their mistress is obliged to labour beside them at the washtub in order to train them up.

In my experience most of the girls are untrainable, said an old lady in black. One finds oneself constantly between housemaids.

This new Masters and Servants Act will give them the whiphand, said the lady on my right, and received nods and murmurs of approval.

I do agree, and they're impudent enough to begin with, said another lady.

Ellen pushed back her chair and walked out of the room. I watched the agitated twitch of her bustle and could only feel grateful she was taking her rage outside. Who knows what she might've said had she stayed.

Most of them should be sent back to Ireland where they come from, said the old lady in black. We'd be better off having bonded labour the way we do with the Kanakas. The company supplies the article and is paid direct. That way it's in their interest to provide us with decent bodies.

You're so right, the other ladies said. They couldn't get enough of talking about 'servantalism' as they called it. Each had a story to tell, one vexing tale after another about Irish maidservants till I found my hands clenched in my lap. Ellen wouldn't listen to this, I thought, and no more will I.

Is it servants we're speaking of? I said before I could stop myself. And didn't I come to this country to be one such myself?

I heard my heart thudding in the silence that followed. There was no need to say what country I came from, my voice did that for me. The ladies hardly knew what to do with their faces.

Willing my legs not to shake, I pushed back the chair and stood up. I must go to my sister, I said.

I escaped from the dining room in search of Ellen, guessing she had gone out on the poop deck. There was no one on board the SS *Boomerang* to shout, Down below, girls! as had happened each evening on the *Kapunda*. We could stay up on deck as long as we liked.

Ellen glimmered in the distance, pacing the boards in her blue muslin gown. I quickened my steps to join her, and we walked together in silence, thinking our own thoughts. And seeing the night sky for the first time since we boarded the *Kapunda* in Belfast, we were both surprised by a queer set of stars. Ellen asked a gentleman sitting in a collapsible canvas chair what they were called.

Why, that's the Southern Cross, he said in an Australian drawl. A remarkable constellation and all our own.

Sure, it looks like a kite, Ellen said, which made the gentleman frown.

We wandered over to the rail and watched the moon rise out of the ocean, spreading a gleam on the black water so extraordinary beautiful it almost hurt to keep watching. The moon rose up slow in the night sky and I felt the dew on my arms and saw fish lepping in the moonlit water. Heard laughter floating up easy and cheerful from the men's smoking-room.

They say your man asked another girl before you, Ellen said.

Who says so?

Oh one of the girls. It was Lizzie Doyle they reckon.

Lizzie was always a bad liar, I said. The moonlight was suddenly sludge to me.

Ellen sighed. She was, she had a tongue forever tripping over the truth.

The notes of a piano stumbling over themselves came up to us from the saloon. Good luck to her anyway, Ellen said. She's a barmaid now.

Is she? I said, but I was thinking—*Lizzie Doyle? She's not even pretty.*

Ellen turned to me. Her eyes looked haunted in the moonlight.

I'll not come with you to the boarding house, Annie. I wouldn't care to. I'll go to the Immigration Depot in Rockhampton and see what I can do for myself.

I saw tears glinting in her eyes. Oh, Ellie, I said, touching her arm.

It's this poxy ship! she cried. What else can I think of except Dev now we're at sea again? Where is he? That's what I need to know. Is he in jail or on the *Kapunda*? The only good thing is he can't drown. Did I tell you he keeps his birth caul in his sea chest, to protect him from drowning?

Well that's good, I said.

Ellen wiped her eyes with the back of her hand. Yes, it is. But how can I get a message to him?

I don't think you can.

Her eyes widened and I added quickly, At least not in the foreseeable future. I'm worried about you, Ellie. Won't you come with me to the boarding house? Mr Wilson has arranged your accommodation.

Ellen gazed at the moon's path on the dark water and made no reply.

The sea with its sorry thoughts for my sister put an altogether different tide in me. I was all the time stitching my new gown and dreaming of Mr Wilson. Remembering the lively light in his eyes. Ellen stayed in our cabin most days so I soon got talking with the other passengers. They wouldn't have let me keep to myself if I wanted. One gentleman walked up to me on the poop deck, a fat man with a ruinous red face.

He tipped his hat.

Day to you, he said. His mouth hardly seemed to move, only the drawly voice came out.

He moved closer. Fine girl you are, he said, looking me up and down. Reckon you're not long in this country, eh? I could show you around, point out the sights.

He put his pudgy fingers on my arm. Oho, touch me not! Where're you going? I was talking to you, you sly piece.

You've got the wrong pig by the ear, I said.

The impudence of the man. I was trembling.

A tall lady who had been watching from under her parasol approached us then, and the man arrested himself in his nonsense.

Alright, I get the picture, he said. Aren't you the right little girleen? Don't wancher anyway.

He waddled off in the direction of the smoking-room.

My name is Mrs Dawbridge, the lady said, speaking through her nose in the English way. I saw that gentleman bothering you so I came over. He has no good name among women who mind themselves.

She gave me a thorough once-over, same as the man had done.

I see by your complexion you are recently arrived, Miss er...

Miss Callahan, I said.

Mrs Dawbridge nodded, considering this. I noticed you last night at the Captain's table. You were with another young lady, I think.

That was my sister, I said, copying her voice.

And are you and your sister friends of the Captain, Miss Callahan? It seems you must be since you were invited to sit at his table.

The waiter showed us to the table, I explained. No one warned us it belonged to the Captain. We don't intend eating there again.

Mrs Dawbridge seemed displeased by this information. But tell me, she said, are you disembarking in Rockhampton or do you travel further south?

We're getting off at Rockhampton.

Ah, she said. Myself also. I suppose you have friends to greet you.

Just the one, I said.

May I ask who that might be?

He is Mr Wilson.

Mrs Dawbridge moved her thin lips in a smile. The shipping Wilsons! she said. Such a numerous family, always travelling up and down the coast with Captain Wilson. I don't know how they do it. Well, no wonder you were invited to sit at the Captain's table while others were not.

My friend isn't a sea-captain.

No? she said. Well there are other Wilsons of course.

Mr Wilson has a horse-breeding farm at Serpentine Water.

She narrowed her eyes. That's nice.

We are to be married, I said.

How splendid! she said. And you have come all this way for the purpose? Such a brave step. My sister has done the same, but she's greatly shocked by the class of servant we have here.

I closed my eyes. Opened them on the same earnest face.

Is that right? I said.

Mrs Dawbridge raised her eyebrows as if inviting agreement from invisible listeners, and moved closer.

You're new here of course, she said. So let me warn you about the slovenly types of females who come out here and pose as servants. You must try to avoid them if you can, Miss Callahan. Not that it's generally possible. They're all we have apart from barefoot girls out of bush huts, and they're no better. Some of the maids run off to get married or any other whim that takes their fancy. It's hard to find an honest girl among them.

Goodness! I said.

My dear, you wouldn't believe the servantalism in this country. If the maids aren't clumsy and breaking the china then they're saucy and think themselves above their work. You'll find Jack's as good as his master in Australia and Biddy is better than either.

She shook her head from thinking on her words, and lowered her voice. And the maids are terrible tale-bearers, Miss Callahan. Remember that when you're in your new home. You must be careful what you say for it's sure to be repeated in their next situation.

Right, so, I said, looking at her cool.

Some even marry above their station, parading about in carriages like ladies. It's quite comical really.

I felt like a mouse must feel when it is outstaring a cat. Mr Wilson owned a carriage and had told me I could use it. Was I to live my married life among people like this woman? The thought unnerved me.

Excuse me, Mrs Dawbridge, I said. I must go to my sister. She is waiting for me below.

Mrs Dawbridge tilted her parasol against a passing breeze. Well feel free to come to me any time you need advice, dear. You seem very young and I know how hard it is when you're a new chum.

Ellen stayed in the cabin while we sailed up the Fitzroy River. She couldn't be bothered she said. But I was all eyes for my first sight of Rockhampton, the town where Mr Wilson lived. Three miles outside it, anyway. It was coming on evening and strange creatures that weren't birds swarmed in lacy dark shawls in the colourless sky.

Flying foxes, Mrs Dawbridge said, though I didn't believe her for one moment. Since when had foxes ever learned to fly?

In the soft evening light reflected off the river the steamer passed the edges of town. Market-gardens and timber cottages with smoking chimneys slid past, half hid among orchards. Great trees rose up behind, tall as giants! We had none such in Ireland. But our dream-like passage along the river was suddenly interrupted by a loud rattle. Sailors letting the anchor down.

The Captain stood at the top of the gangway, farewelling the passengers. Ellen and I heard shouts of Any mail from Home? and How's Baby? as we picked our way along the wharf. Horse-cabs and carriages loaded with passengers rattled past, while all around us the steerage passengers were making their way up a road from the river. We tagged on behind and in short time found ourselves standing on a broad macadam street.

Ellen nodded at a group of native men and their dogs who were gathered on a street corner, dressed up in all manner of mismatched clothes. One man in a red bandanna was imitating the gait of a passerby with exaggerated comical steps, that had the others falling about laughing.

At least some people are happy, she said.

Their skylarking was so entertaining I stopped to watch.

It's rude to stare, Ellen said in my ear.

Chinamen in pigtails loped past on silent slippered feet, and we saw white men in coarse breeches, others dressed smart in top hats, carrying swagger sticks. Dogs of all kinds roamed about, and goats with their queerly beautiful eyes. Some of the buildings were grand, much like the buildings in Belfast we thought. And no man molested us, though that may have been because we wore store-bought gowns and no longer looked like free immigrants. No longer easy targets in our heavy northern clothes.

It was getting on for dark by the time we found Parts' boarding house—a large well lit, two-storey timber building in East-street, the town's chief shopping thoroughfare.

I breathed a secret sigh of relief.

A smell of lamp-kerosene floated through the windows as I trod up the low flight of steps.

Ellen hung back. I'll go to the Depot, she said.

The street light behind her threw her shadow up the steps towards me. I recognised her mutinous look.

Oh Ellen, what hurry is on you? I said from the top of the steps. Mrs Part is expecting us and it's too late to be walking the streets. Come in now, you'll be sure of a good meal and safe bed, which is more than you may get at the Depot.

And who is to pay for the good meal? Ellen demanded.

Well I believe it's Mr Wilson. He told me this is a teetotal hotel and quite a high standard.

Standards are all very well for those that can afford them, she said. So I'll be off now and see you in the morning.

No, Ellen, I'll not let you go. Come in please. Do as I say and don't be aggravating me.

With a bit more push and a lot more shove she agreed, and I knocked on the door which was opened by a pert girl. The parlour maid we learned later. We followed her down the hallway to the room made ready for us, Ellen wiping tears from her eyes and myself marching stiff-backed beside her, as if I was her jailor.

Robbery and Unlawful Slaughter

I WOKE from chaotic dreams, hearing the desperate squawks of a hen, followed by sudden silence. The rush of relief when I realised I was tucked up in bed in Parts' boarding house.

I heard the doorbell ring. Footsteps tapped along the hallway. The parlour maid most likely. Everything seemed to be in order.

I sat up and looked around. At Ellen asleep in the bed by the window, at the bunches of yellow roses on the wallpaper, and said a silent prayer that all would continue well.

In the dining room at breakfast we met Mrs Part, an amiable bustling woman who still had the pink cheeks of England where she hailed from. She had a team of half grown sons—I heard them in the hallway, laughing and chaffing one another on their way to rowing practice on the river—and a daughter about my age with corn-coloured hair.

After breakfast, the daughter introduced herself as Jessie, and offered to show us the way to the Immigration Depot.

It's down by the river, she explained. A pretty spot but you might get lost finding it.

We walked with her the short block to Quay-street and stepped onto the riverbank, following the broad-flowing Fitzroy River downstream.

Keeping to the shade of gum trees where we could. Catching glimpses of sun-silvered water glittering between the trunks.

What season is this? asked Ellen.

Why it's summertime of course, Jessie said. What did you think it was?

Is it hotter than usual? I asked.

Jessie considered. Not really. Though it was 112 degrees in the shade yesterday and I hear birds were found dead under the trees.

Good grief, muttered Ellen.

It's not the heat we're worried about, Jessie said. It's the drought. The City Fathers are getting up an Aboriginal Ceremony for rain next week.

Ellen mopped her brow and said the colonial summer was hotter than Hades.

Maybe so, but it's better not to mention it, Jessie warned. The people of Rockhampton don't like hearing such remarks about their town. We were disgusted by an English gentleman called Trollope when he visited a few years ago. Ah, here's the Depot now.

The Rockhampton Immigration Depot was twice the size of the Townsville one and painted a uniform sludge-brown. We lifted our skirts to walk up the ladderlike steps, Jessie still talking.

The bigwigs held a levee for Mr Trollope at the Criterion Hotel, and made a great fuss of him because he's a famous writer from England. But when his book came out all he wrote about us—Jessie had to wait till she finished giggling—All he wrote was when we die and go to Hell we have to send back to Rockhampton for our blankets.

We were laughing as we stepped through the doorway, and who should be there, the first person to greet us? None other than Dr Salmond, the man who boarded the *Kapunda* in Keppel Bay to hear our complaints about lack of victuals, then lectured us at the Townsville Depot. Large as life and frowning, saying we'd entered by the wrong door.

He showed no sign of recognising Ellen and me, but why should he? We were but two among seventy-seven girls in dun-coloured gowns.

It's Mr Boysen's office you want, he said, and took us outside to point out another door.

In we went by that entrance to have Ellen's particulars writ down, and when Mr Boysen finished scratching with his pen and was standing up, waiting to escort Ellen to her quarters, there was nothing to do but kiss goodbye.

I'll come back tomorrow, I promised.

Don't go drowning yourself in sweat now, that is an order.

Ellen was pale from the heat, but she turned to flash a defiant grin as she followed Mr Boysen down a corridor.

By the time Jessie and I got back to the boarding house I was sweating pretty bad. I went to my room, lay down in my chemise and fell asleep till a thunderous noise woke me. Up I jumped in a panic and pulled on my dress hasty. Was it the French attacking us or something? They had done so once or twice in Ireland.

I scurried out of the room and found Jessie Part in the hallway. What is it? I cried.

She got a fit of the giggles. It's only the One O'clock Gun. I should have warned you.

But was it a cannon or what?

Yes, a cannon on the riverbank, she said laughing. It's to keep the correct time for we can't be believing the Post Office clock that takes its time from Brisbane.

She took me down the hallway to the Part family's private parlour and gave me boiled water to drink. You can't be too careful, she said. Some of the immigrants have died from sunstroke, and not just the immigrants either.

Next morning I went on my own to the Depot and found Ellen lying on an iron bed.

It's only me here, she said, raising herself on an elbow. And some Kanakas in the men's quarters.

I sat on the end of the bed and she jabbed her with her toes.

Want to hear the craic? she said. Rhyming Lynam reckons Dr Salmond is annoyed he couldn't get any men off the *Kapunda*. He tried to have the single men brought to Rockhampton but the Townsville people wouldn't oblige. Rhyming Lynam says the men are wanted here to build a railway. The City Fathers have sent a strenuous letter of complaint to the government men in Brisbane.

She grinned. And guess what? Captain MacFarlane is in *big* trouble for stowing short rations. Rhyming Lynam says he's forbidden to leave Queensland until the government inquiry is over.

Who is Rhyming Lynam? I asked.

Only the wardsman. A nice old fella, you'd like him.

You seem quite friendly with him.

Ellen shrugged. He's someone to talk to.

I looked around the brown-painted room with its rows of empty iron beds. How are you finding the Depot? I asked.

Oh fine, fine. Fine enough anyhow, apart from last night when some foul-mouthed drunkards decided to torment a dog outside the window. Poor little mutt. I shouted at them but they took no notice. A constable turned up in the end and they ran away, so no matter.

Mr Wilson is happy to pay your board, I said, as if it was of no importance. As if I hadn't reminded her three times already.

Ellen shook her head, stubborn as always. I've decided, was all she would say, and told me to go before it got any hotter.

I would be back tomorrow so we parted without bothering to kiss. Hugging we had already dispensed with. It felt out of place inside the tall forbidding walls of the Depot.

But when I returned next morning I couldn't find Ellen anywhere, and went in search of Mr Boysen to learn her whereabouts.

He peered at me over his spectacles. Your sister has gone to Emu Park.

What is Emu Park? I asked, and he said it was a village by the sea.

Your sister has accepted a situation at the Steak-and-Beer Inn. She went off in a carriage with Mrs Stake yesterday. She left a message for you, but.

He handed me Ellen's letter which told the same, and that she had a craving to be by the ocean. It would make her feel closer to Dev, and Rhyming Lynam had told her the sea breezes would make it cooler, and she wasn't going behind the bar. Mrs Stake had promised her that.

Don't be worried I'm in that class of work because I'm not. So take care you eejit and rite soon.

My sister had gone, vanished like a Fairy, and I was heartsick from losing her. When I returned to the boarding house Jessie calmed my fears, saying Emu Park was a great place to live, and not so distant as to prevent visits. A native-born Australian untroubled by doubts, she chivvied me out of my glooms and soon had me smiling again.

Jessie's kindness was a wonder and marvel to me. At home whatever I did was wrong, a cause for New Ma's blows and scolding, and my silence. Our stepmother was afraid Ellen and I would take food from her baby's mouth, and kept nagging our father to send us to the poorhouse. Such a terrible place the poorhouse is for keeping out of. Many a starving creature has heard the doom-sound of its iron door clanging behind them, never to open again, and New Ma was determined we would hear that clang too.

Ah Jeezus! I said to Ellen. We'll starve to death in there.

And God knows what else before that, she said. Remember Dinny Malone.

Who could forget that poor crazed kid? The child who scrambled up a brick wall—with God's miraculous aid it was believed—wriggled through a grill window, fell down the other side and lived to tell his tale. Of rape and murder. So fleshless he could scarcely walk. A trembling terrified skerrick of a boy, but he told his story. There was nothing the guards weren't game for in that soulless place, Dinny told the woman who found him curled up asleep in her turf-shed.

The guards knew they would never be charged with their crimes. Who could know? Who would tell? A week after Dinny squeezed through the window to freedom he was found dead, strangled down at Bolger's Bog. The Anglo-Irish landlords were never going to obey a law made in England, that expected them to house and feed their starving tenants. They housed them right enough, then threw away the key.

But at Parts' boarding house there were no such dangers and it wasn't long before I began to regain my tongue, and was able to chat easily with Jessie. Even to exchange small talk with the lodgers. Ellen would have been amazed to see how forward I had become.

Jessie was curious about Mr Wilson and liked to come in my room and stroke the folds of the white gown where it hung like a chaste ghost in the wardrobe.

Indian glacé muslin, she murmured. So up-to-date modern, and costly besides. He must be a real gentleman to think of buying it for you.

She left off stroking the dress and came over to sit beside me on the bed. You needn't be uneasy, she said, for I see by your face you are.

What do you mean?

Stranger danger, she said, grinning. You're not the first girl to be married off a boat, you know. My dad's a ship chandler and he can tell a tale or two about the men who come sniffing around the wharf. Not even waiting for the Depot to open.

Mr Wilson did it right, I said. He waited for the levee.

But I was remembering what Ellen told me. How he had asked Lizzie Doyle first. And what was it he asked her? Was it to be his housekeeper or his wife? I wanted to tell Jessie about Mr Wilson but had no words to describe the man. All I knew was I liked him. I hardly knew how to explain my feelings, and even when I did they felt too private to share. Jessie would have thought me some kind of man-crazy eejit.

Where is your husband to be? she asked. Has he gone away?

He is travelling by road from Townsville.

That made her laugh. Oh not by road. You'd be lucky to find a track in the bush. If your man's on horseback he'll be weeks in the saddle, which gives you time to look to your trousseau.

Trousseau? Was I to have such a fine thing?

Jessie jumped up from the bed. Let's go down to Stewart & Lucas and get the makings for some dresses. You have only the two I think, apart from those heavy dark things you brought with you.

This struck me as a first-rate scheme, so we fetched our hats and shawls and set off along East-street. The drapery store was only a short walk from the boarding house, an imposing brick building with a glass entrance. In we rustled in our white gowns like proper ladies, and Jessie introduced me to a Mr Floude in Ladies Fabrics, who was another lodger at the boarding house.

Miss Callahan would like to see the summer dress fabrics, she told him. You'll want three lengths, Annie. Patterned, plain, and a silk weave for special occasions.

I gaped at her. But I only intend buying one length.

Jessie took me aside and we stood together in the lee of tall bolts of red velour cloth.

Are you short of cash? she asked.

No, I whispered. But three lengths would be very extravagant.

A necessity, not an extravagance, she whispered back. You really cannot wear a dress more than a day in this weather. If they're not washed regular the perspiration destroys them in no time.

I hesitated. Three lengths would take the last of Dada's three pounds. Two lengths, maybe?

Three, Jessie said firmly.

We returned to the counter where Mr Floude was waiting, pretending not to listen, and with his help and Jessie's advice, I chose a length each of white dimity, white georgette with pink hailspot, and a beautiful slithery white silk-poplin. With buttons and lace to match.

We carried the parcels back to the boarding house and fairly waltzed through the front door. There's a bold one, Jessie murmured as a lady swished into her room. She goes about without a hat or shawl to cover her hair. Mum's wondering should she give her notice.

She giggled and I giggled with her, for no better reason than the pleasure of laughing with a friend. Well tat-ta, she said. I have to get back to the linen sorting.

In the privacy of my room I spread out the delicate fabrics on the bed, to gloat over them. But after a time I fell to worrying. I had spent my half of the money Dada got from selling his horse and cart, and I knew what he would think if he could learn the frippery things I had spent it on.

I thought about Ellen, when would I see her again? And Mrs Dawbridge, what would she think if she could know I was one of the government paupers who marry men rich enough to own carriages?

Then I thought about the man himself and gathered up the clouds of white georgette and pressed them to my cheek.

Samuel, Samuel! Lordsake, man, you're hurt!

It was Mrs Part, screeching in the hallway. I lit the bedside lamp, slipped on my shawl and opened the door a crack. Saw other doors ajar, rimmed with candle-light.

Mr Part was heaving and gasping over by the hallstand, Mrs Part in a tartan dressing gown bent over his leg, and Jessie beside them holding a lamp. A little way off, Mr Floude was watching on in his long johns, next to another man breathing heavy like Mr Part.

Don't fuss, woman, Mr Part said when he got his breath back. Leave me be, it's only a scratch. Leave it I say.

He turned to Mr Floude. Well I caught the rascal any rate and got the watch off him.

That you did, Mr Part, that you did, said Mr Floude. And I'm much obliged to you.

It was mighty fine work, Mr Part, said the other man. You're a fast runner and no mistake, just like your sons.

Fetch the Inspector of Nuisances a glass of water, Jessica, said Mrs Part. And one for your father while you're about it. They are quite done in from their running. Oh dear, it's too dreadful, Mr Floude. You will have to keep your window closed in future.

Then I remembered I was in my nightdress, and closed the door soft. Stood in the circle of light cast by the lamp, suddenly aware of the window and the shadows in the room.

Next morning at breakfast the thief in the night was all the lodgers cared to talk about.

A nice state of affairs, Mr Floude said, addressing the company at large. A fine howdy-do when a man can't sleep peaceful without a hand comes through the window and nabs his timepiece.

He's up before the magistrate this morning and good riddance to him, said Mrs Part, coming through the doorway with the big enamel teapot.

Two kitchen-maids followed carrying platters, one heaped with grilled flesh-meat and bacon, the other with fried onions and tomatoes. The aroma had more than a few noses twitching.

Mrs Part set down the teapot.

We must spare a thought for Mr Part, she announced. He's laid up with his leg this morning, that's the pity of it. If only my older boys weren't away in Brisbane for the cricket they might've saved their father his chase.

She poured out the tea and Jessie carried round the cups. Let's go down to the court-house, she whispered as she handed me mine. It'll be gas watching the thief get his come-uppance.

Never in my life had I done such a useless entertaining thing, so of course I said yes. After breakfast, hatted and shawled, we strolled down East-street and took our seats in the Magistrate's Court among the others chatting while they waited for the entertainment to begin. The heat was terrible as ever. Hardly a breath of sluggish air filtered down from the canvas sail hanging from the ceiling, for all its languid whooshing and creaking, while the hand fans in motion around us served only to move the hot air about and stir up frowsty odours.

The first case was our watch thief, a skinny man with gravel rash on his face. He wasn't in a good way at all. The Inspector of Nuisances I had seen in Parts' hallway stood up first, and spoke his evidence. Then the red-faced Magistrate sitting behind a bench gave the man a lecture about stealing watches.

You wanted time, you shall have time, he said, chuckling at his own joke. And fined the man six shillings, or twenty lashes and a week with hard labour. Whichever he preferred.

I'll take the lash and hard labour, your lordship's honour, said the watch thief. I've not got the money about me right now.

They led the poor fellow away.

While this was going on I heard snuffling noises, and when I looked round I saw a draggle-tailed woman, older than Mrs Part I would guess, and weatherbeaten with it. She was weeping into her shawls, for she was wrapped in a good many red ones, much like the gypsy women we call Travellers at home.

Is that the thief's mother? I whispered.

No, Jessie whispered back. That's Witchety Peg. Shall we stay and watch?

Calling Miss Margaret Purdy, intoned the clerk, and the old woman stepped forward. She had stopped crying by now, and turned her head left and right, sending fierce stares as she hobbled up the aisle.

The evidence that came out about Witchety Peg was curious and affecting, or so I thought. It seemed that Mr Barber, another Inspector of Nuisances, had taken a party of labourers to the main drain, and didn't they find a hundred unregistered goats there and drive them up the Athelstane Range to the Botanical Gardens. And slit their throats for them, every last one.

Yes sir, Witchety Peg said hoarsely to the Magistrate. In the morning I owned a hundred goats and by afternoon they was all laying dead in the Botanical Gardens.

No sir, she said. I never counted them, poor things. They was covered in blood.

When the Magistrate estimated the value of her goats at ten pound she got indignant. Oh no sir! she said. Wherever did you get that notion? They're worth more'n that.

He peered at her as if she was an animal in a zoo. And you live by selling their flesh, do you? he asked, and listened disbelievingly when she told him she only sold their milk.

Mr Barber was put in the box next, and said he was a Special Constable, but Mr Milford who was Witchety Peg's lawyer-man objected, saying Mr Barber wasn't a constable at all. He was only an Inspector of Nuisances and had no power to order the killing of goats.

Mr Barber disputed this point but Mr Milford insisted on being right.

That's enough of your bickering, Milford, ordered the Magistrate. I can't be expected to sit up here all day. The heat in this room isn't fit for man or beast.

He was sweating pretty bad and he banged down a wooden hammer and ordered that Mr Milford had the right of it, and he would give a verdict against Mr Barber, for he was guilty of a wrong and must pay ten pound to Miss Purdy.

At which the old woman cried and said, How will I live? Ten pound is nothing. I can't replace my goats for less than a hundred.

But while she was stomping up the aisle on her gammy legs, she turned her head and stared at me. That bright and knowing her eyes were, burning into me as if she could see into the very crevices of my soul. God almighty, a shiver ran right through me.

I whispered to Jessie who agreed we'd seen enough, and we crept out to give Mrs Part the news about the watch thief.

A Nailer To Gallop

THIRTEEN, FOURTEEN, fifteen, sixteen. Jessie paused in her counting. Oh I forgot to tell you, Witchety Peg called on Mum yesterday. As of next week the town eccentric will be supplying our goat milk.

We were pleating squares of starched white damask in Parts' back parlour, for I had got in the way of helping when I could.

She's a queer one, I agreed.

Seventeen, eighteen, nineteen, twenty, done! Jessie said. Yes, queer enough, but Mum feels sorry for her. The old girl lost another lot of goats in the seventy-four flood. Stuck on top of her humpy down at the main drain, perched on the roof with the ones she managed to save. Save my goats, she cried when a boat came alongside, but they wouldn't of course.

I love animals too but had no wish to have anything in common with a grubby old woman with fierce eyes. Eyes that bored into you till you felt mother-naked.

She was trying her luck, I said. Telling the Magistrate her goats were worth a hundred pound.

She was. She's a cunning old bird.

We carried the starched cloths in trays to the dining room, and moved between the tables, arranging their pleated shapes on the white damask tablecloths. Your man should arrive any day, Jessie said, raising her eyebrows at me.

Yes, I said. It was the twelfth of December, much the time Mr Wilson had said. I was always thinking of him. Wondering when he might come, riding his horse up East-street to Parts' door. King Conan dressed in gold breastplate astride a white stallion is how I pictured him arriving. I was all in commotion inside to see him again.

Sitting by the window in my room a few days later I was going over the same questions. When would he come? *Would* he come? That he might not hardly bore contemplating. If he did come, should I ask him about Lizzie Doyle? I would, of course. I must know the truth, if only to end this disquiet I felt. That's if he could be trusted to tell the truth.

A smell of smoke seeping through the window distracted me, and I pushed up the sash to look out.

The mountains that show their crests above the shops in East-street had thin lines of fire running along their upper slopes, like so many red scorpions. The Berserker Mountains they are called, a queer name though it suits their grandness I believe, and so blue and floating most days you would think they were made of veils instead of rock. Today they were shrouded in smoke-haze, and the shop windows had a yellow glare that I didn't like the look of at all. A burning bit of wind stirred the papers in the gutters, and *Mother of God!* I leaned out of the window.

Who's this clip-clopping up the street in the brassy light? *Mr Wilson!* In a shiny black buggy pulled by two plump chestnut mares.

I ran to the wardrobe to put on my new voile gown, and scarce could breathe for the mad jumping going on in my chest. Twisted up my hair and fastened the black velvet ribbon around my throat that Jessie and I had picked out at Stewart & Lucas. Breathed in deep and said a little prayer on the out breath to compose myself.

Slow down, you're not churning butter, Mrs Part said when I rushed into the hallway. She must have been waiting for me.

Young Winnie has put Mr Wilson to wait in the front parlour, she said. Put a smile on your face, dear. He's not going to eat you. Just straighten your gown and we'll go in.

Mrs Part gave a warning cluck of her tongue and bustled ahead into the parlour.

He was leaner than I remembered. I watched him stand up and bow to Mrs Part, then he bowed to me and said very polite that he hoped he found me well.

I am, yes, I said. I hope you're well too.

We were both staring, giving each other the full examination. I hardly knew how to stop until a sudden thought flustered me. Was he just checking I was the same girl he chose out of seventy-seven similarly dressed ones in Townsville?

Mrs Part settled her comfortable bulk in an armchair by the fireplace. Mr Wilson and I dragged our eyes away from each other and found seats across from her.

Is it dry up north, Mr Wilson, she asked. Or have they had rain?

Only coastal showers, Mrs Part, he said in his deep voice.

It's quite dry here as you may have noticed, she remarked. Moores Creek is in danger of drying up.

Gabbing about the weather while I sat with my hands folded demurely in my lap, watching and listening attentively. Wondering was it true what Jessie reckoned, that some men have the magnetism in them. Mr Wilson slipped me a glance but I looked away quick, as if he had caught me out.

When no more could be said about the weather Mrs Part asked about his journey and who was in his travelling party.

Only my man Harry Roche and a native guide, he said. We had no risk of getting lost.

He hadn't the confident look I remembered in Townsville.

I hear that's true, Mrs Part said. The Blacks know to a hair's breadth which way to go.

Mr Wilson eased his collar with a sunbrowned finger. Duke's good company too.

And nothing untoward on your journey, I hope?

Only the swelling blight on Harry's lip, but that's cleared up.

He turned to me, and Mrs Part said she must find out where the tea had got to. She rustled out of the room and no sooner had the door clicked shut behind her than silence fell upon us. Or rather we fell into silence as into a deep pit. We were all eyes devouring one another and I was desperate to find words to distract Mr Wilson from the naked messages mine were giving out.

He came to the rescue by fiddling with a pouch on his belt and pulling out a sprig of yellow berries. For you, he said.

I held out my hand and he put the berries in it. Chucky chuckies, he said. Good eating you'll find. I picked them for you on the way into town.

I thanked him, and admired the berries until I could no longer put off tasting one. It's a bit like a gooseberry, I was saying with relief when the door opened and Mrs Part returned.

She wasn't going to leave us alone, that was plain. She sat down, adjusting her bustle with a practised hand.

I told Winnie to look slippy, she announced. Tea is on the way.

When the parlour maid brought in the tray, Mrs Part occupied herself with the teapot. Milk? Sugar? she asked Mr Wilson.

Black, two sugars, thanks.

Mrs Part added the sugar. There, she said. Miss Callahan, will you take Mr Wilson his tea?

I carried the cup and saucer with both hands, willing the latter not to shake. He waited in his chair, never taking his eyes off me. Like most men he sat with his legs apart and this added to my distraction. The cup rattled on the saucer as I handed it to him.

Thank you, Miss Callahan.

My back was to Mrs Part, obscuring Mr Wilson from her sight, and the smile he sent me made me feel we shared some secret joke. I returned a small smile that only kept growing. The two of us grinning together.

But we couldn't talk anymore. Not properly. Which might be why, after he drank his tea, Mr Wilson said he must draw his visit to a close or his welcome would become threadbare.

His eyes met mine across the red Turkey rug.

We must call on Father Murlay to arrange the marrying, he said. If it's agreeable, Miss Callahan, I'll come back this afternoon to escort you.

It is agreeable, I said. Thank you, Mr Wilson.

Mrs Part and I went with him to the front door and watched as he ran very nimble down the steps. He was whistling as he drove away and I wanted to wave but he didn't look back.

What a receptacle of good manners your young man is, said Mrs Part.

I made no reply, being occupied touching my hand. The one he had taken and covered with his when he said goodbye. For a time I could think of nothing else—though later I remembered Lizzie Doyle. There was no way I could question Mr Wilson about her while Mrs Part was present, but we would have more meetings before the wedding, surely?

I wasn't such a fool as to go into this blind, and I intended to quiz the man the first chance that presented itself.

Dear Ellen,

I suppose you can't find a piece of paper to write to a sister? I hope this finds you well. I am well here. How are you liking the inn and Mrs Stake? Mr Wilson called today and we went to see the priest. Father Murlay is fine about me marrying a Prodestant. His horse Mickey Free beat Mr Wilson's horse at the June Races so they had a long yarn. Mr Wilson says there is no reason we shouldn't pull well together. We are to be married so soon as the Banns are posted, Januarie 3 which is Leap Year being 1876. Jessie is forever teasing me about it. She is to be Bridesmaid so that is her privledge she reckons.

Mr Wilson plans an excurshon to Emu Park so we shall see you on Saint Stephens Day God willing. He will be away till then on a short cattle drove to Raglan Station. He knows a good deal about horses but little enough about excurshons with Ladies, or fooling with tea-cups in parlors neither. No more at present, your loving sister Annie.

PS. Rite soon and tell me all your news.

On Saturday Mr Wilson called to take me to the races. He came back from the race-course to collect me, for he was up before dawn to bring his racehorse in from Serpentine Water and settle it in the holding paddock. We drove out of town in his smart black buggy with its two carriage horses, padded leather seats and brass side lamps. And no chaperone with us, for Mrs Part had declared Mr Wilson a gentleman of good character and henceforth to be trusted.

How I wished Mrs Dawbridge could see us among the other carriages, making our way out to the course.

The horse in Australia is neither groomed nor cared for, Mr Wilson said as we bowled along. Except racehorses, that is. You'll see some smart ones today, Miss Callahan, my own included.

I asked about his horse and he said it was called Pyrrhus and he had hopes it would do well.

I imported him from India, as fine an Arab stallion as you'll find in the district. Pyrrhus is a nailer to gallop. He should make it hot for the flyers at the June races.

He tipped his hat to a gentleman riding by. A beautiful class of horse then, I ventured.

Indeed. I went down to Sydney to collect him myself and bring him back on the steamer. You're allowed to sleep in the hold with the animal if it's a thoroughbred. I intend standing him next season.

I said nothing to this, being unsure of his meaning. Sitting so close to him had me bashful and uncertain as to what might come out of my mouth. But Mr Wilson seemed unbothered by my silence, and went on talking about horses until we reached a clearing among gum trees.

Crowds of people were wandering about among flag-decked tents, and from everywhere came the shrill whinnies of horses. We pulled up in the shade of a feathery tree that Mr Wilson said was a wattle, and he handed me down the carriage step to the ground.

There was precious little grass underfoot. Despite the Aboriginal rain ceremony Jessie said was got up to end it, the drought continued apace. What remained of grass was yellowed and shrivelled with no flowers to gladden the stems, all the tiny bells that nod their heads in better times and in Ireland are the colour of a sunny sky. But never a flowerlet of any hue to be seen that day among the papery grasses.

Mr Wilson waved a hand at the parched earth.

This is the viewing paddock, he said. Do you see over there, where the flags start? That's the racecourse. On no account step over the flags, you could get lynched for that.

I won't, I promised.

The course was marked out on higher ground, above a lake. A lagoon, Mr Wilson called it, but I hardly had time to take in the throng of people and the vista of the tree-fringed lake before he said he had to leave.

Steward duty, he said, as if that was a good enough explanation. Part of the job when you're on the Arjaycee committee.

The Arjaycee? I said, baffled.

He took a step towards me. Sorry, the Rockhampton Jockey Club. Look here, Miss Callahan, it seems I haven't thought this through too well.

It seemed to me he hadn't thought it through at all. When I failed to answer he added, Don't make big eyes at me, please. You've no call to be shy, you're the prettiest girl in the viewing paddock. Would you like to watch me lead in the horses?

This is fine, I said. I had seen what appeared to be concern on his face but felt no remorse for my tartness.

He thought for a moment, then announced he had a solution. The carriage, he said. You'll be safe there from unwanted attentions.

I think I can decide what to do, I said. I must be free to walk about as I choose.

He was taken aback by my abrupt refusal, I saw that. Of course, he said. Well, if you're quite sure…

I am, I said, averting my face. No way would I let him know how upset I was.

So … he said. I'll come back soon, I promise, but right now I have to take charge of the horses.

He waited for my reply, which didn't come. Then he went away and was lost in the crowd.

For a time I was quite out of countenance until I spotted Witchety Peg. The old woman had a lavender billy goat with her, a colour highly prized in Ireland, and was making her way onto the track among others doing the same. A goat race to begin with it seemed, and men rushing back and forth placing bets. I went over to join the people at the flags.

Off the billy goats ran, their skinny shanks flying, and wouldn't you know it, Witchety Peg's came first. Which to judge by her cackles pleased her greatly, till some lads stole up behind her and grabbed the billy goat's rope from her hand. They scampered down the slope to the lagoon and everyone laughed to see her pick up her skirts and chase after them.

The Swampies have pinched Witchety Peg's lavender, a man in the crowd shouted. What a lark, see her run, called another. Who'd of thought the old girl could kick up her heels so?

She was fleet enough and got her goat back, and a grudging cheer from the crowd. Came up the slope red in the face, taking no heed of their jeers, and would've been chivvied longer only for a bell ringing, and the crowd going off to watch the blackfellows' horse-race.

Let's git, Will Wally, said Witchety Peg to her goat, and stomped off in the direction of town, her red shawls swaying with her uneven gait. The billy's silver beard glinted in the sunlight as he trotted beside her.

I had no idea where Mr Wilson was. The heat was beyond terrible, and that many brawls going on I didn't like standing in the viewing paddock. It was all I could do to keep the face on me owing to remarks made by passers-by. One man barred my way.

Come 'ere, love. I'll give you something to remember.

The reek of alcohol on him, his leering face close to mine, I had to pretend not to notice. Other greetings weren't so repeatable. A strutting fellow ogled my bodice and said in a loud voice, Get a load of the double-barrelled sheila.

My head was beginning to ache and there weren't many women about, and the ones that were had other ladies to talk to, or a man at their side. Time to return to the carriage, I decided, realising Mr Wilson had been right. Apart from being a place of greater safety the buggy had the benefit of shade provided by the wattle tree, and as I soon discovered, its elevated platform gave a better view of proceedings.

From the carriage the Berserker Mountains were visible in their changing blues, while closer to hand horses thundered down the track, half hid in clouds of dust. Spielers in colourful coats lounged under canvas flys, tossing dice to lure gamblers. A card-sharper in a red waistcoat and stovepipe trousers rattled a tambourine outside a tent, calling hoarsely, Roll up, roll up! Try your skill at Spot the Lady!

Past the milling crowd with its fringe of half-starved dogs and wandering goats, smoke curled up from a campfire by the lagoon. I counted ten or twelve dark-skinned people moving around the fire they had made, cooking up something that smelled quite tasty. Aboriginal men and women going about their business, taking no notice of the racecourse crowd.

When I tired of these sights there was the lagoon itself. Pink Lily Lagoon, Mr Wilson said it was called, and lovely altogether under its coverlet of pink waterlilies. I gazed at the still waters and wondered if Serpentine Water was another lagoon, for that would be a fine class of lake to live by.

Mr Wilson returned around midday, waving as he strode toward me through the crowd. Pyrrhus came first in the Hurry Scurry, he called.

That's grand, I said. But what's a Hurry Scurry when it's at home?

A sprint, he said, grinning.

He mounted the step into the buggy at a leap, and pulled a basket from under the seat. Our picnic luncheon, he announced. Prepared by Ah Lin, my cook. The man's a master of his trade so hopefully his efforts will meet with your approval.

He quizzed me with his eyes. You must be famished, I'm sure.

No indeed, I said, polite.

He lifted the lid to display the contents: a variety of finger sandwiches, savoury tarts and fruits. The flask of cordial proved tricky to open, and we were both bent over it when a gentleman appeared and called Mr Wilson away on some pressing matter of weights.

May the Devil fly away with the fool! he exclaimed to the gentleman, who rolled his eyes in sympathy before hurrying off.

Mr Wilson attempted a smile.

It seems I'm needed on a matter of urgency, Miss Callahan. Shouldn't take too long I hope. Don't wait on my account. Help yourself.

And down he sprang from the carriage. I watched him vanish into the crowd, and wanted to laugh. Otherwise, I might have cried.

The fellow's an imbecile, he said when he returned. Calls himself an accountant but as I suspected Dawbridge isn't up to the job. A horse has as much chance of winning under his handicapping as it has of jumping over the Berserkers.

He was talking more to himself but I didn't care. I was content just looking in his eyes. They hadn't the twinkle I remembered in Townsville, but a more fiery spark from thinking of Mr Dawbridge and his numerical failures that I found just as appealing. So I nodded along to his words and wondered if Mr Dawbridge was the husband of Mrs Dawbridge, though in truth I didn't much care.

We settled to enjoy our picnic lunch. Mr Wilson was holding a small green fruit he said was a native plum, showing me how to peel it, when we were interrupted again.

Hulloa! said a breezy voice. I glanced down and saw a gentleman in a silk top hat and embroidered yellow waistcoat standing beside the carriage, looking up at us. A handsome man with gleaming black eyes, and muscular to go with it.

Mr Wilson's face lit up in a grin. Jack! he said, leaning down to clasp the gentleman's hand.

Paddy, the gentleman replied, smiling broadly.

I thought you were at Emu Park, Mr Wilson said. Weren't you competing in a rifle tournament?

Got knocked out in the semi-finals didn't I? Big setback. But who have we here? the gentleman said, giving me the stare.

Let me do the honours, said Mr Wilson. Miss Callahan, may I introduce a colleague of mine, Jack Royce. He's on the Arjaycee committee with me, and a good friend. Best friend dare I say. Jack, this is my fiancée, Miss Callahan.

Mr Royce stroked his moustache. Miss Callahan, he said with a fine careless air, and lifted his silk hat.

So this is the young lady who has stolen your heart, he remarked to Mr Wilson. No wonder you've been hiding her away.

And shall continue to do so, Mr Wilson replied. Damned if I'm fool enough to introduce Miss Callahan to some of the fellows I know.

Mr Royce laughed. Peabody to name one, he was saying, when a woman's shrill voice cut across the crowd's babble. Looking round, I saw an argument going on between a down-at-heel couple—a paunchy, beetle-browed fellow and a small dilapidated woman.

Some horse of a woman bawling in the viewing paddock, Mr Royce said. This I must see.

The woman was shouting, asking the man for something, which made him angry. He set upon her, beating her with his fists, and in no time a small crowd gathered to cheer him on. The poor bedraggled creature made no attempt to defend herself, only smiled in a sneering way each time the man hit her. It was dreadful to watch.

I wanted to curl up in shame for her, and felt myself shrink into her shame and inhabit it with her, for not having the courage to go to the woman's aid.

Mr Royce watched the beating with amused interest.

Hey! What you looking at? the woman shouted, noticing his cool stare. Something stirring under your breeches, cock?

Not only a loud woman but a lewd woman, he retorted. Not a flicker of expression on his face.

She bared her broken teeth in a snarl.

That chap knows how to deal with cantankerous females, Mr Royce remarked. You must give them a kick and they'll soon learn to be amenable.

One way of looking at it I suppose, Mr Wilson said. Though I can't say I agree.

Well you wouldn't, Mr Royce said with a laugh.

Why wouldn't you? I wondered, searching Mr Wilson's face. *Because I'm here?*

By now the man had lost interest in beating his woman, or was too hot to continue. He was content to harangue her and pull her hair, which made the crowd restive.

Why does no one go to that woman's aid? I asked Mr Wilson. Testing him.

Mr Royce smiled. I think we know why, don't we, Paddy? None of our business, that's why. Which is how we like it.

Mr Wilson looked at Mr Royce as if trying to fathom his meaning. The thing is, Miss Callahan, he said after a pause, that's his woman the fellow is chastising. So unfortunately, legally, Jack is correct.

A bell clanged, causing most of the onlookers to drift off towards the flags. Hell's bells! Mr Wilson said as the clanging continued. He let out a mirthless laugh.

It seems I must leave you again, Miss Callahan.

He turned to Mr Royce. Is your horse in this race? he asked. If not, could you stay and keep Miss Callahan company till I get back? Not the best neighbourhood for a lady at the moment.

No it's not, yes I could and no it's not, answered his friend. It will be my pleasure, old boy.

If that's alright with you, Miss Callahan, added Mr Wilson.

Not caring to speak, I nodded my agreement. His steward work obliged him to leave me, regardless of what I might wish, though surely he had noticed my distaste at Mr Royce's remarks about women.

Good, that's settled then, he said. And down he leapt from the carriage and in seconds was lost in the crowd.

Aren't you going to invite me to join you? Mr Royce asked teasingly when I didn't speak.

He was a flash man as they say in Australia, all kitted out in his silk bell-topper and embroidered waistcoat, not to mention the cream cutaway coat. And himself to be Mr Wilson's best friend. I had half a mind to gainsay his request, but then he would be obliged to stand in the dust beside the carriage the length of his stay. So against my better judgement I relented, and invited him to sit in the buggy.

He sprang up the mounting step, a quick man despite his stocky build, and lifted his coat-tails to sit across from me. Well, this is a delightful spot, he said, glancing at the tree we were parked under. And if I may say, delightful company to share it with.

Again I got the stare from his dark eyes. Taking in my white georgette gown spangled with sunlight and pink hailspot, and my new straw hat which I had trimmed for the occasion with a matching pink velvet ribbon.

Easy to see how you threw dust in Paddy's eyes, he drawled.

Perhaps it was the other way round, I said.

He laughed. *Touché!*

Mr Wilson is a lovely man, I said. Unlike you, I thought. But I don't need to tell you that since you're his best friend. You must know all his virtues.

Oh I do indeed, Miss Callahan, he said, smiling. His virtues *and* his vices. Well this is a turn-up for the books. A girl with spirit, not quite the meek miss your looks would have me believe. And to think I almost didn't come today. It was a coin flip between putting in an appearance as a member of the committee or staying at home, dosing myself with the poison of my choice.

What poison would that be, Mr Royce?

He pulled a wry face. Brandy, dear lady. When you lose in a pigeon shoot you had every expectation of winning and the duties required of you in this world seem overly burdensome, you need a few drinks to fortify yourself. Have you never felt that way yourself?

Not that I can recall.

He tilted back his head and laughed. Then you've missed out on one of life's pleasures, Miss Callahan.

I said nothing to this. Occupied myself moving the picnic basket out of a patch of sunlight. When I looked up from my task he was examining me.

I suppose it's in order to offer my congratulations on your sudden engagement? he drawled. The wedding is all arranged, I take it?

It is, I replied, letting him hear the tartness in my voice.

Pardon, didn't mean to offend, he said, the amused smile back in place. A man can but live in hope. Wedding bells ringing out at Saint Pauls no doubt. Reverend Locke *will* be pleased.

He was asking whether I was Protestant or Catholic. The people of Australia don't come out with a direct question the way they do at home. Matters of faith aren't so important in the colonies. There's not the same painful history attached.

It will be at Saint Joseph's church in Alma Street, I said.

Eh? How's that? Paddy *has* fallen in a big way.

Mr Royce leaned back in the padded seat with a lazy smile. So what's it like being engaged to our mutual friend? he asked. Must be hard work I imagine, listening to all the horse talk. He can be a bit of a bore in that regard.

I don't find him boring at all.

Give him time. Your man's a source of entertainment to those of us who love him, what with his Irishisms and obsession with horses. The joke going round the billiard rooms is to imitate his delightful brogue giving advice on how to rear colts. Paddy's stricture is to treat them as gently as you would a child, would you believe?

Surely his friends aren't so petty, I said.

All too true, I'm afraid.

I held his gaze. It might be better not to repeat their jokes.

Oh, don't worry. I'd say the same to Paddy's face, and have done many a time. All in good fun you know, we like to rag one another. That's how it is with us men, Miss Callahan, and damn me if I tell a lie.

Would you like a savoury tart?' I asked, to change the subject. Or a sandwich? They were packed in ice and are still fresh.

Don't mind if I do. He lifted the basket lid and examined the finger sandwiches. Devilled egg and watercress? Hmm. Cheese and pickle. And what's that? *Cucumber*! No meat then? Think I'll pass on that one. Ha ha. Thanks but no thanks.

You're welcome to try the jellied fruit, I offered.

Not a great jelly-eater either as it happens. Hold on, here's your man coming back. Time to relieve you of my tiresome company I think.

His eyes lingered on my bodice before travelling up to meet my gaze. I sent him a look that said, Did your mammy never teach you manners?

He returned the faintest nod. It's been a delight meeting you, Miss Callahan, I really mean that. Hopefully I'll have the pleasure of doing so again.

Another lingering look, then his polished boots descended the mounting step and he was striding toward Mr Wilson. I watched them stop to talk, saw them laughing together till Mr Royce clapped Mr Wilson on the shoulder and continued on his way.

How bold I had been, chipping him. Never in the world would I have spoken so to a gentleman in Ireland. To an ordinary man perhaps, if he was impertinent, though never to a gentleman. But already in this land of easy manners I was growing more outspoken. It made me wonder would I ever learn to become quiet Annie again.

Mr Wilson arrived to distract me from further thoughts of a rebellious nature. I was careful not to mention his friend's remarks about 'Irishisms' and how to train colts, but I did ask a few questions of my own. What does Mr Royce do? was one of them.

He's a surgeon, reputed to be the best in town.

Goodness! I said. I'd never known a doctor before, not to speak to socially.

Mr Wilson gestured as if presenting his friend. The man's an artist on horseback, a wordsmith and punster besides. Always good for a joke and loyal to a fault. If it came to the pinch I believe I'd lay down my life for Jack.

We spent a whole hour together before he had to return to his steward duties. The last set for the day, he promised. Which made me smile, too thankful to hide my relief.

When we got back to the boarding house we sat awhile in the buggy. I won't come in to pay my respects to Mrs Part, he said. Have to get over to the Cri for the settling.

The Cry?

Sorry, the Criterion Hotel.

I made no move to climb out of the carriage. Would he take my hand? I stole a look at his fingers curled around the reins. As they should be, of course.

Do you have family in Australia, Mr Wilson? I asked.

No. His glance was wary. My people are happy enough to stay in Ireland. I miss them at times.

They must miss you too.

Mother would be delighted to have me home, not so sure about the old man. I did go back once, and couldn't stand it. Australia spoils you with its endless space. The land of sirloin steaks they say, but for me it's the open plains.

He broke out a smile that sent flutters through my chest, and added, Preferably seen from the back of a horse.

Do you have brothers and sisters? I asked, unable to stop the questions now I had started.

Two sisters, Sarah and Meg. He was silent a moment. Meg's married now I hear, to Thomas Quinn. That caused a bit of fuss.

Why so? I made so bold as to ask.

Well, Tom's a Catholic.

Do your parents know about us? I asked in the pause that followed.

No and I don't intend telling them. Not until I have to. Father has no tolerance for Roman Catholics, you know how it is.

I did, of course. My father was no different about Proddies, but it was hurtful all the same, learning our marriage was to be kept secret from his family.

It's nothing personal, he said. Meg hasn't set foot in Father's house since she married Tom. It's not only yourself will get the cold shoulder, believe me. Well, better see you to the door, I guess, or I'll be late for the settling.

Was that regret in his voice? If so, I failed to hear it.

Can you apologise on my behalf to Mrs Part for not coming in?

I will, yes, I said.

He jumped down from the buggy and handed me onto the footpath. Walked with me to the front door.

I hope you had a pleasant day, he said.

I never had a day like it before, I replied. Cheeking him politely.

Should I take that as a yes or no?

By the glint in his eye I knew he was cheeking me back.

Then away with him down the steps at a trot and leapt in the buggy like a man just beginning his day. I watched the buggy till it disappeared round the corner. He was going away droving to Raglan Station in the morning. Two whole weeks must pass before I saw him again and I wondered how I would endure the wait.

Pig-headed as Ever

SAINT STEPHENS day took forever to come, and no sooner for the lacklustre Christmas spent daydreaming about it. The boarding house had become a ghost of itself. Most of the lodgers were gone, fled away to their families in the bush or decamped to the south for the holy season. The Parts were occupied in the back parlour with their own family rituals, and celebrating the return of their eldest son from Brisbane. Jessie was nowhere to be seen the length of the day, or next to never.

On Christmas Eve my thoughts turned to Ellen, how she must be feeling, alone in Emu Park with no family around her. If we were at home with Dada and New Ma, we'd be calling on our neighbours now. Tramping through snowfall to share a night made merry with music and dancing, whiskey and cake. The latest gossip gone over, babies brought out and jiggled.

To distract myself from these bittersweet memories I ventured out after dinner to join the family groups strolling the footpaths. Stopping with them to admire the displays of greenery and mottos in the shop windows. The butcher's shop had a paper star shining on the roof—the star of Bethlehem I guess it was meant to be. Luminous against the indigo sky anyway, and so hopeful and glowing I couldn't stop looking at it.

Later, when I was in bed and the smell of the warm night came through the window, my thoughts turned to Mr Wilson and my body grew hot and desirous. Burning inside like the candlelit star. I forgot my fears about him then. That he was a stranger only made him more attractive.

On Christmas morning, I put on my new georgette gown and went to early mass. Walking the deserted streets at dawn felt queer, knowing I had no family to go home to. Knowing Ellen must be feeling the same. My first Christmas Day in Australia was a lonely affair with little comfort in it.

Next morning I woke early. The promised day had come. Saint Stephens Day, or Boxing Day they call it in Australia. I was up and dressed before dawn, and Jessie too, for she was coming with us. Mrs Part considered it improper to make a journey of such length without a chaperone, even if the gentleman was my intended. And we would be staying overnight so that settled the matter, she said.

Mr Wilson arrived in the pre-dawn dark on a big black stallion he called Caractacus, and his man Harry Roche in the buggy to drive Jessie and me. We made quite a party when we gathered on the footpath. Lit by the amber glow of the carriage lamps we said goodbye to Mrs Part.

Mind the basket stays under the seat, the sandwiches will go off otherwise, she told Jessie. Now, Mr Wilson, she said, turning to his shadowy figure, you must promise to take care of my girls. And no sampling on the way if you please. Do I have your word on that?

We'll not stop for any sampling, Mrs Part, he said in his deep brogue. Only tea at Gritty Hannah's Half-way House if the ladies wish. They'll come back safe to you, never fear.

Then away our carriage rolled through the sleeping town, white mist lying on the flats and ribbons of golden light unfurling in the great arch of sky, till we came to the Fitzroy River and went across on a punt—Jessie and myself still perched in the buggy, gazing down at the smooth flowing water—then bowled along the Yaamba Road all walled about with trees.

After a time the road veered east and we followed Mr Wilson into deeper forest. The air alive with the calls of birds. Any amount of warblings and sweet whistlings filled our ears as we jolted along behind Mr Wilson's horse.

He has hypnotised you, Jessie said. Can't you take your eyes off him?

Would you look at that? I said, pointing at some flowers to distract her. Harry Roche was at the reins with a pair of ears on him under his wideawake hat, and might repeat what he heard. They were queer flowers I showed Jessie, hanging from a tree like so many yellow insects dangling.

Oh that, Jessie said. That's only a tree orchid. They're everywhere in this bit of old scrub.

Clumps of white lilies grew in the shade of trees, seeming to glow with their own light. Huge ferns hung from gnarled branches, green waterfalls you'd think them. How could this be called scrub?

It's pretty, though, I said.

But already we were leaving the forest and emerging into sunlight.

The bush affects newcomers that way, Jessie said. Some carry on about the ring-barked trees—her voice went up high and mincing—Their weird and desolate appearance, they reckon. Weird and desolate my eye! They're just dead trees aren't they?

I saw no ring-barked trees, though stumps showed where trees once stood. Smoke curled up in lazy spirals from the chimney of a small slab hut. Its fresh-hewn timber glowed red in the long bars of morning light.

There's a grand sight, I said. The humble farmhouse had made me think of home.

Jessie laughed. I hope you're not going to turn into another new chum rhapsodiser, Annie.

I believe Mr Wilson has led a bush life, I said. He must be used to dead trees by now.

He carries the country with him, that's easy seen. Even in his town rig there's no mistaking him.

Do you like him, Jessie?

We were whispering so Harry Roche couldn't hear.

He don't look like he's got much fun in him.

Why do you say so?

Oh you know, nothing really. He's just so correct is all.

Mannerly ways are better than coarse ones, I reminded her.

After that we were silent for a time.

We passed Gritty Hannah's Half-way House, a tumbledown shanty with a roof made of bark, set back from the road among gum trees. A few miles further on, Mr Wilson called a halt beside a creek among more gum trees.

The men went off to forage for firewood while Jessie and I spread out Mrs Part's picnic rug in the dappled shade, and knelt on it in our white summer gowns, unpacking the cups and sandwiches. Mr Wilson returned to drop an armful of kindling on the ground.

Your first billy tea I think, he said. I hope you will like it, Miss Callahan.

I watched his hands at their work, breaking and laying the firewood. He knew what he was about and had the water boiling in no time.

Will you be Mother? he said when the tea was brewed.

Be mother? I asked, startled.

He stood up from his squat by the fire, at ease in his rolled-up sleeves. He seemed to be struggling not to laugh.

Give the ladies their tea, he told Harry. I'll see to Caractacus and the buggy horses.

He was a long time attending them, loosing the mares—addressing them as Zillah and Willow—and leading all three to the creek. We drank our tea without him, and a delicious brew it proved.

Eucalyptus smoke, Harry said in his Australian drawl. That's the secret.

In the afternoon we came to the crest of a hill and got our first view of the ocean, calm as a bog-lake and blue and innocent as if it could never rear up in tumult the way it had on the *Kapunda*.

Hooray! Jessie cried, and Mr Wilson reined in his horse.

Your sister is down there somewhere, Miss Callahan. You will soon be reunited with her.

Air flowed into my lungs, buoying me, and I realised what I was feeling was simple happiness. Something I hadn't felt in a while.

We rattled down the wooded slope to the sea-village called Emu Park. Timber cottages peeped out behind banana trees, dogs lay sprawled asleep on the road, and the great attraction, the glittering blue bay, was crowded with tents along the foreshore. For the Christmas campers, Harry explained.

He pulled up outside the Steak-and-Beer Inn, which had a quantity of carriages and waggonettes and spring-carts outside, and as many horses tethered to the hitching posts.

Mr Wilson dismounted from the black stallion and handed Jessie and me down from the buggy.

The Emu Park pubs do a roaring trade this time of year, he said. I'll get along with Harry to ours now and see about stabling for the horses. Walk yourselves over when you're ready, ladies. That's our hotel across the road, the one with the stuffed crocodile on it.

So there was. A crocodile right enough, hanging on the outside wall, under the shelter of the upstairs verandah.

Your sister is resting, Mrs Stake said when she was fetched by the maid. It's a very great nuisance but she's not been well these past few days. Mr Stake is quite put out. It couldn't of happened at a worse time, we're run off our feet. The maid will show you where to find her.

Her sharp eyes took in our white gowns. No, better I do it myself. Come this way, please.

She led us down a hallway to the back door and showed us a shed in the yard. Its corrugated metal walls were all but surrounded by a litter of broken bed-springs, cracked chamber pots and rotting tea chests.

The servant quarters, she said. Door number three. I must get back to the bar so I'll bid you good day.

Ellen was lying on her back in a narrow bed, stretched out under a stained cotton sheet. The room was oven temperature. My goodness! Jessie said from the doorway. Should we open a window? Is there a window?

Well don't just stand there, Ellen said, pulling herself up. Give us a hug, you eejit.

What's wrong? I whispered.

She grimaced. Nothing much. Just the pains at times, and the weakness.

Her face was pale under a film of sweat. Dark half-circles cupped her eyes. I put a hand on her forehead.

You're feverish.

It's my bones feel achy, she muttered. I'd be right otherwise. Mrs Stake reckons I shouldn't have stayed so long in the sun on my day off. I did get hot that day but I wanted to be by the sea. Dev's out there somewhere.

Her voice grew dreamy. I could swim out maybe and—

How long have you been like this? I demanded. And in this dreadful hot room. Has the doctor been? What does he say?

Mrs Stake's been dosing me regular with laudanum and brandy. It fixes most things, she reckons.

But how long?

Three days, five. I don't know.

You must come back to Rockhampton, I said. You must see a doctor.

Ellen sank down on the pillow. You always was a fusser, Annie. Let me look at you, she said. A sight for sore eyes you are, glad as a rose in that white dress.

She would hear no more talk of doctors so I gave her my parcel.

Only a day late, I said.

I helped her sit up so she could undo the wrapping. Her hands trembled as she took out the white gown. You big bostoon, she said. This is the voile you bought in Townsville, and you're giving the dress to *me*?

I couldn't stop smiling. I wore it once, I confessed.

Ellen's eyes glistened. It's lovely, Annie. You must have been stitching for weeks and I've nothing to give in return.

I was hoping you'd put it on so we can see if it fits. I wasn't expecting to find you like this.

Ah well, I'll get better and then I'll wear it.

She lay back on the pillow and flashed a glimpse of her old grin. They have dances here on Saturday night, did you know? I should make quite a stir in this.

So you're liking Emu Park?

Apart from getting sick, it's fine. I've had my share of offers from the local men. Rhyming Lynam even, he caught the mailcoach down to propose. But I let him down gentle by telling him the truth: that I will never marry any man unless it's Dev.

Jessie was hovering in the doorway. I'll say goodbye, Ellen, she said in a carrying whisper. You two will be wanting to tell each other your secrets. See you at the hotel, Annie.

Take care now, we chorused, smiling as we waved her off.

As soon as Jessie was gone, Ellen asked if I'd written to Dada.

Not yet. Have you?

She shook her head. Don't write you're marrying a Proddy. You'll only give New Ma satisfaction when he chucks your letter in the fire.

Don't worry, I won't tell Dada. What he doesn't know can't upset him.

In the night all cats are grey, Ellen quoted. And in Australia all men are Catholic, or so our father must believe. I wonder what shade of grey your cat will be, Annie. Dev now, he was a great shade.

Can't you forget him? I said. It does you no good to be always fretting.

Christ, she groaned. It's hard work forgetting. I don't think I ever shall.

I wish you'd come back to town with us and see a doctor.

She heaved up from the mattress to give me the full stare. I'm better off here. This place is like Paradise must be. The men bring up yellowtail and snapper from the sea every day. Oysters off the rocks when the tide's out. And the colonial men are more amiable. Not so fighting wild.

She sent me a sly look. Let's hope your man don't prove too wild. Rhyming Lynam reckons he's called Mad Paddy.

Mad Paddy? What was that supposed to mean?

Then his name must be Patrick, was all I could think to say.

I fumbled for words. Ellie, what was the ... that story you told me, about him asking Lizzie Doyle to marry?

Just that. I heard it from Polly.

Polly, I said dully, and dropped the subject. If Polly was the one who reckoned he proposed to Lizzie then likely the story was true.

We spent the afternoon together. I brought water for Ellen to drink from a barrel I found in the yard, but had to tip it out. It wasn't drinking water, she said, and she had already been scolded for using it.

Then how are you to drink?

Ellen pointed at a pail in the corner, which on inspection turned out to be empty. Take it to the scullery, she said. The kitchen slushy will fill it.

I did that and brought back the filled bucket. Poured a tumbler of water for Ellen and used water from the barrel to rinse her nightdress and undergarments. The whole room stank of sweat and manky clothes. It seemed no one was attending her.

I went over to stand by the bed. Now, Ellen, I said, I'll pack your clothes for you. You must come back with me to Rockhampton.

I'm not coming so you can forget about it.

Ellen was pig-headed to a fault. Always had been.

But you're sick and you haven't seen a doctor, I argued. Brandy and laudanum may be beneficial for giving relief, but what do they do to combat the cause?

Ellen's lips turned down in a sneer. Oh big words! That's fine coming from you, Annie. You're all fixed up with your fancy gentleman, just like Dada set himself up with New Ma after Mam died. But what about me? I have to make a life too, and hanging onto your skirt-tails isn't my way of doing it.

I swallowed the lump suddenly constricting my throat. It hurt me to see my little sister so unhappy and angry.

Oh Ellie, who said anything about skirt-tails? All I'm suggesting is you come up to town and see a doctor.

Well I'm not coming so forget about it.

We would have kept arguing only for the shadows creeping through the doorway. The time had come to say goodbye. Promise you'll rest and get strong, I said. Make sure you write and tell me how you are. Tell me you're fighting fit, that's what I want to know.

I'll tell you how many proposals I've received since last we met, Ellen boasted, and we laughed very merry. More than we usually did. Hiding our feelings to ease the pain of parting.

Mr Wilson and the others had just returned from watching horse-races on the beach when I arrived at the other hotel. I found them sitting in armchairs in the entry parlour. Jessie was flushed in the face.

A touch of sunburn, she said, laughing.

Harry was all smiles too. He had bet on a winning horse and won three guineas, and he insisted on taking the gold coins from his waist pouch to show me.

Never had a guinea in my hand before and now I got three, he said. Dinner's on me tonight, he told Mr Wilson, who smiled but didn't answer.

The others kept up their talk about the races and were still gabbing about them when the dinner bell rang. A waiter showed us to a table by a window, through which we heard the hushed, murmurous roar of the ocean. Around us a low rumble of voices and the chink of cutlery on china. From my seat by the window I saw the broad bay glinting in the moonlight. The shoreline was that close I wondered how it would feel to walk barefoot, and have sand squish between your toes.

The most comical thing, Annie, said Jessie, interrupting my thoughts. They use sand in the saddle-bags for weights, did you know? But some lads made slits in them and when the horses took off you couldn't see them for the sandstorm. It was a gas to watch.

Mr Wilson stiffened. Even his voice seemed to bristle. There was nothing comical about it, Miss Part. Sand is bad for horses' eyes. Personally, I'd like to whip the scoundrels responsible.

Jessie slipped me a look as if to say, See what I mean, your man has no fun in him, but I wouldn't smile back.

Our meals arrived, piled high and smelling delicious. The sea air had sharpened everyone's appetite so no one said anything much until we were all sitting back, our plates scraped clean. Harry broke the satisfied silence by telling a long-winded joke that wasn't very funny about a lady in a crinoline who went to sea in a rowboat.

Jessie and I laughed politely and Mr Wilson said, You never cease to amaze me, Harry. You have a story for every occasion.

Harry reddened, the blush moving up his face in waves. Stories stick to me like burrs, he said. But he was pleased with Mr Wilson's words, you could tell.

After the waiter removed the last of the dishes Mr Wilson's eyes sought mine across the table.

Did you enjoy your visit to your sister, Miss Callahan?

I might have enjoyed it better, I said, if not for finding her ill with fever.

His face turned sombre. I'm most sorry to hear that. What does the doctor say?

He hasn't been called.

I could have a word with the Stakes if you like, he offered. If time permits. It's worth reminding them that your sister requires medical attention. It's their job to look after a bonded servant's health.

That's very kind, I said. Thank you, Mr Wilson.

He nodded and took a silver watch from his waistcoat pocket.

Time to check the horses, he announced. The stabling was taken so Caractacus and the mares are loose in the hotel paddock. I don't want any larrikins borrowing them.

Yeah, no, Harry agreed.

Can you not refuse to lend them? I asked, but Mr Wilson said borrowing was Australian for stealing. He pushed back his chair and stood up.

Good night, Miss Callahan. Sleep well. Good night, Miss Part. He inclined his head to each of us and took himself off, followed by Harry who grinned and dipped an imaginary hat.

Jessie and I went upstairs to our room soon after, and were happy enough to do so. It's the sea air, it always makes you so-o-oh sleepy, Jessie said, yawning as she unpinned her long tawny hair, which shone like gold in the lamplight.

But later, in bed, all I could think of was the moonlit walk on the beach that Mr Wilson and I might have taken. The kiss we could have enjoyed.

Horses, one. Annie, nil, I told myself. Making a joke of it to ease my disappointment.

In the morning, before sunrise, I heard someone calling. A deep voice, his own voice, I knew it. I slipped out of bed and tiptoed across the floorboards to peer through the doorway. Not wanting to go out on the verandah and be seen.

It was himself right enough, in the hotel paddock, calling out *coo-up coo-up* in the Irish way. The way Dada called when he wanted our mare. Come up come up, *coo-up coo-up,* he'd call, like a dove cooing to its mate, and Birdie would trot up the paddock to be yoked. And Caractacus doing the same. Mr Wilson stroked the black stallion's mane, then called up Zillah and Willow for their share. And afterwards stood in the dawn light, whistling and looking about. A lithe man with the stance of a dancer. I watched him till he went inside.

A tap on the door startled me, but it was only the maid with a lamp.

What is it? I whispered, opening the door a crack.

Your breakfast call, miss. Mr Wilson ordered it for five.

I never got to see Ellen again. Mr Wilson had requested sandwiches prepared for the journey, so by six we were on our way to Rockhampton. It was two days nearer our wedding day and God forgive me, I hardly spared a thought for my sister as the carriage rolled along.

Why Are Ladies Called Ducks?

AND SO it came time for our wedding. January 3 in the leap year of '76. I couldn't sleep the night before. A murderess waiting to be hung in the morning couldn't have been more alert. And nothing better to do than look at the familiar wallpaper. I stared at the bunches of yellow roses for what seemed an age, and mighty queer they looked with the moonlight slanting on them. Not at all like their daytime appearance. When that didn't work I tried counting the bunches, which wasn't to be done; they were all the time jumping about and I had to start again. Then I counted the ceiling boards till I fell asleep and woke in the morning with the fright on me.

How do I know he's not a drunkard or wife-beater? I asked myself, and tossed about among the pillows for a time. Wait a minute till you think, I thought. Isn't he a jewel of a man and a gentleman besides? Why would I think of jilting such a one as him? I'd be mad if I did, but I'm not mad and I am going to marry him.

Up I jumped and went over to the wash basin to splash my face as if it was everyday, and Jessie came rustling into the room. She was already dressed up in her best gown of apple-green organza on account of it was to be a morning wedding to avoid the heat.

Let's get those dratted curlers out, she said. She brushed my hair and twisted it up very complicated, all the while pursing her lips and considering. The two of us peering at the mirror to judge the effect. For though I take little interest in such matters as a rule, I took plenty that morning. Jessie buttoned me into the shimmering white gown, then circled around me, alternating between frowning concentration and fits of giggles while she pinned the lace mantilla her mother had loaned me to my hair.

Ellen had sent a letter saying her health was improving, along with a pierced scallop shell tucked inside to be my wedding token. I turned the pale pink shell in my hand, breathing its salty perfume—the smell of the ocean that had brought my sister and me to this country.

Jessie fixed the shell to my bodice, nestling it among the froth of lace on the neckline. So pretty, she said, but where is your something blue?

And off she ran and returned with a blue ribbon for my garter, to be that article. Then we went out to the back parlour for the viewing by Mrs Part.

She was spreading a white cloth on the table when we came in. The good woman wouldn't hear of anything but to give a wedding breakfast. It would be her pleasure she said, and she was only sorry to be losing such a useful body about the house.

Let me look at you, she said, swishing out from behind the table in an imposing gown of green ruched silk. And made me turn about and turn about until I began to feel like a cow on market day.

So muggy this morning, she said, dabbing her face. Mr Part swears it will rain and Heaven knows we need it. As for myself I judge the heat not vicious enough. I've lived in Rockhampton sixteen years, as long as the town has existed, since the first crazy days when gold was discovered at Crocodile Creek. So I ought to know.

Oh Mother! Jessie said.

Next Mrs Part sent for Jessie's brother Willy to be our escort, which vexed Jessie greatly.

Mother, she said, he's sixteen and we're much older. We don't need him along.

He'll do well enough, Mrs Part said. It always looks better to have a man with you, and William is a sturdy lad and tall enough to pass for that article.

69

So with Mrs Part waving from the steps we set off along East-street to Saint Josephs church. I was wearing three borrowed or given articles and Willy had added to my store of threes by making up the bride's party to the same number. *1 for Sorrow, 2 for Mirth, 3 for a Wedding and 4 for Death* is how the old rhyme goes, and you can't be too careful where a marriage is concerned.

We stepped inside the little wooden church and saw Mr Wilson and Harry Roche waiting at the altar. Harry swivelled his head to watch as we advanced up the aisle.

Mr Wilson and I knew not to look at one another. We both stared ahead as if turned to stone.

But the queer part about it, when Father Murlay came to the words *Who gives this woman away?* everyone looked around, and realised there was no one for the job.

It appears Miss Callahan is giving 'erself away, Father Murlay said and laughed at his own joke.

In the end it was Willy who was made to come forward, red-faced and scowling, to say he was the man. He was the one handing me over.

Bien, Father Murlay said when the words were all spoke, and lifted his surplice to waft a breeze under it. Red as a rowan berry the poor man was, from the unnatural heat.

And now, ze ring if you please, he said.

Harry looked uncomfortable, like Willy, and rummaged in his pockets. It's in here somewhere, he said, and ended up dropping the gold band on the floor.

Willy picked it up and handed it to him, and Harry passed it to Mr Wilson, who put it on my finger.

It has taken four men to get this ring on my finger, I thought, and in the queer dream-state I was in I thought I heard Ellen's snorting laugh behind me.

Mr Wilson gave me a chaste kiss.

Voila! said Father Murlay, and led our little party across the gravel sweep to the presbytery to sign the marriage papers. He ushered us into the green-shuttered parlour with its bars of watery sunlight quivering on the ceiling.

I made sure to write my age in the marriage book—twenty-four— and made sure to read what Mr Wilson wrote. *Thirty-five*, he put for his age, *Kilbeggan, Westmeath* for birth place, and *Overland drover* in the space for occupation. I stored the last piece of information away for future delving. For father's occupation he wrote *Clergyman*, and signed his name *Edward* and not *Patrick* as I had expected.

So then I knew a lot more about him than I had known before.

Under clouds heavy with rain, we drove back to the boarding house, Jessie and myself in Mr Wilson's buggy. Harry Roche followed on his horse with Willy perched behind. But when we pulled up at the kerb Harry announced he wouldn't come in.

I don't care for parlouring and going among women, he told Mr Wilson. I'll get along now and see you later.

No you won't, Mr Wilson said back to him. You'll come in with me like the flash man you're always blowing you are.

At that Harry Roche gave him a despairing look and followed behind with his bow-legged horseman's gait.

While we were at the church the boarding house cook had put on a very good spread in the back parlour under Mrs Part's direction. Cold turkey and other cold meats, mayonnaise, salads, cut fruits and cream and sherry trifle, with cold cordials and iced tea to follow. We sat down at the dining table, Mr Wilson and myself made to preside at the head.

Mr Part came in the room and fetched two bottles from the sideboard.

Oh Mr Part, said Mrs Part, it's much too early for drinking. And we are a teetotal hotel.

Nonsense, woman, this is a special occasion, Mr Part said, and added in an undertone, Don't fret about the lodgers, Dorothy. We're quite private here.

Now what will you have, gentlemen? he asked. Brandy, or a drop of this new whiskey they're making out at Gracemere?

Mr Wilson declined but Harry cocked his head.

I'd be a pie-eyed wallaby if I ever touch the Gracemere brew again, he said, but I'd surely appreciate a brandy if one's on offer.

In no time he was on his second nobbler and talking a blue streak, as they say in Australia, and it might have been better if he had got his wish not to come in the house. The stories he told were diabolical, though I do believe he thought they were suitable for female ears.

Why are ladies called ducks? he asked, looking round the table. And went on a rambling tale about how not all of them were tame, how a good deal of sport could be got from the wild ones, how they could be captured and plucked, how they were always dressed for the table but needed a good deal of buttering, how they had long bills and so on and so forth—with Jessie rolling her eyes and kicking my feet under the table.

And are you married, Mr Roche? asked Mrs Part when he finished. I believe you must be for you appear to know a good deal about women.

Not as yet, ma'am, he said. But next year I might look over the heifer-paddock in Brisbane and take my chances.

Do you not find the Rockhampton women suitable then? she asked, frowning.

Well ma'am, females ain't too plentiful hereabouts, Harry muttered. With that he fell silent and not another word could be dragged from him.

Mr Wilson announced it was time to make tracks before the storm hit, and goodbyes were said, and hugs exchanged on the footpath, and a few tears shed also. Mr Part hoisted my ship box onto the jump seat and shook Mr Wilson's hand. Harry crept round the back of the carriage to attach a couple of tin cans, while Mrs Part examined the clouds and gave as her opinion they were rainless and we would make it home safe.

Mr Wilson handed me into the buggy while Mr and Mrs Part, Harry Roche, Jessie and Willy—and Winnie the parlour maid who had followed us down the steps and was adding her waves and smiles—stood in a row on the pavement, waving goodbye.

See ya, mate, Harry said.

Mr Wilson flicked the reins and we set off for Serpentine Water.

PART 2

Serpentine Water

I WOKE up in the lonely bed and memories came rushing at me like a herd of startled cattle. Himself kissing my nipples sticking up in their fright, his body on mine, I scarce could breathe from wanting and fearing what was to come. The thrusting, and pain so sharp I cried out. Blood seeping on the sheets, himself getting up afterwards, saying he didn't like to sleep on wet sheets, and going off to another room.

The howling that came through the window, enough to curdle your veins. Like lost souls in torment, in Purgatory maybe. I was sure it was wolves.

I lay on the blood-caked sheets, creeping my fingers down to feel below. The night just passed streeled through my head like one of those picture-books you riffle to make the figures move. I heard all manner of noises. Creakings and settlings in the timber house, cattle bellowing far off, dogs barking, birds screeching and other queer cries that might have been human.

After a time I got up, gathered the sheets and night-clothes in a bundle and carried them through the house, fearful someone would see me. And glad to find the washplace outside, on a bench under a tree, and put the linen to soak in the water I found in a barrel.

When that was done I looked about.

A black man was letting out a milch cow from the house-paddock and smoke drifted up from the native people's camp by the lagoon. But I wasn't thinking of any of that. I was remembering the night and what went before.

Us driving through town in the buggy, passing Rutherford's Livery Stables and Mr Wilson saying I mustn't go there because ladies shouldn't be seen stravaging about in a horse bazaar. Then the queer wooden cottages perched on posts along Dawson-road, and such a terrible smell coming from Pattison's boiling-down shed with its big black pots and heaps of bullock bones. Then the first lagoon, the Yeppen Yeppen, and all the birds, so many of them, and a big brown snake that slithered across the road. Crows cawing, and a queer class of animal with faces like deers that Mr Wilson said were kangaroos. They watched us, swivelling their ears one way, then the other.

I heard laughter then and returned to my senses. The dark-skinned children, the piccaninnies Mr Wilson called them, were splashing in the lagoon while their mothers sat by the fire, keeping watch. Yesterday the women were in the water with their children, diving down to bring up water-lily roots and stuff them in woven bags.

I turned to look at the house and saw smoke rising from the kitchen-house chimney. Saw Dinah sweeping dust through the doorway in leisurely strokes. Yesterday she was waiting on the front steps in the same ragged red dress, a smile on her face like the sun after rain, and her eyes that are bright as two jet beads giving out their welcome. Ah Lin was with her, grinning too, shuffling down the steps in his embroidered slippers to help with my ship box.

I looked at the ring-barked trees like skeletons in the paddocks— so big the paddocks were you couldn't see the finish of them—at the huts for the men, the meathouse with bullock skins stretched on its roof, and the Berserker Mountains softened by distance into a dream of themselves. Then I went inside.

Mr Wilson came in the house at dusk. I was helping Dinah set the table and couldn't look at him after the night just passed.

Ah there you are, Mrs Wilson, he said in his deep voice. I believe Dinah can see to that. Let's sit outside for a time, shall we?

It wasn't a real question, so we went out on the verandah. And spent a time standing in the evening light, him with his arms round my waist, looking at me soft. Myself trembling as if a small engine was inside me. Then he went away and flung himself down in a chair.

Come and sit by me, he said. This is the time we enjoy the cool.

I went over and sat beside him, in a wicker chair that was there. Everything go alright today? he asked.

Yes, Mr Wilson, I said to the floor.

Oh you can't be Mr Wilsoning me anymore. It must be Annie and Paddy between us now.

Or Mad Paddy is it? I thought. Yes, Mr Wilson, I said, keeping my head down.

You'll soon get used to it, he said. Try it for me now.

I thought your name was Edward.

No one calls me that in Australia, he said. I'm just another Paddy here. So will you say it for me?

Paddy, I said, though it felt like swallowing a lump of gristle.

He went in the house and came back with a tumbler of brandy, and we sat together, looking out at the paddocks, and the first faint stars in the sky. Orion's Belt was upside down I noticed. Fireflies flittered above the waterlilies on the lagoon, and every now and then Mr Wilson's cattledog Banjo thumped his tail on the floorboards. The buckets of burning cattle-dung Dinah had lit earlier stung my eyes from their smouldering, but I didn't mind. It was worth it to keep off the mosquitoes.

A couple of workhorses must have thought so too, for up they trotted from the house-paddock to stand close to the verandah railing and have some ease. Frogs croaking in the lagoon and insects adding their din, and every now and then you would hear a little plop as a drop of water fell from one of the canvas waterbags hanging from the rafters.

After dinner we sat in the parlour, the drawing-room he called it, himself reading a newspaper and myself writing to Ellen at a little desk that was there.

Dear Sister,

I receved your welcome letter and pretty shell, thank you for sending it. It got good use for the Something-new you will be pleased to hear. I am glad you are better in your helth, I have been praying for you. Please stay out of the sun in fucher, that is an order. Well Ellen I am a marryed woman now. My husband is reading a newspaper beside me at this moment. I have a woman to help in the house, she is a Half Cast and marryed to the cook, he is a Chinaman. We have a gentleman coming to call soon, he is Mr Wilson's partner Mr Praed. He has a cattle farm on Port Curtis Island and a Wife. She may come too.

Hoping you remane in better helth. No more at present, your loving sister Annie.

PS. I call him Paddy now.

Mr Wilson put down his newspaper. Well, I don't know about you, he said, but I can't keep my eyes open.

He yawned and ambled out the door. But when I came in the bedroom he was lying on the bed with his eyes open. Waiting for me.

I never saw him next day till evening. He was gone before I woke up. But Dinah and I got on well enough without him, and I liked Ah Lin also. The food our cook served up was better than anything I ever ate previous, or after for that matter.

One cartridge, two bird, he said the first night when he brought in a roast duck on a platter. Grinning till his eyes almost disappeared.

Dinah was watching from the doorway. *Pho*! Shoot him duck, she said, giggling. Number one husben, that fella mine.

A very good shot, agreed Mr Wilson. That will be all now, Dinah.

Well then, he said later, looking at my clean plate. You enjoyed that I see.

I did, yes, Mr Wilson, I said. For he was Mr. Wilson to me still, whatever I told Ellen. I couldn't call him Paddy, though it was lodged in my heart like a secret.

Dinah and I became friends. We were a good deal together in the house, and she was a great help to me about the centipedes and snakes, getting used to them I mean. Our house at Serpentine Water had many such creatures, but Dinah had no fear of any of them and taught me the same. One time she caught me staring at the ceiling, trying to guess what was lying on the other side of the stretched canvas, making it sag.

Old man possum sleep there, she said and laughed at the face I pulled. I had no idea then what a possum was.

Dinah was a big laugher. I never knew anyone with a laugh so catching, we were often at it together. Mr Wilson came in the house early one day and found us in fits of laughter in his office-room, astonished by the pictures in a medical book, they were that rude. He only looked at me then, but later when we were sitting on the verandah he said I mustn't be familiar with Dinah that way.

It's not that she's an Aborigine, but that she's a servant, he said.

I like her, I said. I didn't say I was killed for someone to talk to.

One can never become friends with servants, Mr Wilson said, and went off to get his brandy. But I was thinking of the Depot in Townsville and Mrs Morphy's words about wages, so when he came back I asked what Dinah got paid.

He took a sip of brandy before replying. Nothing in the way of money. She gets her food and clothes. Baccy of course. If she's sick I get her medicine, a doctor if needed.

But servants are paid in Australia, I said. For I knew they were.

Not the natives, he said. Now don't make eyes at me, Annie. It's a mistake to give them money. They only make themselves sick, buying opium dregs from the Chinese or rot-gut from grog shanties.

And the white men? I pursued. Do you pay them?

Well Harry and Tom are different. They're drovers so they get the going rate. What a solemn little questioner you are, he said, and told me not to bother my head with such matters.

He talked about the weather then, how the drought was drying up the milkers and Ah Lin reckoned the hens had stopped laying. He looked at the sky that had not a cloud in all its blue. We're overdue for some rain, he said. Ah Lin wants me to bring in a few scrub turkeys for the pot, but they're thin on the ground lately.

Mr Praed that was Mr Wilson's partner drove out from town one morning, jolting up the track in an American buggy. He must have hired it at the horse bazaar for it had Rutherford's Livery Stables painted on the side. I wasn't too fascinated by the pink-faced gentleman in his white boater hat. He talked through his nose and looked about him distasteful, at the women sitting in the dirt with their dogs, at Dinah and myself waiting on the verandah. And never troubled to greet me. Went striding off with Mr Wilson to inspect the outbuildings and hadn't a word to throw me the length of his visit.

I tried to learn more about him afterwards. Sundown was the best time to talk to Mr Wilson, himself sitting in his squatter's chair, gazing at the paddocks. They were covered in pink cockatoos that day, pecking at what was left of the grasses and looked like nothing so much as pieces of the pink sky fallen to earth.

Mr Praed's wife didn't come with him, I remarked.

The woman has babies and stayed at home. Praed's concerned about her of course.

Why is that? I asked. I was curious about the woman I had hoped to meet.

Port Curtis Island is a mass of flames at the moment, but she's a bush-girl it seems. Praed's confident she'll take care of the station.

It's a wonder he didn't rush home to her, bush-girl or not, I thought.

He's a queer enough customer, Mr Wilson said, rubbing Banjo's back with his boot. He's only here to make money and take it back to England, like most that come to the colonies. Good luck to him I suppose. He helped me set up Serpentine Water, so I'm hardly complaining.

He left off pleasuring Banjo and put his feet up on the leg-rests of his chair.

The visit went well, he said. Praed was pleased with the improvements, the fencing and out-buildings. The horses are my affair, I don't bother him with that sort of detail.

And he began talking about horses, how he was getting another two up from Sydney, a stallion called Clansman and a Clydesdale called Dainty Davie.

We'll have first-class breeding stock when they arrive. Pyrrhus for racing, Clansman for gentleman's hack and Dainty Davie for carriage and dray work. We should make good money standing them next season.

He went on talking about horses, and I understood most of it. I was getting educated from hearing so much about them.

The Forgiveness of Trees

B UT NOW it comes time to tell the next bead in memory's string, and hard bitter work it will be in the telling. Yet tell it I must, for memory is all I have now. Dinner was cleared from the table and myself pinning out the dimity on its slippery polished surface. I was wanting to get the gown finished because I had only the one cool one, having given the white voile to Ellen on Saint Stephens Day. So I'm pinning the dimity, Mister Wilson sitting across from me reading the newspaper in his leather armchair, when on a sudden he looks up and stares at me. A queer enough stare it is too.

Annie, he says, and clears his throat. Come over here will you? Sit by me a moment.

What's this about? I think, and go over and sit beside him.

He clears his throat again, looks at the newspaper and puts it down. What is it? I say, thinking for the love of God give it out, man.

Is it about your horses? I ask.

Not the horses, no, he says, and looks at me in the same queer way. Then I know it's bad, whatever it is.

Well then, he says, maybe it's better you read it yourself.

He stands up and gives me the newspaper. Points with his finger where I must read. I'm trembling now and don't want to, and can't anyway. The print jumps about and the letters won't come together. Then they do and I read it all, despite the big words—like rocks strewn in a field the long words were—till I come to a bare patch. And know.

I have the notice from the newspaper still, with the date on it: 2nd February, 1876. I keep it in an old biscuit tin along with the letter Ellen sent me and the ones I wrote to her, that were sent back after. Strange to take out the newspaper clipping and see how it has turned yellow, like an ancient manuscript must look.

We believe the immigrants who venture to this country are not given sufficient warning about the hazards that prevail in the Colonies. It is hoped that in future, public moneys spent on bringing out labourers from the Mother country will be directed in part towards educating them about the circumstances they find themselves in. It has come to our attention that a young servant-woman named Ellen Callahan died yesterday at the Steak-and-Beer Inn in Emu Park. It appears the deceased suffered from pains in her limbs for several weeks prior to her demise. A doctor attended after her death and certified that she died of sunstroke complicated by infection from contaminated drinking water. We can only repeat: It is high time immigrants are given adequate information regarding these ubiquitous colonial dangers.

Then my new husband is patting me and telling me I mustn't cry and put myself about, and he goes out to the kitchen to tell Dinah to make tea.

I heard their voices, they must have been standing on the verandah, their words came drifting through the open door. My head was that dizzy I only heard bits of it, I was drifting myself. She is morbid from overstrain, the Doctor was saying ... a fair dose of laudanum ... yes, asleep now ... pull herself together ... *that was Mister Wilson* ... guilt eating her ... but she won't eat ... give her time ... time ... the voices drifting, swelling and shrinking ... the curtains swelling and shrinking and suddenly Ellen comes running up from the turf-lake, four years old again. She has a bog-lily in her hand and I see the dimple in her cheek that's long gone, I had forgot it was ever there, the faint down on her ear lobes, the specks of mud on her chubby fingers, I see it all, everything in every tiny detail, Ellen laughing her fat chuckle, the dimple coming and going, and she gives me the bog-lily and stretches out her hand because she wants it back, and I'm laughing with her and taking her hand, and we go up through the grasses, and there's the brown horse, not Birdie, the one we had before, munching, munching. And Ellen gives him the bog-lily to eat but he doesn't want it.

It was the opium in the laudanum gave me that vision, though I didn't know it then.

Tom Creed that is Mister Wilson's general man drove me into town for mass. Mister Wilson doesn't like me to travel alone, on account of the black men and worse still, he says, the white men I might meet on the way.

In the little timber church I lit a candle for Ellen and knelt down to gaze at its flame. I thought about Dada, the letter I must write, the grief it would bring. The candle flame wavered and threatened to go out. I knew I wasn't forgiven. It might have been better if I had lit more candles for my sister when she was ill. She might be alive now. Oh why didn't I insist that day? Convince her to come back with us and get proper care. I was too busy thinking about Mister Wilson and my new life with him to fight her on it. That was the reason.

After mass I asked Father Murlay would he give me confession, but when I tried to tell my sin he said there was none. It was God's will and so on and so forth. I had to go back to the buggy carrying my sin as heavy as before.

Dr Callaghan rode out from town a second time. He is a friend of Mister Wilson, they are both big men for the horses and both Protestant besides. He sat in Mr Wilson's chair on the verandah and I sat beside him.

We have the same name I believe, he said, and told me he was an Ulster man born not so far from my county of Cavan. So then I knew Mister Wilson had been talking to him about me, for how else could he know where I came from?

He said he often thought about Ulster and was I homesick for the old country, and I said I was.

You're not alone you know, he said in his gravelly voice. You can talk to me any time. Just get in the buggy and come and visit me in my rooms. Or at home if you prefer. My wife and I will be glad to see you. And you have your husband to lean on, remember that.

I looked down, watching my fingers at their work, pleating and unpleating the folds of my gown. It was because of Mister Wilson, in a way, that Ellen was dead. She would never have taken up work at the Steak-and-Beer Inn except for him. I might still be together with her, still hear her laugh and wicked tongue. He might not have intended this to happen. It wasn't done deliberate, I wasn't so demented as to think that. But none of this would have happened after we landed in Australia if Mister Wilson hadn't come to the Immigration Depot in Townsville and asked me to marry.

Give yourself time, Dr Callaghan said. You'll find life worth living again. It will all come out right in the end.

He took up his hat, inclined his head polite, and went down the steps to his horse.

Another day Jessie Part drove out from town with her brother Albert. I was blacking the stove when their pony trap pulled up, so I couldn't hug her as she wanted. She brought a big pot of soup her mother made and messages from her also, but I couldn't think what to say, so after a time they went away.

I stood on the verandah, watching Albert flick the reins to start the pony. Jessie waved and I waved, then I went inside.

I heard a curlew that night, the first one I heard in Australia. Some say the cry of the colonial curlew is a ghostly sound, it chills them to the bone, but it wasn't that way for me. It was my own voice I heard in the darkness, crying its lament. In the morning Dinah told me the curlew had come for someone. Someone was going to die and the curlew would show them the way to their new home.

Did a curlew come for Ellen? I wondered. Did she hear one the night before she died?

Sure enough, a terrible wailing broke out in the dead of night, coming up from the native camp by the lagoon. It continued for hours. Dancer, the house cowboy, gave me the news when he brought up the milk-pail in the morning.

Piccaninny bong, he said. Bad spirit make her bong. Blackfellas go now, no good this place, missus.

He didn't look happy at all. No more did I probably, we were a pair of long faces together.

Later I saw the people burying the dead child, the men wailing and striking their chests with knobbed clubs. A truly pitiable frightening sight. The women no less violent, belabouring themselves with sharp-pointed yam sticks till their naked bodies glistened with blood. Afterwards, the men covered the small mound with sheets of paperbark while the women circled them, uttering high-pitched fluttering cries.

They dragged the wood off the fire and stamped out the embers with their feet. The women rolled up their possum-skin rugs and the men gathered their spears, then they went away, into the forest. The men first, women and children following. One moment they were there, walking through the trees with their easy economical gait, their bodies tattered by flickering light and shade, the next melted into shadow, as insubstantial as the bark peeling off the gum trees.

Dancer went with them.

Dinah and I stood in the kitchen doorway, watching them depart. Dinah was from a different tribe, so she had no reason to go with them. For which I was very grateful.

When Mister Wilson came in the house he said it was a damned nuisance about Dancer. He would have to go into town and find another man.

He had a letter for me when he returned.

A message of condolence, I expect, he said, watching while I opened it.

He was always peering at my face after Ellen died. I knew he was worried for me, but I could never give him the smiles he wanted, and I had set my heart against him anyway, because of Ellen. The letter was from Sergeant Lynam, the wardsman Ellen had made friends with at the Immigration Depot.

Dear Missus Wilson,

I am v. sorrow to learn the melancoly news of Miss Callahan's demise. Your sister was kind to this cranky old fellow if I may say. She was a v. fine class of lady, a good strict lass if you follow me, but it is not for me to tell you who is her sister. These surely are times would take the heart out of you when such a one as Miss Callahan is took so sudden, it is the trecherous world we live in, there is no saying otherwise. That is my say to you Missus Wilson, may your shadow never grow less.

Yours v. respectful, Sergeant Phineas Lynam.

I put the letter in my pocket and Mister Wilson began talking about headstones. He had spoke to the stonemason he said.

The words now. What would you be wanting?

He didn't mention Ellen's name. I suppose he had no wish to see a female shedding tears again. I thanked him and said I would think on it and give him the words in the morning. I was grateful to him in my heart but that didn't lessen its heaviness.

Mister Wilson had taken himself off to another room after he gave me the newspaper. I couldn't abide having him touch me was the truth of it. But as weeks turned to a month he showed himself less forbearing, and let me know he wished to return to his marriage bed.

Am I likely to be kissing my wife tonight? he would say. If so, I'll have the full bath.

I always shook my head, and he would go away without another word, which I believe many another man would not show himself so considerate.

We kept up our custom of sitting on the verandah at sundown. Himself sipping his brandy, myself listening to the voices of insects and beasts and the swamp pheasants making their low soft calls. And when the last bit of sun dropped behind the hills and green frogs croaked in the fern-baskets, and the starlight grew strong as the lights of town, then the tears lodged in my heart were not so heavy as before.

I told Tom Creed after mass I had a call to make at the Immigration Depot, which he agreed to, guessing maybe it had to do with Ellen. For Tom was thoughtful in his quiet way; I saw it in his eyes sometimes under the wideawake that never left his head. He drove me down to the Depot on the riverbank, and I looked about to find the wardsman's dwelling-place, which I knew was nearby.

It was one of those colonial cottages made of timber, with a red iron roof and a narrow front verandah. A modest house you might think, but sitting square in a yard big enough to be a small field at home. A man of middling years was digging with a spade out the back, so with Tom content to smoke his pipe I climbed down from the buggy and went over to the fence.

The old fellow planted his spade in the ground and ambled across in his flannel shirt and breeches. A strong built man with a good girth to his chest and a look of health on his grizzle-bearded face.

Why, I do believe it's Miss Callahan's sister, he said. Come in, ma'am, come in. You can be no other with them eyes. You are like to her in all but size.

Bless you, Sergeant Lynam, I said. I am yes, the same, come to thank you for your kind letter.

He took me to his front verandah and installed me in a wicker chair. Brought out a tumbler of water and sat in a nearby chair, watching and nodding while I drank it off.

It was shaping up to be another scorcher, as they say in this country, but somehow the latticed light on the verandah and the lush green ferns spilling out of cut-down kerosene tins made the possibility of fierce heat feel less likely. Sergeant Lynam was half hid by curling fronds of ancient ferns and bracken.

Your sister often spoke of you, he said. She reckoned you was the Fairy in the family and she had the true word. You are a small woman, Mrs Wilson.

I leaned forward to get a better view of him.

Sergeant Lynam, I said, for it had to be said, I want to thank you for befriending Ellen in her lonesome days at the Immigration Depot. She told me of your kindness.

He parted the fronds. You can never know when you'll be prostrated, he said. And her so young, that's the sorrowful part.

She was just turned twenty-two, I thought.

And so light and quick on her feet you'd want a greyhound to catch her.

I nodded, remembering Ellen, her skirts hitched up, legs flashing.

Lively, too. Liked taking the mickey if she could.

You're right there, I said. The words were out before I knew it, the corners of my mouth lifting in a smile.

I sat in the wicker chair, drinking in his words which were everything I wished to hear. After he said his fill I checked the light starring the latticework.

It's warming up already, I said. I'd better take my leave before Tom Creed gets struck by the sun.

We walked outside into the sunlight. Sergeant Lynam stood at the gate while I climbed in the buggy, and lifted his hat in a half salute.

May God and His Blessed Mother watch over you, he said. Take care, ma'am.

And yourself, so, I said, giving him a small wave in return.

Piccaninny belong Baiami, all same now, Dinah said when we were spreading wet sheets on the bushes. She pointed to show me where Baiami lived, somewhere in the sun-bleached sky.

The mother, it must have been her, came back to the lagoon and took up her child from under the paperbark cover. I watched her from the house. She wrapped the tiny body in her blue government blanket and carried it into the forest.

I walked down to the deserted camp in the afternoon. It was blistering hot, not a breath anywhere, not a leaf rustle or bird twitter. I looked at the strewn ashes and the small mound where the little girl's body had lain, and wondered if the native people were right. Was this a bad place? Was a bad spirit sending these deaths? Then the stillness took hold of me, the stillness of the bush, and gave me some ease.

It was what I needed, that stillness, though I hadn't known it.

I stayed there a long time, thinking about Ellen if I thought about anything at all. The ring-barked trees in the paddocks seemed almost human the way their leafless branches stretched up like arms to the sky. The lagoon was like a mirror, reflecting the ti-trees along its banks. Their papery branches hung low, sometimes touching their reflections in the water. In the shadow of the trees the water looked black, slushy with reeds and dead logs poking out. It was a melancholy place right enough, but it felt good to be there. I knew I was in the right place at last.

Rosa Praed's Passion

MR PRAED and his wife will be in town next week, Mr Wilson said at dinner one night. You shall want a new dress for the occasion. Mind you get the best now, we're to go among the *bon ton*.

I worried should I go excursioning so soon after Ellen had died, but Paddy, I was calling him that now, said he knew of no mourning period for sisters, and four months seemed a reasonable period. We were in the bedroom when he said that, and he came up behind me and put his arms round my waist. Besides, he said, we can't deprive the piano-owning class of the sight of your new gown.

Paddy, I said as his hands went higher. Not now, not when my hair's done up.

Very fetching, he murmured, squeezing my breast.

He was in his town rig of white linen coat over white shirt and cream moleskins, and when I finished dressing I had on a rose silk gown, made special by the Misses Tannock. In quick time they stitched it when Jessie explained the hurry on me. The Misses Tannock are the best sempstresses in town, but it was Jessie who told me about them. So I was pleased with my new gown, knowing I could trust its handiwork, all the pin-tucking and beading and lacework, not to show me up before the ladies.

We set off in the buggy to meet the Praeds, having eaten first, for it wasn't to be dinner, only music and craic. We drove along the Port Curtis Road in the cool of the evening. The air that fresh from recent rains, the Berserker Mountains moody in the distance before us—the moon showed them up well enough, and clouds chasing their shadows across them. They were on the move, those clouds, with more rain promising.

The scent of gums and cedar blossom perfumed the air, and every now and then little rustles came from the grasses. Pademelons most likely, going about their night business. Above us a great swishing of wings: flocks of wild geese making their way through the firmament.

You must order carbolic acid for the mosquitoes, Paddy said as we rolled along. Smoke's not enough to stop the bloodsuckers since the rains.

I knew that was so. At dusk the horses rolled in the grasses to thwart their tormenters, or galloped round the paddocks, snorting and kicking for the self-same reason. The work-horses, that is. Paddy made sure the racehorses in the stables had their own buckets of burning cow dung.

At the edge of town we turned up the hill that is called the Athelstane Range, and in no time were pulling up outside a big white-painted house. All lit up within, piano music tinkling, and a good few people sitting or standing on the verandah, flapping their mosquito-whisks.

And who should be there to greet us? None other than Mrs Dawbridge, the lady on the steamer. She fell upon me with a cry, calling out to some ladies that she had met me before, that this was the Miss Callahan she'd told them about. Some of the ladies tittered and gave me the full stare.

But not Miss Callahan anymore, I believe, she said with a coy smile. And you must be Mr Wilson, she told Paddy. Mr Dawbridge often speaks of you. You're a colleague of his in the Jockey Club I believe. Well do come in. We have the Praeds waiting to meet you.

She took us into the drawing-room and looked about but couldn't see Mr and Mrs Praed anywhere.

The men were dressed in white like my man. The women wore pale gowns and carried pretty painted fans. I hadn't known I should bring a fan and Paddy having gone off somewhere I didn't feel comfortable, so I took myself back to the verandah and found a seat in the darkness among the others. Voices lifted in song drifted through the open doors behind me. The ladies and gentlemen were taking it in turns to sing, English songs they must have been, for I didn't know any of them.

Two gentlemen sitting further up the verandah were talking about the native people, saying it was time to do another dispersal. I had heard that kind of ugly talk before, on the SS *Boomerang*, so I moved away out of earshot. Even so, their voices were that loud I couldn't help overhearing some of it. But luckily Paddy came in search of me, and saved me from hearing more.

Suppertime, Mrs Wilson, he said, and we went inside and ate melon slices and sliced cake and strawberry guavas, and were offered drinks by maid-servants in white mob caps. One stout-bellied gentleman wandered over to us and Paddy introduced me.

Mr Praed, he said. My wife.

In the lamplight, without the white boater hat, I hadn't recognized him.

Evening, Mrs Wilson, he said in a plummy English voice.

As soon as I heard him speak I knew. He was one of the gentlemen I'd heard on the verandah. I had no wish to talk to him. But he went away soon after, and Paddy began pointing out the guests he knew, for he knew one or two he said.

The young man over there by the piano is the son of old Birkbeck of Glenmore Station. The woman talking with him is Nina Bourcicault, an actress. Her father owns the *Northern Argus*.

How proud I felt standing there, listening to my man. But after supper he disappeared with the other gentlemen to smoke on the verandah, while we ladies—I suppose I was one now—sat down on the chairs and sofas in the drawing-room. And no sooner seated than wouldn't you know, they began gabbing about servantalism.

It's getting so disgraceful, said Mrs Dawbridge, you know every girl you hire will prove useless.

Though sometimes, said another lady, after nineteen bad ones the twentieth proves a treasure. It has happened to me and an Irish one at that.

I do agree, said a girl with eyes a bit sticking out. Of all the people who come to the colonies I never saw any to equal the Irish. Slips of girls without shoes or stockings but so quick to learn. Father always employs them in Brisbane.

The other ladies looked doubtful.

That may be so in Brisbane, Mrs Praed, said Mrs Dawbridge, but it is certainly not the case in Rockhampton.

I looked at the girl in her buttery yellow gown. So *she* was Mrs Praed. I liked her style of talk. It gave me the courage to have my say too.

I am Irish myself, I said to the ladies. Wouldn't the girls you speak of be home-grown, never knowing that one day they'd be expected to behave like lesser people?

The ladies looked shocked. Some whispered behind their fans, and I saw Mrs Praed having a little laugh to herself. The gentlemen trooped in from the verandah then, saving us from our difficulties, and Mrs Praed got up from her chair and came over to sit beside me.

A gentleman with a face like a pink dinner plate tinkled a bell for silence. Mrs Dawbridge's husband, I guessed.

Hrrhrrm, he said. Mr Birkbeck has agreed to favour us with a reading from his recent publication. What's it called again, Henry? he said, turning to the young man by the piano. That's right, *Cupid and Psyche*, printed by none other than our very own Mr Bourcicault here.

Everyone turned to look at the black-bearded gentleman with a letter-box mouth, and clapped politely. Then Mr Birkbeck stood up and read his poem, which seemed to be about arriving in Australia. He handed out copies after, so I still have mine.

Immortal nymphs – so sudden, great the change
Of scene and place to me, since yester-night;
I know not what to think; or if I see
With waking eyes, or dream. Tell me, I pray
What place is this, by whom I'm hither brought?

And so on, for the poem went on a terrible long time and Mr Dawbridge and another gentleman fell asleep and began snoring.

There is nothing of Australia in that poem, whispered Mrs Praed. Oh why doesn't that young man take flight in the colonial ether? That's what is wanted, don't you agree?

Ether is it? I whispered, not knowing what that article was. But you're right about Australia, Mrs Praed. There's nothing of it in his poem.

Then you do see, she said as the clapping began. I thought you might. You have a wicked sense of humour if I may say, Mrs Wilson, the way you set the ladies on their ears just now. Do call me Rosa, she said. One day *I* shall write about Australia, and it won't be like Mr Birkbeck's poem.

She was clasping and unclasping her hands. Australia is the mother of heroes, she said, and it's time someone told their stories.

Please call me Annie, I said.

Her eyes were shining. I suppose you've heard the colonials complain about our land, she said. They're fools, Annie, mired in old sentiment, and haven't the wit to see the brave new world we live in. When I write about Australia I will teach people to love it as I do.

I see that you love it, I said.

An excitable class of woman, this Rosa, I couldn't help warming to her. She gabbed on, lower this time, for it was about womanly matters. Her home on Port Curtis Island mostly. She came to it as a bride, same as myself at Serpentine Water, and was terrible lonely to begin with.

But now I have little Maud and Bulkely it's better. And Mr Praed gets back from the mainland when he can. I suppose you don't see much of your husband either, do you?

He is mostly about the place.

Then you're fortunate. She was downcast a moment till she became lively again. He's an Irishman, isn't he? My husband tells me so. Such a romantic breed, the poetry in their souls, I like that tremendously.

Sure now, I said, a bit doubtful. I didn't think Paddy had poetry in his soul but it pleased me to hear her speak well of the Irish.

Before long Mrs Praed, or Rosa I was calling her by then, was telling me she might write to me on occasion, in the long hours she spent alone on the island. She was a great letter-writer and meant to add me to her list. It was after I told her about the baby coming she had the thought of doing so.

Paddy came over to greet Mrs Praed and inform me it was time to leave. I could tell he was pleased seeing me getting on so famous with Mr Praed's wife.

Isn't that the queer thing? I said as we drove home. Mrs Dawbridge from the steamer to be the one giving the party?

Paddy said it was no surprise. Praed was thick with accountants, he needed men like Dawbridge to juggle his investments.

Clouds slid across the moon, hiding his face.

Mrs Praed reckons he's away from the island quite frequent, I said.

He's a number of irons in the fire, and keep this to yourself now, but I hear he's a bit of a ladies' man.

But he's married with children!

Men must take their fun where they find it, I suppose.

And yourself, so? I asked. Is that the way it will be with you?

His deep voice sounded in the darkness. I'll not be giving you the run around if that's what you mean.

We fell silent, rattling along the road, with only the frail light of the buggy's side lamps to show the way. I thought about the baby growing in my belly, would it be a boy or girl, and was Paddy likely to abandon me in the bushfire season. I didn't think he would, but Mr Praed now, it was nothing to him to leave his family among the fires. I felt sorry for Mrs Praed who hadn't got a husband as good as my own.

Then I told Paddy in the darkness what I hadn't been able to tell him before, about the baby coming. He was well pleased with the news.

Mammy-Palaver

THEY ARE fled from memory now, the days of my confinement. I was sunk in lethargy like a cow in a bog-hole and hardly noticed what went on. But I remember the night Harry was born, I remember that well enough. Nine months after the wedding he came into the world, our native-born son. I had a nurse for the lying-in, for it's the custom in this country to have a woman in the house for a month. Dr Callaghan chose her and Tom Creed brought her out in the buggy a week before the baby was due.

Mrs Methpotter her name was, and didn't she have a moustache on her, poor woman. She was the one who helped Harry into the world.

We were struggling awhile to get him out, Mrs Methpotter running back and forth to boil water and give orders, myself doing the huffing and puffing. But he came out at last, my beautiful boy. Yes, we got the baby out between the two of us and a fine strong singer he proved, bawling himself into a red rage. I loved him from the start.

Mrs Methpotter and I were the ones doing the work and Paddy pacing the rug in the drawing-room, so he told later. But I saw him through the window between my pains, cantering on Pyrrhus in the house-paddock, for all the world to see.

He was proud enough when he held Harry in his arms, he dropped a tear or two you may be sure. September, Harry was born, and Paddy celebrated in grand style in October by buying seven mares and another two in foal, brought up by steamer from Sydney. Only this time he didn't go down to choose them, not liking to be away from the house now he had a son. When he came in at night he went straight to the bedroom to steal a look at the baby that one day would ride with him around the paddocks.

Who's the son of my heart? he'd say, lifting him in the air. Who's my broth of a boy?

He was stretched for sleep—we both were—but he always had a smile for Harry, even when his son's urgent cries woke him night after night. One thing we kept up despite the new baby-palaver was our custom of sitting on the verandah at sundown. Frogs still croaking in the lagoon but myself not heeding them, keeping an ear open for Harry's snuffles instead.

I ran into Milford at the races, Paddy said one evening.

The lawyer-man? I asked, remembering the day Jessie and I went to see the watch-thief get sentenced. A Mr Milford it was that spoke for Witchety Peg.

Paddy shot me a glance. You know that do you? he said, and told me Milford thought we should use my name to get more land. Which he would need if he was to make Serpentine Water the best stud farm in the district.

I asked was land costly but he said it would be a government grant. All I had to do was sign my name on a bit of paper.

What a fine country this is to have land for the asking, I marvelled, forgetting where that land came from. God forgive me, I was young then and knew no better. I couldn't wait to tell Dada in my next letter, and put the thought of emigrating in his head.

Fine when it doesn't break you, Paddy said. It's broken me in its time.

When I asked what class of brokenness that might be, he said it was nothing that need concern me. Right so, I thought, and took myself off to find better company with Harry.

And in my pride didn't I celebrate Harry's first Christmas in grand style. A pine-tree put up with the Star of Christ on top, green boughs over the doors—we were very festive. Paddy had a gift for his first-born to put under the tree. A saddle was his thought for his child.

He lay in his basket on the verandah on Christmas morning, waving his little fists, more pleased by the crows in the sky than the gifts he received.

Those crows are maybe looking for a dead beast, I thought. It was likely one was about. Ah Lin had given up working in the vegetable garden, his pumpkins vines drooped lower till they withered entirely. Flesh-meat we never were short of, three times a day we had it on the table, but by Christmas day there wasn't a single vegetable in the kitchen garden fit to be ate.

Ah Lin sent Dinah to search along the edges of the lagoon for pigweed and fat hen that are native greens and good eating. She brought back a bucketful and Ah Lin found any amount of ways to prepare them, braising and frying and I don't know what else. The man was a miracle-worker. We had a table fit for a lord thanks to Ah Lin, Harry Roche and Tom Creed along with us, very gay.

Saint Stephens Day fell on Sunday and I thought I would take some pigweed to give Rhyming Lynam after mass. Tom Creed drove me down to his cottage and waited on the river bank. He liked to sit with his back against a gum tree, smoking his pipe. I gave Rhyming Lynam the pigweed, which he was well pleased with, and he brought out tea to his front verandah.

The old fellow had sad news to tell while we drank our tea. Dr Salmond had taken his job off him. So that's why you're looking so glum, I thought.

Sure now, I said, whyever would he think of doing such a thing, and you so long in his employ?

It ain't his doing, Mrs Wilson. It's the government. They're not bringing out immigrants no more so they want a married couple. Cheaper, see.

That's terrible news, I said. But why have they stopped bringing out immigrants?

Rhyming Lynam rubbed his beard. Maybe you ain't noticed, Mrs Wilson, he said, living out of town as you do. Men are tramping the roads in numbers and going west in drays. It surely would help if I had a wife in these dull times. Not someone fancy dressed up in stays. Just a decent woman who keeps the old ways.

Listening to him, suddenly I understood how he got his nickname. Rhyming Lynam laced his speech with rhymes, knowingly or not I couldn't guess.

I seen your man on Saturday, he said when I didn't speak. On one of his nags in Kent-street, at the hotel races they have there. A fine sight he made with his coat-tails flying, he won by a nose if I'm not lying. Some of the lads chaffed him a bit, but.

Did they not like him to win?

Well, your man's a swell ain't he? Got an earl or two in his ma's family they reckon, and a swell don't go down well, not with the Rocky lads. Your man took it in good part any rate, he was after being everyone's mate.

He gabbed on but I only half listened. It was a queer enough notion that Paddy was an earl, but rumours are apt to be fanciful, and I was sure this one was no different.

I might have told Paddy what Rhyming Lynam said, but he had news of his own at dinner. He had fixed for Harry's baptism, he said.

The minister prefers ten o'clock. Does that suit you?

Minister? I said. Where is the priest in that?

Minister, priest, call him what you like.

I wasn't too fascinated by his news, though I had half expected it. It is the custom in this country for the boys to go to their da's church and the girls to their ma's. But I worried for my child, the way his soul would be in peril, and I said as much.

Paddy looked at me as if I had gone soft in the head and told me the Church of England was a Catholic church like mine.

Indeed and is that so? I thought. *Such lies!*

It has the same Communion, the same service. It's not a Protestant church, it never protested anything theological. That's the Methodists and Presbyterians you're thinking of. You can make yourself easy, Harry's soul will be fine.

But why do you care? I said. You never go to church yourself.

I've made up my mind, he said, and that's the end of it.

So Reverend Locke it was who did the baptism in his little timber church in William-street. Stonemasons were putting up another church alongside while we waited in the grounds with Harry Roche. We were waiting for Dr Royce who was one of the godfathers. Harry was the other, and a very good hand with a baby he proved. He can soothe the squallingest one.

Reverend Locke waved a hand at the sandstone walls going up beside his little timber church. Coming along splendidly, he told Paddy. Yes indeed, we'll soon have the first cathedral in Rockhampton.

Myself nodding along to his words, hoping Father Murlay wouldn't come by and see me in this godless place, nursing a Protestant baby in my arms. But clip-clop, clip-clop, a horseman was trotting up the broad street. I squinted into the glare and was glad to see it was only Dr Royce.

He twitched the reins and cantered across to us. Am I late? he called.

Right on time, Paddy said.

Dr Royce laughed and jumped down from his horse. Mrs Wilson, he said, bowing. His eyes held mine longer than necessary and he never so much as glanced at his godson in my arms.

Well, come along, come along, said Reverend Locke in his fussy way, and we went into the church.

We stood around the font while the minister talked through his nose. On and on he droned, till Harry Roche fell asleep and toppled back into a paper screen behind the font and disappeared altogether. He was only lately back from the droving and had celebrated in town the previous night, so he was in what you might call a delicate state. Reverend Locke stood affronted while the rest of us hid our faces owing to the foolish smiles on them.

Harry dusted himself off and came back to his place at the font, and Reverend Locke talked on. On and on, till we began to feel drowsy, then quite sudden and unexpected he says to Harry and Dr Royce: What name do you give this child?

The gentlemen looked at him startled. Their minds were roaming and gone to other places, and Reverend Locke frowning at them over his spectacles, till Harry remembered. And how could he not?

Harry! he said, pleased with himself, instead of saying Henry Edward as he should. Reverend Locke must have thought him quite unsuitable to be a godfather.

When we got back to Serpentine Water, Paddy said we must wet the boy's head and being the mother I must stay for the celebration.

He poured brandy for the men and Dinah fetched in the tray of sandwiches and fried morsels Ah Lin had fixed earlier, and soon the men were sitting back in their chairs, talking about horses.

A few more brandies and Harry was asking Dr Royce how many toes has a pig and that gentleman saying, Take off your shoes and count 'em, and all of them laughing. Paddy telling jokes and Harry wiping his eyes, declaring they would bring tears to the eyes of a turnip, then standing up, saying he had an announcement to make.

I am thankful to have had the chance of visiting a Protestant church today, he said, for I'm soon to become a Proddy myself.

Eh? How's that? Paddy said.

Honest truth, mate. I have met a young lady who has done me the honour of agreeing to become my missus.

Well now, Paddy said, raising an eyebrow.

The best woman as ever trod shoe leather begging your pardon, Mrs Wilson. Mary-Jane Hampton that resides in Mount Morgan. A good strong woman but misfortunately a Protestant, and won't have me unless I become the same.

Come now, said Dr Royce. You must put your foot down. Show her who's boss.

I did not hear that, Dr Royce, Harry said. That never was spoke in my presence. Mary-Jane is as fine a woman as ever baked bread, Mrs Wilson, a lady like you.

I admit I'm surprised, Paddy said. How did a quiet lad like yourself get talking with a young woman in the first place?

Oh I got on the soft side of her, Harry said. It was her beauty went to my head like strong drink and gave me the courage. She was stepping out of the draper's store as I was coming in, in one of them kiss-me-quick bonnets the ladies wear. So there it is, I'm to be married to Mary-Jane and count myself the most fortunate man in the colony. She's a country girl and knows a thing or two about porridge.

Harry ruminated into his glass awhile. If there's one thing I can't abide it's lumpy porridge, he said. But never again come our wedding day, so here's to Mary-Jane.

He lifted his glass, and Dr Royce and Paddy raised theirs, and afterwards slapped him on the back and wished him happy.

Here's to your two heads on the pillow, Dr Royce said, with a sly glance at me.

I must see to the baby, I said, and took myself off. I heard them as I went down the hallway, Paddy saying something about mothers and their mammy-palaver, and himself and Mr Royce chaffing Harry unmerciful.

Same Like You, Brother

AFTER HARRY went away to be married Paddy couldn't find a good man to take his place. I never thought Harry would have the courage to wed any woman, he said, and now he's done so I miss him sorely.

A Mr Crinzian he chose next, but that gentleman proved useless, it seems. If he wasn't losing the cattle in some gully he had a talent for stampeding them by shooting himself in the foot.

By now the drought was upon us in full measure, and the men kept busy boiling up prickly pear to keep the horses in good heart. Yet you might have thought everything dandy the way Paddy kept handing out money. First it was the fences to be put on the new land, next it was carpenters to fit glass in the windows, brought up by steamer from Sydney.

I couldn't complain. I got a wash-house with walls and a roof, and shelves for the blueing powder and scrubbing brushes.

And Paddy kept buying horses. There was one I remember—a swishy-tailed stallion called Trump Card. He was that fond of it he employed a warty-nosed man called Cabbage Smith for the training and to be its jockey at the races. For Paddy never rode in the general class of races, only the Corinthian that is for gentlemen. He was an amateur rider he said, which meant doing it for love, but he had high hopes of doing well out of Trump Card with Cabbage in the saddle, doing it for money. And maybe a bit of love as well.

Paddy reckoned Cabbage would pay for himself several times over, but in the upshot he had to sack the man because of his habit of getting disqualified for riding short weight and other dirty tricks.

In September Paddy put notices in the papers announcing Pyrrhus and Dainty Davie and Clansman were available for servicing. But not so many takers as he hoped, owing to the dull times brought on by the drought. The banks were foreclosing on the big men who would have been his best customers, the cattle barons out west with their thousands of acres and their mansions on the Athelstane Range. One or two ended up shooting themselves after the banks foreclosed on their cattle-stations, but most rode into town to put up at the Squatters Arms and find themselves situations as auctioneers or stock and station agents.

To hear Paddy talk you'd think none of this was happening. I wasn't a farmer's daughter for nothing, and with another baby growing in my belly I had a few thoughts of my own. Often enough when we sat on the verandah I wanted to give out my tuppence worth. He was more likely to listen when he had a brandy in his hand and Banjo looking up at him adoring, beating a tattoo with his tail. But it wasn't my business to tell him what to do, so I kept my thoughts to myself.

Our little girl was born in October, the same month the native people returned to their camp by the lagoon. We named her Annie Eliza, or I should say Paddy did. For her two grandmothers, he said. Annie for your mother and Eliza for mine, but Annie must go first.

My mother's name first? I said, pleased and surprised.

In honour of you my dear, for you're another Annie and a very clever one to give me such a beautiful daughter.

I lay back on the pillow and felt my heart swelling. I don't think I was ever so happy. My little girl safe in my arms, himself smiling at me with the soft look in his eye. Sure, I was in Heaven at that moment. Mrs Methpotter came in the room and said Mr Wilson must remove himself, but I didn't mind. I lay there smiling, inside as well as out it felt like.

Though not so happy when I learned our daughter was to be baptised a Protestant. And no gainsaying Paddy however hard I tried. So much for the custom of the girls going to their ma's church, I thought. I was vexed altogether. One thing I got out of him though, was that Jessie Part be asked to be godmother.

Annie Eliza, our daughter was christened, though we always called her Cissie. She was a colicky baby but I loved her dearly. She was six months old and the cooler weather setting in, when Boney the house cowboy ran off with one of the women from the camp.

The men set up a great hullabaloo and came up to the house looking for Boney, but he was long gone with the woman he stole, back to the other side of the Fitzroy River where his people lived. Boney was a different tribe to the ones by the lagoon, for they are the Darumbal people, named for the waterlily roots they like to cook up and eat.

With Boney gone, Paddy had to go into town for another man. He came home with a town Black, not a skinny man but a well set-up fellow called Douglas. The grin on him wide as Dinah's the way it flashed out at you. Such a smile he had you fell into it as into a bear hug. And he proved the best stockman Paddy ever employed, so he told. There was nothing Douglas couldn't do on a horse if my man was to be believed.

The two of them became friends in a way, riding together in the paddocks, Paddy in his moleskins and blue shirt, Douglas in a pair of old breeches and the red Crimean shirt Paddy had given him. On droving days they would start out at dawn with a great deal of noise, Banjo barking, stockwhips cracking, as they drove the breeding bulls to better pasture by the mere—an arrangement Paddy had made with the Archer brothers. Then they'd bring them home around sundown.

I would hear the men coming up the track, the horses' hooves making pat-pat sounds on the dry grass, the clink of stirrups as they lifted off the saddles. Their voices easy and low. Douglas's footsteps going away to his hut. Paddy would come in the house and often as not fall asleep after dinner.

Dinah told me Douglas was from her own clan, the Warraburra people that reside in the Gracemere district and are named for the warra or guava fruit. But from not living with them anymore she got it wrong.

In the upshot I learned a different tale from Douglas. He came up to the house with the milk-pail one morning and said his tribe was from another place further out, somewhere on the Dawson River.

This fella piccaninny tumble down longa water, he said, meaning he was born there I suppose. But he ran away when he was small and the Warraburra people found him hiding in the bushes and took him in.

Why did you run away? I asked.

Pho! Pho! Douglas said, miming squinting along a gun barrel. Whitefella shoot blackfellas. Blackfellas fall down. All finish now.

No words would come to me from hearing his words. Such a terrible tale, I could only look at him, not knowing what to say.

He was with us only a year, then we lost him during the June races. Paddy was up early on Saturday to take Trump Card to town, and he gave Douglas two shillings and sixpence at the slip-rails, for he was to follow and would need the money to get through the gate. Then away my man cantered, the sun shining on his cabbage-tree hat, the winter sky blue as rinsing water above him, the Berserker Mountains a dreaming blue ahead. A very pretty picture. I was watching from the new wash-house, and later I noticed Douglas ambling up to the house.

That was queer. He never went to the house unless it was to bring the milk, or the horses for saddling. I hope he's not thinking of running off with Dinah, I worried, remembering Boney. And herself alone in the kitchen gathering the dishcloths and towels to bring down for the wash. For we kept Mondays for linen and clothes only.

But Dinah arrived with the basket so I thought no more of it till we had the cloths spread on the bushes and were back in the house. I fed Cissie next, and afterwards went in Paddy's office-room to do the dusting, which was when I found the cash box open, and coins scattered on the table.

Paddy didn't come home till late. He always went to the settling at the Criterion hotel in town, and afterwards stayed for billiards, so it wasn't till Sunday I could tell him. And himself enjoying the spectacle of his sturdy son smearing porridge on his face when I gave out the news.

He flew in a rage at once and leapt up, saying he would give the man a thrashing.

Wait a minute now till you think, I said. Nothing is proved. It will do no good to you or anyone if you act hasty.

I knew from his face he would be using his whip, the way gentlemen do when they wish to chastise one another.

It's no good blinking things, he said. The fellow's a thief and must take what's coming to him.

And off he went at a pace to Douglas's hut. He was gone only a little while, and next I heard him calling. When I went out on the verandah he was standing at the foot of the steps, Douglas woebegone beside him. The two of them looking up at me.

Dear to goodness, have you hurt Douglas? I asked, and Paddy said if it wasn't for me he would have slung the whip harder. He was breathing hard but not the raging devil that rushed out of the house.

Admit now! he said to Douglas. You took my money didn't you? Mrs Wilson here will be our witness.

Don't be dragging me into it, I thought.

Yes, brother, Douglas said, getting his smile back. I took 'em money alright.

Damn and blast you! I didn't expect this of you.

All same like you now, brother. Flash man like you.

So that's how you spent my money, Paddy shouted, and I saw Douglas was dressed up smart in new clothes.

Speak out, man. Is that how you spent my money? Paddy demanded when Douglas remained silent. Looking at the ground, the smiles gone from his face. I believe he had no idea why Paddy was angry with him.

Yes, brother, all same like you. Proper stockman now.

Saddle the horses, Paddy said. We're going to town. Well, don't just stand there! Bring up the horses.

I had to go into town to give evidence. We sat in the courthouse, Douglas miserable in the box before us while the charges were read out. He had admit them already but they read them again. The money he stole, how he took Paddy and a constable to the different shops to show where he bought each article. A hat and coat and trousers at Face & Co, a pair of boots from Henderson's, spurs from the saddlers. Douglas couldn't repeat the oath they wanted him to say. It was a drawn out affair with big words in it and he failed from his English not being good enough. But he wasn't a Christian, the Magistrate said, so it didn't matter.

Suppose you tell a lie, where will you go? he asked Douglas.

This fella not know, Douglas said, that low it was hard to hear.

I suppose you know what jail is, the Magistrate said, but Douglas shook his head. What? You don't know what a jail is? Suppose you tell a lie you go to jail, understand. Where will you go?

That made Douglas smile. This fella go bush, he said, at which the Magistrate stopped explaining the oath and called for the evidence. I couldn't look Douglas in the face when I stood up to give mine, and after Paddy and the policeman told theirs the Magistrate found him guilty and sentenced him to six months hard labour.

Pleasure-Horses

B Y NOW the drought was so bad our milch cows that brought us fourpence a quart for their milk were getting stuck in bogs formed around the lagoon. Australia is a friendly country and there is never any shortage of neighbours to help pull out a beast in its difficulty, but before long the breeding bulls were in the same trouble. Paddy went into town to see the bank manager, to raise money to put a fence around the lagoon, but Mr Vaunce wouldn't oblige.

He had a letter for me when he got home, but it wasn't from Dada. It was from Rosa Praed, the first letter I got from her, and the last.

Dear Annie,

What a long time since we met at the Dawbridges. The years slip by so quickly, don't you find? But we may soon have the pleasure of meeting again. My husband has formed the plan of returning to England and must arrange his affairs before we leave. He is going up to Rockhampton to settle some business with your husband, and I have asked to accompany him. I can't tell you how glad I am to be leaving the island and its mosquitoes. You have no idea what a trial it is keeping the children safe from them. One got under Maud's mosquito-net the other night and the poor child is covered in bites…

It's from Mrs Praed, I said, passing Paddy the letter. She says Mr Praed is coming to town.

So I've heard. He scanned Rosa's words. Well, I don't know if Mrs Praed is right about coming too, he said, handing me the letter. Praed never mentioned her in his cable.

I hope she will, I said, thinking how fortunate we had glass in the windows. It would give me better countenance to receive her that was a lady.

But just as Paddy suspected, Rosa wasn't on the boat. He rode down to the wharf to meet Mr Praed and couldn't find that gentleman either until he thought to look in steerage and found him there. And he never brought him out to Serpentine Water for Praed hadn't the time for gallivanting. He had financial matters to settle in town, Paddy said when he came home.

We were on the verandah, himself studying his brandy as he swirled it in the glass.

Well then, Mrs Wilson, he said, meeting my eyes, I've news for you. As of today you're looking at the full owner of Serpentine Water. Praed has sold me his share.

I wasn't sure whether to be glad or not. Then you have the money for it? I asked.

It'll be tricky. I must raise the cash but the new lot of breeding bulls should just about cover it once the market improves.

That could take a time, I said.

Oh I made that plain. Praed's given his word he won't draw out the money until I can sell the bulls at a fair price. I've no way of meeting the mortgage otherwise. We had Milford, naturally, and Praed's man D'Arcy, to see it was done by the book.

So all in writing then?

Naturally, all in writing. Except Praed's undertaking, but I have his word on that. A gentleman's word is worth more than any piece of paper.

Which gentleman would that be? I thought. I didn't doubt Mr Praed was a gentleman but trusted him no better for it. I would put my trust in a good few men that weren't gentlemen before Mr Praed—Harry Roche, Tom Creed, Sergeant Lynam. Any one of them might be better depended on than the manky article I heard giving out his spake on Mrs Dawbridge's front verandah.

God help us, I thought.

The beginning of November Paddy signed the papers in Mr D'Arcy's office and by mid November he had the milch cows up for sale without reserve. *Owing to the dissolution of the partnership of Messrs E. Wilson & Co*, the advertisement said. Praed was in Brisbane by then and Paddy in simple faith he wouldn't quit the country till cattle prices improved. Another two weeks and all was up with Serpentine Water. Praed drew out the money and took himself off in a steamship to England with Rosa and their children. We saw their names on the passenger list in the newspaper.

Well, what could Paddy do? He was obliged to sell the breeding bulls at drought price but the money he got was far short of the needed. He went to see Mr Vaunce at the bank and told him about the agreement with Mr Praed, how that gentleman had promised not to take the money till cattle prices improved, and in charity could the bank not give him an extension.

Mr Vaunce said he would like to help but first Paddy must get rid of his pleasure-horses.

What are pleasure-horses? Paddy asked, genuinely puzzled. At which Mr Vaunce said he was sorry but could give no extension.

So that was the end of Serpentine Water.

What upset Paddy most was selling the horses. They all had to go, all the racehorses and thoroughbreds, except for his gentleman's town hack and another two kept for the buggy. He was in a fine rage against Mr Praed and cursed him quite frequent, and cursed the bankers as well, saying they had no soul to be damned and no arse to be kicked. I believe he was troubled with his liver from time to time, through eating so much beef. What went down his gullet would give a pig indigestion. When I tried to make him drink buttermilk he cursed that as well.

It will soothe your heartburn, I said.

Even if you're right, he said, what matter how soon I go to the devil now? Australia has beaten me, twice it's done for me. Only a fool would throw his hat in the ring again.

I put down the glass of buttermilk and sat down, waiting for him to tell me what he wanted to say.

He told a story then about a sheep-station he once had, way back in the 1860s. He was pacing the floor by now, talking to himself more than me. Near the Isaacs River the station was. A wild bit of country. And himself travelling overland with bullock-drays and men, to clear the trees and build the first shelters, till he had a big concern going. Sheep in vast numbers, shepherds' huts, a woolshed, orchards and vegetable gardens planted out. Everything as it should be. The money for the sheep came from another man but Paddy was to have a half share of the profits for doing the work, and he named the station *Rookwood* after his uncle's estate in Ireland. For the good memories he said. The good times he'd had riding to the Hunt there.

So all up and running. And never any trouble from the myalls.

I asked what were myalls. Wild Blacks, he said, and *Rookwood* had more than its share because they'd been chased off other stations.

Why would anyone want to chase them? I said. I didn't understand. The native people at Serpentine Water were nothing but friendly and helpful to us.

Paddy stopped pacing to look at me. The way they'd be spearing the sheep, he said curtly.

I suppose they thought, if the sheep are on their land—

Now look, Annie, get this straight. It's not their land. These people don't have a fixed place of abode. They're wanderers with no more claim on the land than anyone else. But I kept on their good side. I'm Irish aren't I? Why wouldn't I know their feeling for the land? So I gave them the run of it and overlooked the odd sheep that went missing.

But not Douglas, I thought. *There was no overlooking for him.*

The big flood of sixty-four was what did for me, he said. I was in Rockhampton getting supplies when the rains came or I might have got the sheep to higher ground. Who knows? Any rate the man I left in charge didn't succeed and the sheep were drowned. The bank wasn't long in foreclosing after that.

He stopped speaking then.

Sit you down, I said. I'll fetch you some tea.

Like a child that does what it's told he sat down, and was still staring at nothing when I returned with the tray. The memory of *Rookwood* was bitter to him, that was easy known.

Our last weeks at Serpentine Water were sad days. Only if he had the baby in his arms or was playing with Harry did a smile come on his face. Hush now, go to sleep, he'd tell Cissie. Poor little pet, you don't know what it is to suffer.

It grieved me to leave Serpentine Water too, and from knowing I would never look on them again I began seeing more clear the wheaten-coloured grasses in the paddocks and the waterlilies on the lagoon. The heart has many dwelling places they say, but only one home, and Serpentine Water had that honour for me in Australia. So I watched the brown-skinned children playing with the kangaroo dogs, and at dusk I looked up and saw white cockatoos winging their way home, their breasts turned ruby by the setting sun.

But want was our master and leave we must. A man from the bank came out to take particulars of the house and outbuildings. Paddy asked Tom Creed would he walk the land with him, for he hadn't the heart to do it himself. Ride the land I should say, for you'd be days finding its mearings on foot. Then Serpentine Water was put up for sale and the time came for leaving. Dinah and Ah Lin were already gone to live on Moores Creek with a brother of Ah Lin's, and Tom had taken up work on a cattle-station outside Alpha.

Now it came our turn.

The new glass windows flashed in the sunlight as we climbed in the buggy, Cissie on my lap, Harry beside me, Paddy upright at the reins. An eagle hung in the sky, fixed like a sign in the blue. Not a bird call broke the silence. Not a movement anywhere except the smoke curling up from the campfire by the lagoon. The Darumbal people weren't going anywhere, and I envied them, though I knew they could be dispersed at a whim by whoever bought the farm at Serpentine Water. Hadn't their land been stolen from them by the English, same as the English stole ours in Ireland.

Paddy flicked the reins, and we left Serpentine Water forever.

Three years I lived by the lagoon yet it seemed only yesterday I came out in the buggy on my wedding day. Mam used to say grief counts the seconds and happiness forgets the hours. She had the true word.

South Esk Cottage

WE MADE our new home in a rented house, *South Esk Cottage* it is called, across the road from the railway station in Stanley-street. It was smaller than the house at Serpentine Water and put me in mind of Rhyming Lynam's cottage, only instead of vegetable beds out the back it had stables. Harry and Cissie got woke from their naps the first day by the One O'clock Gun—I had forgot about that article—but they soon got used to it, and we settled into our new dwelling-place quite snug and comfortable.

Paddy saddled his horse the first morning and went off to see Jackson & McPherson that are stock and station agents, to enquire was there droving work to be had, and he came back in the afternoon to say he had signed up to a Mr Kelman.

He was mighty pleased with himself, bouncing on the balls of his feet. What a flowery land we live in, he said, where a man can find employment the first day he enquires.

Who is Mr Kelman? I asked, and he said a station-owner who wanted sheep brought up from the colony of Victoria.

I'll be gone awhile, he said. You might get lonesome at night.

Don't fret yourself, I said. We'll do well enough without you.

But my heart skipped a beat from learning I was so soon to lose him.

I'll have a yarn with Callaghan and ask will he drop by occasionally to check you're alright.

Dr Callaghan is welcome to call, I said.

Paddy grimaced. I don't like the neighbourhood over much. Maybe I'll leave you one of my pistols, Annie. I hope you're a good shot.

St Patrick save us, I thought. It's a bad business when you must hope a thing like that.

He smiled at the face I pulled, and said when the dust settled over the mortgage we should have enough money to move to the Range. I needn't think I'd be spending the rest of my life living opposite a railway station.

Paddy didn't begin his journey till New Year, time enough for him to fix for a woman and her husband to live out the back in the loft above the stables. The buggy horses would be wanting the man's attention, he said, and I would require his services as yardman, to split the firewood and do the messages, and his wife to help with the wash now I had babies to care for.

That was true. I couldn't be in the wash-house all morning and my little ones alone in the house. So I was to become mistress of a town servant, same as Mrs Dawbridge and her lady friends, and I wondered how that would work out.

On Christmas Eve we took the children to East-street to admire the green boughs and mottos in the windows. Quite the proper family we made among the others. Harry got excited by the star on top of the butcher's shop and couldn't stop saying Tar, tar for days. But then it came New Year and time for farewells. And plenty of games beforehand between Harry and his father, them chasing each other around the sofa.

We went out on the footpath, Harry along with us. Be a good boy for Mammy now or she'll strop you, Paddy said.

I will not indeed, I said. Don't be frightening the child that way.

He picked up my hand like it was some object only happening to be attached to me. And you, Annie, he said. Take care now.

The cross of Christ between you and harm, I said, looking back at him steady.

Is that all I'm to get from you. No kisses then? And he pulled me to him with no shame or mercy, and planted a kiss on my lips in full view of any passer-by. And myself no better, kissing him back with no thought for the proprieties.

See you in May, he said and sprang on his horse, and was trotting down the road with Banjo following before I could gather my wits.

He turned in the saddle to wave goodbye. How happy he looked that day. He was going to the bush, the place he loved best, and would be in the saddle for months. I never could compete with any of that.

I missed him right enough. It was a surprise learning how much I wanted him. I had no fear he'd get lost, he was too long in the bush for that, and besides, he was taking a native man and another man with him, and a tent he had made waterproof by pouring boiling grease on it. But he must travel without roads, in lonely parts where the sun is the only watchman by day, and the moon by night. Gardiner's Lantern, Paddy calls the moon, named for a bushranger who lived in these parts. I prayed Gardiner's Lantern would shine clear and show him safe in his tent. I prayed he would come home to my arms.

Mrs Shout, the woman that lived over the stables with her husband proved a cheerful class of woman. She was about ten years older than me I would guess, a native-born woman with a laugh on her loud as any man's. She told me to call her Jemima and I said she must call me Annie in return.

I will not, Mrs Wilson, I will not indeed, she said, her cheeks red and shiny from the flat iron she was wielding. She put it back on the stove and looked at me where I was feeding Cissie her porridge. You're a new chum ain't you? she said.

I am, yes.

How are you liking Australia? she asked.

It's agreeing with me fine.

Well that got her started, she was off like a hound after the fox.

There are some folk don't think so, she said. They look down their noses at us in the colonies. There is one I worked for never stopped complaining of colonial servants. I declare I will slap her face if I meet her on the street. Let her come and take my place for work and scrub out the kitchen and make the beds, and feed the hens, and chase the larrikins through the scrub when they pinch the firewood. She wouldn't have breath left to complain then, the silly old cow.

I believe I've met ladies like her, I said. That was my mistake. I shouldn't have encouraged her, but I was new to the business of being a mistress.

I would bet a year's wages the one I'm speaking of ain't got a set of drawers that don't need mending, Jemima said, thumping down the iron. And her ruby necklace? Did she pay for it? Or her Paris gown? Half them nobs on the Athelstane Range never pay their bills as everyone knows. And she had the gall to tell me I mustn't go to dances dressed like a lady. The cheek of her! There's no law to prevent servants wearing white dresses that *I* am aware of.

It's to be nothing but talk of servants in this town, I thought, the one side or the other. But I liked Jemima. She said her mind and was never sly, and very fond of Harry and Cissie besides. I knew I could go to mass on Sunday and know my children were safe in her care.

What with babies and sewing and the rest my hands were quite full, but even so I began a vegetable patch out the back. Rhyming Lynam, the green-fingered man, put me right on the colonial seasons, and Mr Shout, or Bob I was calling him by now, he grubbed out a bit of ground for me and dug the trenches. Jemima came out from the kitchen to watch, and said he was making a right hames of the job and must add horse manure from the stables and spread hay on top.

I believe Bob was a little afraid of her for he never said boo to a goose, only went off at once to do her bidding.

That woman next door is badly mated, Jemima said while we watched Bob shovel the manure. But she has made her bed and must lay on it. Her husband run off with some strumpet and good riddance to him, he never was worth the bother. Never put a sausage on the table. Here, what's your dodge? she shouted at a boy who was peering at us over the fence. Don't come here pinching any more firewood on me, you little larrikin. I'll have the hide off you if you do.

The boy ran away, but not before he held up a stick and pointed it at her. Bail up! he shouted, very brazen. Your money or your life!

Thinks he's Ned Kelly, Jemima said, watching him scamper off into the scrub. Yairs, that Carmel I was speaking of, her peacock turned out to be a jackdaw and no surprise. She's a dirty woman who never cleans her house, so what can you expect? And she got another man already to judge from the goings on I seen last night.

117

Jemima was right about the woman next door, she was right about most things I found. The neighbour-woman's husband came back one evening and found his wife entertaining a man in the kitchen, and a big barney broke out. With all the shouting and crockery smashing going on the wonder was it didn't wake Cissie and Harry. The visiting man ran out of the house and stood on the footpath, turning the air blue with his curses.

I'll be up with me mates tomorrow! he shouted. I'm not finished with you yet.

After that it got nasty, the husband chasing him down the street with a stick and using him desperate to judge from the screams.

Jemima gave out the news in the kitchen next morning. That Carmel ain't got the sense she was born with, she said. She's gone and told her man she's had enough of him and he's took on terrible about it. There'll be trouble now. That new bloke she's got is a fair dingo. Likes to hunt in packs he does.

Sure enough, next night a party of men arrived at the neighbours' house and broke in through a window. Are you ready for your hiding, you bastard? one of them kept yelling, and the husband saying No, no, very meek. And all the while Carmel screaming, Don't bash him, don't bash him!

If I don't bash him I'll have to put a bullet through him, the visiting man shouted.

Don't do anything rash! Carmel screamed. Then more shouts and thumps till the man and his mates ran off and we could get some sleep.

By my Maker, Jemima said in the kitchen next morning. That new man of Carmel's was fair boozed last night. Coming round here depriving decent folk of their shut-eye, and what for, I ask you? Only for the dirtiest woman in town.

Maybe I should think about learning to use that pistol Paddy gave me, I thought.

But we had no more trouble after that. Carmel ran off the same day and we never saw her again. A fortunate day altogether, because in the afternoon Bob Shout brought the mailbag from the Post Office and didn't I find a letter in it from Paddy. I knew it was from him because the postmark said Wangaratta, and very thankful I was to see it and know he wasn't murdered by bushrangers or eaten by cannibals.

To begin with it was all I could wish, love words for my eyes only. But only a few endearments, the rest was all news. His man that was with him died from a snake-bite. It was awful hard to know what words to use for the burying he said, but he was a clergyman's son and said a prayer over the grave, and spoke what parts of the service he could remember.

When he rode into Wangaratta to find another man the town was in commotion, reporters and police swarming everywhere, owing to Ned Kelly had paid a visit two days previous. Paddy wrote the police had Buckley's chance of finding the Kelly gang, and the Black trackers from Queensland likewise, for rain had washed away their tracks. Besides, he said, the Kellys had that many friends to shelter them it would want the best regiment from Melbourne to find them, and then it would not.

And he said he expected to be home in June. That was the part I was waiting for. I worried, knowing his man was bit by a snake. I knew Paddy could take care of himself most ways, the tough timber that was in him, but any old snake might get it into its head to cuddle up alongside him at night. That was out of his hands entirely.

Witchety Peg poked her head over the back fence one morning and saw me on my knees in the vegetable bed. She was passing by in the scrub, on the way home to her humpy most likely, for the main drain is that direction.

You again, she said, quizzing me with her beady-bright eyes. You're like an India-rubber ball you is, down when you're not up. I thought you was a lady but you're not dressed smart enough.

Why would I want to dress fancy when I have to be up at dawn to rake out the stove ashes? I said. I'm not that kind of Cinderella.

She had a bit of a cackle to herself when I said that.

What you adoing in the dirt then?

Digging up potatoes, I said. I was pleased with my crop. I like to be dabbling in the dirt and might be back on the farm at Ballyconnell when I'm at it. Often am in my mind.

My father growed spuds in England, she said.

And my Da in Ireland also. He's still doing it.

You're lucky, she said. Mine ain't. Turned up his toes in England, Pa did. Ma too.

She nodded at the potatoes. What you gonna do with all them spuds? You got plenty there I see.

You're welcome, I'm sure.

Hand 'em over the fence, she said. My goats could do with a feed of them spuds.

How are your goats? I asked while I dropped potatoes in her shawl. I hoped she had no sad story to tell, for I read in the papers she was still having fights in court on their behalf, trading sharp words with the Inspector of Nuisances.

Still bleating, she said, no thanks to the men hereabouts. They is no better than beasts some of 'em.

She turned down her mouth and said she spoke ill of beasts, there being plenty of two-legged animals in town doing deeds no four-legged ones ever would.

You have the true word, I said. I had heard the screams of animals.

Day to you, missus, she said when the potatoes were safe in her shawl. And off she stomped into the scrub, half my crop departing with her.

Witchety Peg wasn't wrong about two-legged animals. Some men were that accustomed to slaughtering beasts at the abattoir it may be, they thought nothing of further killing at home. And there was a good deal of sickness about, diphtheria and whooping cough and measles, to carry off the children. One poor woman lost all three of hers to diphtheria.

Big George the firewood-man gave me the news while he stacked logs against the stable wall. Likely the woman never used Greathead's Sulphuric, he said. If she had of, her kiddies might still be running around.

After that I made sure to have Greathead's Sulphuric in the house.

Even so I worried. It was all my thought for Paddy to come home and take us up to the fresh air on the Range. It wasn't for his sake only I wanted him back.

And come home he did one bright June morning, trotting his horse down the side of the house to the stables. I ran out to greet him and so fit and brown he looked, so grand altogether my legs near gave way under me. The cut and swagger of him. And a great bush of a beard that

120

never was on his face before, which he said he must keep as he was of an age to wear one now.

Cissie didn't know him when he picked her up, she screwed up her face and screamed, poor mite, and her father no happier at the greeting he got.

His sweet embrace afterwards. Mad for it he was and mad for me, and myself no better. The lovely smell of him, I buried my nose in his armpit just to lose myself in it.

The Camptown Races

PADDY WAS always a quick man, a doer and rusher, and by August we were living on nobs' hill in a house among the others. It was one of those wedding-cake house, all white paint and latticework with verandahs all round to make it airy. The kitchen wing under the same roof, very modern and convenient. Pressed metal ceilings in every room to keep out the possum piss, we couldn't have been more comfortable. For icing on our cake-house the Shouts came with us, to live above the stables out the back. I was that glad to have Jemima by me, for I liked her quite as much as Dinah.

We were hardly settled in our new home when Paddy announced he was taking up employment with Jackson & McPherson as a stock and station agent.

Ah, man, I said, that's grand altogether. When you're away we feel the want of you.

I'll still have to travel at times, he warned. I'll be away a couple of weeks this month.

I looked up from feeding Cissie. It seems only yesterday you came home, and already you're leaving.

I have to graft as hard as the next man now, he said. It's only my wages put food on the table.

Within a week he was saddled and ready to depart. The packhorse loaded and waiting, Banjo looking up at him with one ear cocked. But no farewell kisses this time. His lips brushed mine, then he was up in the saddle, looking down at me.

See you in a fortnight, he said, and away with him down the hill, Banjo and the packhorse following. The morning sun stretched my shadow on the road as if it was trying to reach him.

The Athelstane Range isn't a mountain range but a hill shaped like a hairless caterpillar that sits above the town flats. Being near the eastern end of the caterpillar, a stone's throw from the hospital, we had a good view of the town and the winding Fitzroy River, and beyond that the Berserker Mountains.

Even so, I liked the back of the house best. Houses were built far apart in the 80s, with paddocks between and patches of scrub, and Paddy's horse-paddocks ran down towards the northern lagoons— Crescent Lagoon, Pink Lily Lagoon and Murray Lagoon. Their waters shone like mirrors in the morning sun, when they weren't covered in ducks and every feathered creature in Christendom. Sunset was another good time to be out the back and watch the lagoons turn brazen gold in the powdery gold haze covering the plains. A great croaking of frogs after rain, and the sky would turn dark with flocks of wild geese coming and going to the lagoons, till your heart lifted up like a bird itself.

I was pulling up carrots in the kitchen garden when a different flock rose up from the grasses along the crest of the hill.

Butterflies!

Millions of them if they could be counted. Yellow in colour and a good size too, they rose in a cloud and flew low to the ground with a festive fluttering air, as if on their way to a dance. Before I knew it they were all around me, the whole world was nothing but butterflies tickling my face and feathering my arms as they hurried on to their destination.

Mother of Mercy! Such abundance I had never seen in my life. I had to come to Australia to behold such marvels. All around me in the deep Sabbath silence, a world made suddenly of butterflies.

Mrs Wilson!

I turned to see who was calling and saw it was Dr Royce, trotting his horse down the driveway through the tail end of the butterflies. Slashing at them with his whip. A phantasm got up by Fairies to lure mortals to the underworld you might think the spectacle. For a moment I hardly know where I was, and only sorry to lose the butterflies.

Good morning, dear lady, he called, cantering towards me through the last of them, the silk of his top hat gleaming in the sunlight. A handsome man, certainly, but a mite too pleased with himself on that account in my estimation.

From knowing something of horses by then, I couldn't help noticing the small tug he gave to the curb rein, at the same time touching the mare's flank with his off spur. A light enough goad, but it made the surprised creature rear up, curvetting and snorting her indignation. And made himself look very grand sitting astride her, controlling her.

I was hoping to find you at home, he said from the height of the rearing horse.

But his spur had served its purpose, and now he was patting the mare's neck to calm her.

Mr Wilson is out of town, I said.

So I've heard, he said. Fine for him but hard lines on you, Mrs Wilson, left languishing on your lonesome.

Stroking the tips of his moustache. I have come to invite you to *Richmond House.*

Oh I don't think— I began, but he cut me off, saying, To take tea, this afternoon if that suits.

Thank you, but as you see I'm busy.

Busy? On a Sunday?

Sunday is a day like any other so far as plants can know, I said, wishing the carrots weren't dangling from my hand.

Wouldn't you like to come?

I'm sorry—

Dr Royce kneed his horse, sidling it closer.

Naturally, my wife will be present. Paddy suggested you might benefit from a little socialising, so I thought you'd like to meet Ephie.

Would you care to come? We have a crate of luscious oysters brought up fresh this morning from Keppel Bay.

There was no gainsaying the man, and by now I no longer wanted to.

Thank you, I said. What time would Mrs Royce like me to call?

As to that, I dunno. Ephie don't fuss too much over civilities. Shall we say three o'clock?

I would have to ask Jemima to give the children their afternoon tea and put Cissie down for her nap. If you like, I said, a bit doubtful.

Splendid! His eyes took in my Sunday rig: the old boots and blue cotton gown I kept for gardening. His gaze travelled upwards. When he got to my face I was waiting for him with the full stare.

He cleared his throat. If I may say, Mrs Wilson, the wench style rather suits you.

You may not, Dr Royce.

Till the appointed hour then. He wheeled his horse about and cantered up the driveway.

I watched his easy slouch in the saddle. He was a flash man right enough. All blow and fancy waistcoats and riding tricks, but likely his wife might be different. We might even become friends.

Near my feet on a blade of grass sat a butterfly with a broken wing, a casualty of Dr Royce's whip it must be. It had lost its tribe and would never fly again, and I could do nothing for it. I turned away from the trembling creature, remembering the fluttering host it was once part of. If only Jemima had been there to see it. And what would she say, what would she think when I told her I'd been invited to *Richmond House*? Such a grand brick two-storey building that Jessie had pointed out the day we went to the courthouse to see the watch thief.

So up with me to the kitchen to toss the carrots in the sink and go in the bedroom to shake out the folds of my new gown. It had to be the watered silk, I knew, because it was made in the latest style with a dropped waistline and I was slender enough to look well in it. After four years living like a hermit the prospect of going among company had me on fire. From the old ship trunk in the box room I took out the Rose of Tralee shawl Mam wove for me on winter evenings. Such a beautiful cream-coloured shawl she wove in those long ago quiet hours, and its border of crimson roses would set off the moss-green of the watered silk.

Strewth! Bob said when I came outside to get in the buggy. You're dressed up smart, missus.

I'm taking tea with the Royces, I told him.

And why shouldn't you deck yourself out if you want? Bob said as if to himself.

I climbed in the buggy and we rattled down the hill, myself staring at the stubby hairs on the back of Bob's neck while thinking about Mrs Royce. What would she be like and would we get on? When we pulled up in East-street I stayed in the buggy, examining the big house.

Small trees and shrubs grew along the sides, making a green corridor to keep it private from its neighbours. I liked that, an elegant touch in East-street that doesn't go in for fripperies like vegetation. Upstairs, on two wrought iron balconies, potted ferns made a fine show of green against the red bricks. The ground floor had two matching green doors, like the doors of a giant doll house, each with a shiny brass knocker.

The plaque on the left-hand door must surely mean it led to Dr Royce's surgical rooms. The door on the right was probably for his dwelling-place.

Perhaps if you come back at five, I told Bob. I'm not sure, but maybe that's the correct time.

Righty-oh, he said.

Then there was nothing for it but get down from the buggy. Pulling the folds of Mam's shawl closer around me, taking courage from the love she wove into it, I approached the right-hand door.

A young woman about my age with green eyes under auburn ringlets opened the door to my knock. Come in, come in, she said, drawing me into the hallway and planting little popping kisses on my cheeks. Her voice was Australian like Dr Royce's, only more refined.

So kind of you to invite me, Mrs Royce, I said, taking in her pale pink silk-taffeta gown. I had been right to wear the watered silk.

I drew off my hat and she took it from me and hung it on the hallstand.

You find us at sixes and sevens I'm afraid, she said, dimpling smiles. An undesirable gentleman has taken up residence in the parlour, but we mustn't let that bother us must we?

I put out a hand to clasp hers. I'm that glad to meet you, Mrs Royce.

And I you she said, taking my hand between hers. For something tells me you're a country girl like myself. But you must call me Ephie, please. All my Sydney friends do. We call everyone by our pet names, Sinbad or Queenie or Puss, so you'd better call me Ephie at once for I won't be called anything else.

Then you must call me Annie, I said when she drew breath.

I followed her down the hallway to a candle-lit room. The blinds on the tall windows were mostly drawn so the light was needed. Reclining in leather armchairs under a chandelier crowded with lit candles, Dr Royce and two gentlemen paused in their chat to look up.

The black-bearded one, a thickset fellow with a gold watchchain draped across his waistcoat, stared at me with bold probing eyes. The sandy-haired one was distracted, wiping something off his moustache. Liquor, I suspected. He was your specimen of sporty townsman in his mustard-coloured suit and hair slicked flat with pomatum.

I am saved from having to do any work today, Ephie Royce said with a little laugh, seeing me look askance at the array of glasses and the cigar smoke coiled up under the ceiling.

She gestured at the black-bearded man. Mr Bignal here is taking care of our evening meal tonight. He shot some ducks at Pink Lily Lagoon, clever fellow, and Jack bet him he couldn't cook as good a roast duck at *Richmond House* as it seems he does at *Paris Villa*.

So that explained the delicious smell wafting into the room.

My grandmother taught me how to cook, Mr Bignal announced in heavy tones.

Five guineas says you can't do it, said Dr Royce from his chair.

Mrs Wilson, may I present Mr Bignal, his wife said, ignoring him.

Mr Bignal examined me from under thick black brows. Pleased to meet you, he said, or should I say growled it out.

And Mr Timms. Ephie tilted her head at the sandy-haired man.

How d'you do, Mrs Wilson. Charmed I'm sure, he said in a nasal English voice.

Do take a seat, invited Ephie. Where did you get that gorgeous shawl, I wonder? I shall have to find out later but we mustn't bore the gentlemen with girl talk now.

It seemed a presumption to take the remaining armchair so I sat on the sofa across from the gentlemen. Dr Royce was occupied trimming his cigar, and Ephie tripped over to the windows to pull down a blind, abandoning me to the two gentlemen's inspection.

I looked back at them steady enough I hoped, and cast a few glances of my own. At the gilt-framed pictures of pansies and passionflowers on the walls, the soft-lit lamps and pretty china bowls, and bronze statuettes of naked women and prowling lions dotted about the room on spindle-legged tables. And gave a woman's eye to the Turkey rugs and tabletops to satisfy myself how clean Ephie Royce kept her house. Not as well as she might it turned out. Though perhaps she was 'between housemaids' as one of the ladies on the SS *Boomerang* had put it.

Ephie returned on silent feet. What will you like to drink, Annie? she asked.

Tea would be nice.

Tea? I don't know if … She glanced about. We have champagne opened. A glass perhaps, to celebrate our meeting. Fetch a glass for our guest will you, she said to her husband, contriving to look coy and pert at the same time. There now, my pretty—turning to me—Are you happy with that?

I have vowed never to drink alcohol, I confessed.

Ephie clapped her hands. A teetotaller! How marvellous. Well, that makes a change, wouldn't you say, Mr Bignal?

The look she sent him was almost as flinty as Mrs Morphy's stare. You and Jack were kicking up your heels at *Paris Villa* last night I hear, she said. What do you think of his complexion today, Annie? Rather sallow, wouldn't you agree?

Mr Bignal does look a little pale, I said.

So would you be if you'd been sinking grog till the wee hours.

Ephie went over to the remaining armchair and snuggled into it, curling up like a cat. Her house shoes peeped out under the hem of her gown. Pink silk ones, I noticed, decorated with whorls of tiny glass beads.

Dr Royce had wandered over to the sideboard during this chatter, and he brought back a stemmed glass of cordial chinking with ice. His fingertips brushed mine as he handed me the glass. By accident I was sure, but even so my hand tingled.

Look at that, Ephie said. Jack is on his best behaviour. I do believe he wants you to like him, Annie.

No surprise there, said Mr Timms, smirking. The lady looks appetising enough.

Ephie pouted. The candlelight here does rather flatter a girl.

Maidens like moths are ever caught by glare, Mr Timms intoned. Lord Byron of course. Can't claim it as my own *bon mot*.

I was feeling more and more uncomfortable and must have shown it on my face, or made some awkward movement, for Ephie's laugh ran up the scale.

Oh dear, Annie's going serious on us, she said. Don't take offence, dear, it's only us maniacs, we can't help ourselves. Mr Timms doesn't mean to offend.

And so it went on, the bright chatter. I was a fish out of water in their company and knew it. The one who stayed silent and listened while they bandied jokes and occasional barbs over their champagne and oysters. I had declined the offer of oysters, having taken an instant dislike to their slithery grey appearance. Even thinking of swallowing one made me feel queasy.

Ephie's eyes rested on me. But there, she murmured. We are boring poor Annie.

Don't, Ephie, you're embarrassing her, Dr Royce said, and turned to me.

I'm afraid we've been forgetting our manners, Mrs Wilson. Too much gossip but at least nothing about horses, eh? I'm sure you get enough stable talk to last a lifetime from Paddy.

Ephie tinkled out a laugh. You're a one to talk. A stable boy among gentlemen and a gentleman among stable boys, that could be your epitaph.

You're so sharp you'll be cutting yourself, Dr Royce said. Do shut up, Ephie. If the Lord meant you to talk He'd have given you a prettier mouth.

He did give me a pretty mouth, she said back. And people who tell lies cannot go to Heaven. Remember that when next you speak.

Dr Royce frowned. Will you stop prattling and think of our guests for a moment? What music have you planned for our entertainment?

I'm sure I don't know, and what's more I don't care, Ephie said. It's your party, not mine, Jacky boy.

Sing us a song, dear Mrs Royce, said Mr Timms. In his haste to persuade her, he stood up from his chair. Please do, he begged. I would be delighted to accompany you. It's such a pleasure hearing you sing.

At least we have one gentleman in the room, Ephie said, uncoiling herself from her chair. She went over to the piano and struck a pose, one dimpled white hand resting on the glossy black piano top, the other draped across her pink taffeta bodice. Mr Timms lifted his coat-tails and sat down at the keys.

Oh were I but a drop of dew, a pearl upon the snowdrop small, Ephie sang in a sweet languorous soprano, drawing out the mournful notes. And so on and so forth. Her eyes rested on Mr Timms as she sang, Were I a moonbeam of the night, with kisses white would I alight upon one sleeping forehead fair.

Bravo! that gentleman cried when she finished. You are a true *artiste*, Mrs Royce. You should be in the theatre.

Don't exaggerate please, Mr Timms. I fluffed a note, remember. So now, who is to be next?

Ephie looked around. You, Jack?

Dr Royce shook his head.

We all declined. No one could be made to stand up, the gentlemen pleading exhaustion from the night previous, and myself out of shyness claiming a sore throat.

Ephie stamped her foot. I declare, that's too bad! Then we shall just have to dance.

On a Sunday? I looked at the others, but no one seemed bothered, let alone shocked.

Ephie went over to a carved sideboard and took a sheaf of music from a drawer. Stood with her back to us while she leafed through the sheets, then swung around.

The *Camptown Races* to begin with!

Dr Royce and Mr Timms who a moment ago were too tired to sing were already down on their knees, rolling up the Turkey rugs. Mr Bignal inclined his head. May I have the pleasure? he growled.

Oh, how I longed to dance, Sunday or not. It seemed years since I had tripped across a dance floor. You may, Mr Bignal, I said.

Dr Royce sat down at the piano and began pounding out the *Camptown Races*, which proved a grand toe-tapping tune. Ephie and Mr Timms wasted no time moving onto the floor and Mr Bignal took my arm, guiding me in the same direction. But he whirled me about and whirled me about to such a degree I began to feel dizzy.

Where has Paddy Wilson been hiding you? he said. You're a fetching armful of female flesh if I may say, Mrs Wilson. If not for your husband I'd run you down and put my brand on you myself.

Dancing up close with a man is always chancey that way, but I was made of sterner stuff than to simper at such impertinence. I grew up in the Corcashel townland after all, and said in sugar-sweet tones, Such a pity, Mr Bignal, since I haven't the slightest desire to put my brand on you.

He made no reply and we jigged around the floor in blissful silence.

Dr Royce led me on the floor next and made an exhibition of himself you could say, for he danced with wild hops like a wind-up toy. It was all I could do to keep up with him. We dipped and turned and progressed by leaps across the polished floor. Meanwhile Mr Bignal was thumping the keys and Ephie skimming along in the arms of Mr Timms, doing the heel and toe.

I might have been back in Ballyconnell the way the music had me hopping. One thing I learned in Ireland was how to dance. It was Up with you, Mrs Wilson from Dr Royce, and May I have the pleasure? from Mr Timms, and I never dreamed of saying no. It was like the Palace of Dance all over again. Better, because I never had to sit out a dance.

Are you enjoying yourself, Mrs Wilson? asked Dr Royce as he escorted me to the floor. I believe you must be for your cheeks are quite flushed and your eyes are shining.

Such fun, I said. I love dancing. Thank you for inviting me.

The feel of his warm hands, one pressed lightly against my back, the other holding mine, sawing away with it as we stepped out to the music, added to the pleasure of the moment.

You're very light on your feet, he said, looking into my eyes. I believe it would take a leopard to catch you if you had a mind to run.

I only have a mind to dance, I assured him, smiling as we twirled about and almost collided with Ephie and Mr Timms.

We skipped across the floor, laughing as we pranced.

Don't let your partner take liberties, Ephie said later, gliding alongside with Mr Timms when I was dancing with Mr Bignal. She leaned in to whisper, He's known as something of a lady-killer in town. He tried to abduct me once.

Deluded woman, growled Mr Bignal. Who'd want to run away with you?

You'll have me wild in a minute, she said. Shouldn't you be checking the oven?

Why? he shot back. Have you a bun in it?

I say, Bignal, that's no way to speak to a lady, said Mr Timms, but he sniggered when he said it.

Pardon I'm sure, said Mr Bignal. The door was open and I couldn't resist running through.

Ephie was upset by Mr Bignal's remark, and for some reason her tightened lips made me think of the time. I pulled away from Mr Bignal.

What o'clock is it? I said. I am being collected at five.

It's five on the dot, Dr Royce said from his seat at the piano. He got to his feet, an athletic man in his movements, a dancer you might think him except he was not. In that case, Mrs Wilson, he said, if you're ready I'll escort you to your carriage.

Please don't leave your guests, Dr Royce.

Dear me, quite the gentleman aren't we? Ephie's face was flushed as she looked from her husband to me. Do come again, Annie, she said, pressing my hands. Would you like to? Just us two without any of these gentlemen? I have a feeling you and I will find lots to talk about.

Thank you, yes, I said.

Good. I'm so often left alone in the house by Jack and will like it too. Which reminds me, Mr Bignal, I would also like to eat tonight and it's high time you basted the duck.

Our farewells apparently completed, Dr Royce walked with me down the hallway, leaving Ephie and Mr Bignal to continue their bickering. We stepped through the doorway onto the pavement and as if on cue Bob Shout appeared in the buggy, clip-clopping round the corner from Fitzroy Street.

We stood together in the brief Australian twilight, watching the buggy advance up the empty street. Dr Royce made a dashing figure in his cutaway coat, there was no denying it.

I hope you enjoyed your visit, he said.

I did, thank you.

Now the ice is broken we should do this again, he said. You're looking a little peaky, if I may say, Mrs Wilson. An outing might put some colour back in your cheeks. A picnic perhaps, at the Botanical Gardens.

Well I—

I'd consider it an honour while your man's out west. He'd do the same for me, I know. Shall we say this coming Saturday? My wife will take care of the catering.

The buggy creaked up to the kerb. Bob loomed above us on the box seat, clucking the mares to a standstill.

Thank you, yes, I said.

He handed me into the buggy. Till Saturday then. We'll call for you at ten.

A Danger To Herself

WITH OUTINGS and company suddenly to look forward to, the only thing missing was my man. But he came into town quick enough when he got the message about Mr Praed. That gentleman was still causing trouble it seemed, sending letters from England about money he reckoned was still owed him. And as well it was only myself heard Paddy's ranting, for his language wasn't fit to be repeated.

Wearing out the rug, venting his spleen. There's nothing worse than a liar, he cried. A black liar I'd call him!

He was a man for sudden rages, it's why they call him Mad Paddy, I believe.

Mr Praed had brought an insolvency case against him, and myself dragged into it owing to the government land Paddy had applied for under my name.

He flung himself down in his chair. The hearing's in Brisbane, he said, looking into his glass—to avoid my eyes maybe. You'd better fix with Mrs Shout to take care of the children while we're away.

I said I could never leave Harry and Cissie, which put him in another temper.

But my mettle was up too. I'll take care of the children, I said, and they'll want my care I'm thinking when their own father thinks nothing of abandoning them.

Do you want to drive me out of my reason? Paddy cried. Hold your tongue can't you?

I'll hold my tongue, I said. I'll shut up. Never a word will I say about a man that tears a baby from its mother's breast.

What on earth are you blathering about? Cissie is weaned, she's three years old for Christ's sake.

It was back and forth between us, myself was and yourself ought to, there were shouts aplenty, and more Shouts having a good listen in the stables. For I knew Jemima wouldn't fail to do so.

He gave in at last and said he would obtain a nurse to travel with us.

Such a rare day when I got the better of him, why wouldn't I want to savour it? I had another engagement, I said, to let him know he wasn't the only one inconvenienced. And told him the Royces had invited me to a picnic on Saturday.

Paddy was unable to hide his surprise. Mrs Royce? he exclaimed.

Yes.

You must keep away from her, Annie. She was a barmaid in Boolburra when Jack met her, and not only that, the woman has no father.

I stifled a laugh.

No known father, he said, frowning. Now look here, what's all this about? Have you been visiting *Richmond House*?

Only the once.

What on earth were you doing there?

Nothing would make me admit to dancing on Sunday. Taking tea, I said. What did you think?

It might be better not to go there again.

I bit my tongue to stop the words that rose to it. If Ephie Royce wasn't a fit companion then nor was I in the eyes of the ladies on the Range, if they could know my true story: a hungering girl obliged to travel to the ends of the earth to escape a bad death in the Ballyconnell poorhouse.

And for all her skittish manners I quite liked Ephie.

Paddy was studying my face. You're new here of course, he said, so you can't know how your reputation would be damaged by associating with Mrs Royce. She's known for her eccentric manners, and for worse misdemeanours I believe, if rumours are true.

He smiled to soften his words. For both our sakes, it might be better to discourage any further intimacy. Shall we agree on that?

Inwardly mutinous, but obedient as women must be in the main I suppose, so long as it doesn't concern their immortal souls or the welfare of their children, I was muttering my assent when we heard a knock on the door.

Paddy went out to investigate and I heard Jack Royce's voice in the hallway. Up went my hand to my hair, smoothing it.

—left your pipe in the bar, Jack was saying as they entered the room. Thought you might be needing it, given this latest gambit of Praed's.

He laughed and Paddy managed a grin.

Evening, Mrs Wilson, Jack said, and took up a stance beside the fireplace. Everything about him gleamed in the lamplight. His riding boots, black hair, dark eyes.

Paddy returned to his chair. On top of everything else, he said gloomily, I have to put up with people laughing at me. Royce here was telling me people are saying I'll be glad to be declared insolvent, because then I won't owe anyone a penny.

They're only words, I said. Can't you forget them?

How can I forget? he flashed back. They're even saying I made you sew money inside your bustle. Isn't that right, Jack?

Surely people aren't saying such things, Dr Royce?

All too true, sadly.

I held his gaze. Some things are better not repeated.

That's as maybe, Paddy said. At least I know now which men are blackening my name. A coterie of D'Arcy's toadies no less, and I'll tell them so to their faces. Knox D'Arcy may fancy himself as a lawyer, but he forgets I have lived in this district fifteen years and can bring fifty men to vouch for my name.

Jack had followed this rant closely. D'Arcy's a jackass, he said. Everyone knows you for a straight shooter, Paddy.

He stood up from his lean on the mantelpiece. Well, better keep going, I s'pose.

Oh, before you go, Paddy said. Mrs Wilson will be coming with me to Brisbane for the hearing, so can you pass on her apologies to Mrs Royce? I believe there may have been an outing planned.

That's right. We had thought of a picnic in the Botanical Gardens but my wife will quite understand. Well, goodnight, Mrs Wilson, I'm away now. No, don't get up, Paddy.

I'll see you to the door, Paddy said and they went out together.

Mr Praed must have been quite put out in England when he learned the judge in Brisbane threw out his claim. By then we were home, and straight away Paddy had to go back to the bush. I didn't see him for another two weeks.

Harry was grown a sturdy child, a pupil at the Central Boys, and after school he liked nothing better than playing in the bush below the horse-paddocks. I rang the cow-bell one afternoon to tell him to come home, and went back to shelling peas. It was only when they lay green and glistening in the colander that I realised he hadn't returned.

So out with me to the verandah to ring the bell again and scan the grey-green line of trees. Looking for the tell-tale movement, the flash of blue shirt that would signal he was about to appear. But nothing. Not a movement, not a sound. Bob Shout had gone off with Jemima to a bible meeting in town, so it was myself must run down to find Harry.

Quick down the steps I went, picked up my skirts and ducked under the fence, and was halfway across the training paddock before I stopped to call out.

Harry! I shouted, shading my eyes against the lowering sun to stare at the forest. Fear scratched my heart, zigzagging and bright. The trees in the lower paddocks joined up with others in our neighbours' paddocks; they went all the way down the hill to the houses on Racecourse Road. Beyond that was wilderness.

What chance had I of finding Harry if he was lost? It would soon be dark. Oh, where was Paddy when I needed him? Sick at heart, I ran into the forest.

Then I saw Harry, bent over a log with two other boys. They ran away at the sight of me, and Harry looked up angrily. His school shirt was covered in dirt and leaves.

Who were those boys? I demanded as we walked back to the house, and he told me Billy Stapleton and Micky Coogan.

Billy's teaching me how to trap snakes, Mummy. He knows everything about them.

Snakes indeed! I said. There'll be no more snakes and no more getting lost. Your father will have something to say to you, don't fret yourself.

I wasn't lost, he said. I knew where I was.

That's enough of your spake! I cried. Go up to the house and clean yourself.

Such a look he threw me, but started up the slope as bid.

Jemima had plenty to say next morning about playing in the scrub, and none of it any good. We were in the kitchen, herself thumping bread dough and myself settling a fresh log in the firebox, when Harry came bouncing into the kitchen.

Why is Cissie still in bed, Mummy? he asked.

She has a nasty cold, sweetling.

Then she has to have nasty medicine, doesn't she? he said, and stuck his fingers in the sugar bowl.

Here, be off outa that, Jemima said. Mr Shout is waiting for you in the buggy.

Please, Mrs Shout, he said. Can I have some sugar? I'll let you kiss me if you do.

No fear, she said. Old birds ain't caught with such chaff.

Just the one then, I said, closing the firebox.

He crammed the sugar in his mouth quick and skipped out the door.

Jemima made sure to see the back of him before she had her say.

I didn't like to say nothing before him, she said. He's gone now—for we heard the back door slam shut—so I'll tell you. That son of yours is a complete boy, Mrs Wilson. Not rousing nor smacking can change him. Between you and me, you want to stop letting him take Cissie to the scrub. She's growing into young womanhood and a danger to herself from the roughs around here.

Whatever do you mean? I said. Cissie is a child. She's still playing with dolls.

Wait till you hear what I'm saying, Jemima said between thumps. It's the girl-children them larrikins like to do dirty things with. And the Stapleton kids and their mates in the Swamp Push are beyond anything. Always stravaging about on the lookout for mischief, wasting their days like flies on a cowpat. You can't go a step through the scrub to the Racecourse Road without them tykes jumping out at you like wallabies.

Are you saying Cissie is in danger from them? I said, greatly amazed. They are children themselves.

She stopped kneading to lock eyes with me. They're lads some of them, and getting bigger by the day.

Yes, but—

Only I'm saying I'm glad it was Harry and not your little girl they put in danger yesterday. It's not only grown men puts their mickeys into girl-children if they find them on lonely tracks. Not by a long chalk.

She slammed down the dough as if it might be a Coogan under her hand.

I had to sit down. My heart rose up and stuck in my throat. Even to think of anyone doing that to Cissie, bringing fear and hurt to her, weakened my limbs. I swore then and there, to Jemima and myself, never to let Harry take Cissie to the scrub, though they loved playing there more than anything, Cissie in particular. It was her favourite game, playing Ladies under the trees, pouring out the tea Harry boiled up in his father's old billy can. But it was a game she would never play again. I would make sure of that.

Visitors from Ireland

THE DAYMEN were slaughtering goats at the Botanical Gardens while Mrs Methpotter and I were getting the new baby out. The pitiful cries of the dying goats got mixed in my mind with my own. I believed I was dying also, such a hard time I had of it with Ada. Much worse than the first two. Paddy didn't go back to the bush for a month after Ada was born, but he might have been away for all I cared. He couldn't tolerate being startled awake by baby cries and had taken himself off to another room to get better rest. A different story to when Harry and Cissie were babes, but those days were long gone it seemed.

Jemima and I were in the kitchen, cutting up melons for jam when she gave me the benefit of an older woman's counsel.

You're quite down in the mouth, if I may say, Mrs Wilson, she remarked. It's a pity you didn't go to Miss Part's wedding. That might of put some cheer in you.

Oh Jemima, I said, how could I with the belly I had on me then?

Well you might of. You wasn't showing on her wedding day.

And with Mr Wilson away on business?

If you weren't a lady you might of gone on your own, Jemima said. It's only ladies that have to be so particular.

Yes, I said dully. I suppose I'm a lady now.

It's true I was unhappy missing Jessie's wedding. It was herself stood by me on my own marriage day and it grieved me not to be a witness at hers. I shouldn't have taken on so. I knew well enough the better times I had of it in Australia than people were getting in Ireland. They would be glad to have a potato to put on the table. But rather than count my blessings I fell to moping. I missed the pleasures of company was the truth of it. Paddy was away on stock and station business, Jessie confined to her house on account of the baby in her belly, Rhyming Lynam out west looking for work, and the ladies on the Range never paid calls, owing to what I said at Mrs Dawbridge's party, most likely.

But wait. Memory is playing tricks on me. I did have someone besides Jemima to talk to. How could I forget Mrs Lynch that lives on the Lion Creek Road? A Tipperary woman married to a butcher-man, though I never invited her to the house. She was too able for gossip and I had no wish to make myself the topic of her scandalous tongue. Mrs Lynch liked to detain me on the footpath after mass, and it was from her own mouth I heard something of the married life of Jack Royce.

That wife of his, she said. That Ephie now, she's a pert piece. Don't know enough to keep her mouth shut before a man. I hear he abuses her fine for it. Whopped the Devil out of her last week.

He never? I said, all ears at once.

Mrs Lynch laid a finger on her nose. Honest to God, Mrs Wilson, didn't she have two black eyes on her when she come in for her bit of steak. Not that I got any time for her, she was a barmaid in her father's pub in Muttaburra when Dr Royce met her they reckon. That class of woman can't never be much chop, isn't that right, dear?

The poor woman, I said, thinking—*Ephie Royce*? Surely not? *Jack*? I was loath to believe Mrs Lynch, and likely she had it garbled. Hadn't Paddy said Ephie was a barmaid in Boolburra and had no father?

If you ask me, said Mrs Lynch, there ain't much to choose between the pair of them. From what Cabbage Smith tells me Ephie Royce don't have a woman's decency in certain departments.

Cabbage used to work for Mr Wilson, I said, thinking it better not to mention Paddy had sacked him.

And doesn't he work for Dr Royce now and live in the man's stables and see for himself what goes on? Not that I'm saying I got time for Cabbage. He's had a dog tied up at Mr Lynch's shop this past six months.

Oh dear, that's a long time for a dog to be tied up, I said, and thought, In a butcher shop too, where it's all the time tempted by smells and newspaper packages oozing blood.

Oh Mrs Wilson, she said, laughing till her bosoms shook. You're that comical. Don't you know nothing, dear? That's Australian that is, for not paying your bill. So anyway, like I was saying, Cabbage reckons Ephie Royce ain't exactly clean as a starched pillow herself. He surprised her with a gentleman in the stables once. Bold as brass, doing up her bodice when he came in.

If he is to be believed, Mrs Lynch, I said coldly.

Paddy had to go out west again, but before he departed he came home with a name-plate for the house. Bob Shout fixed it beside the door and the three of us stood on the front verandah to admire it. *Rookwood* it said in green Celtic letters raised up on brass.

You're like other folk now, Bob said. All the houses on the Range have 'em.

That was true. Most of the houses had names, the one next door that belonged to our bank manager, Mr Vaunce, was called *Fairbairn*, and I saw others when Bob took me to town in the buggy

It's an odd one but, Bob said. It'd be named for a forest I guess.

It's a place name, was all Paddy would say. He didn't like to be questioned by his yardman, or anyone else for that matter. The sheep-station he had lost wasn't a topic he cared to discuss.

Not long after, Mrs Vaunce was taking her morning stroll. She never gave so much as a nod if I was on the front verandah, which was most days since I kept an eye on Ada when I put her out for her airing. So imagine my surprise when I saw Mrs Vaunce lower her parasol and peer at our new name-plate. Then at myself sitting under it, darning Harry's socks.

I am Mrs Vaunce, she said, coming up to the gate and smiling with all her teeth.

I put down the darning egg and stood up. And I am Mrs Wilson, I said, trading smiles with her.

I see you have a name for your house, she said. We have one too, you may have noticed.

I have, yes.

Now, *Rookwood*? she said. That's unusual. It must be a name from home, surely?

It is Irish, I said.

Now isn't that the strangest thing? she said. Mr Vaunce was only telling me at breakfast this morning there's an Irish lady and her husband arrived in town, and the address on their luggage is Kilbeggan, and the wife signed her name Eliza Cuffe Wilson. Which surely must mean she's related to the Kilbeggan Cuffes. We looked them up in an old copy of Debretts and it seems they're titled people. Would there be any connection, Mrs Wilson? That you know of?

I was that surprised I could only gape at her.

Well I just thought I'd ask. The Reverend Wilson and his wife? It's such a coincidence, is it not? And yourself a Wilson too.

It must be Mr Wilson's father and mother, I said. But it's news to me they're in the country.

Oh, they've only just arrived. Putting up at the Criterion Mr Vaunce told me, in one of the family suites. Well, how lovely to have them come all this way.

It is, yes.

I'm so pleased to have met you, Mrs Wilson, she said. Now that we know each other I shan't neglect to call on you with my *carte de visite*.

Mrs Vaunce gave a wave and more smiles and continued her walk. As for myself, I hardly knew what to do first. See to the house or press my best gown? The house! I thought, and told Jemima we must do a spring-clean.

We were at it all day and were beating the rugs in the backyard when Paddy came riding down the driveway. I must tell Mr Wilson, I said, and ran across to the stables where he was unsaddling his horse.

Paddy! Paddy! I cried. How fortunate you've come home. Do you know your mother and father are in town?

Who told you that? he said.

The lady next door. She had it from her husband this morning.

What? Vauncey? He doesn't miss much, Paddy said, and told me we'd better talk inside.

But when we were in the house he sat down in his armchair with a face on him like a man who's lost sixpence and found a turd. Aren't you the queer article? I said. And your mother and father travelled all this length to visit you.

Well, you see how it is. I had to rush back to town without finishing my business.

Mr McPherson won't mind, I said. He'll be glad for you. But they may call any time. If it's to be today I must get back to the cleaning.

He said they weren't coming to the house, he had seen them already and that wasn't their wish.

Ah sure, I said. They're getting on in years. But I knew by my heart beating more steady the relief that was in me. My housekeeping wouldn't get a mother-in-law's sharp eye cast over it.

It will be no harm to Ada to travel in the buggy, I gabbled. She's a sturdy child and never been sick the once.

Paddy took up his pipe. That's good of you to take it so well. I had half a notion you might be offended.

Indeed and I'm not. But when are we to call?

He was knocking the dottle out of his pipe with methodical taps, and took a while to answer. Well that's just it, he said when he finished tapping. There's no we about it. They're all agog to see the children, that's of course, but they'd rather … uh, that you, uh … don't come with them.

Not come? I said. Why ever not?

He told me then what I already knew, that his father had no tolerance for Roman Catholics. He was also a frail old man who mustn't be upset. I thought it odd all the same. If Reverend Wilson wouldn't see his daughter that married a Catholic, why had he travelled this length to visit his son that married another one?

I grew quite tired of hearing Harry and Cissie's prattle about the excursions they took with their grandparents. If it wasn't pineapple ices in the Cremorne Gardens it was lions at the circus, and one day they didn't get home till after dark. A steamer on the Fitzroy River was the outing that day. Paddy along with them, for Mr McPherson gave him time off. They were both on the Arjaycee committee so he was thick with my man and apt to show him favour.

We saw a rude man on the boat, Mummy, Cissie said at breakfast next morning.

Well now, Paddy said, he wasn't so rude, pet.

Oh Daddy, he *was* rude. He put his hand on a lady's bottom.

He squeezed her bum, Harry added, grinning.

Hold your tongue, ordered Paddy. You'll get a thrashing if I hear language like that. You may leave the table. And Cissie, you're finished I see. You may go too.

They slipped off their chairs and went out of the room, Harry working his legs like pistons and giving out whistles. Trains were all he could think of, owing to an excursion to Westwood he had taken with his grandparents.

Such guttersnipe language the boy's picking up at the state school, Paddy said.

Most likely he learned it from me, I said. What's wrong with saying bum anyway?

He looked at me that distasteful I was sorry I spoke.

You must stop that immediately, he said. You're teaching the children bad habits. Oh botheration, don't make eyes at me. I was only setting you straight.

If we're to speak of teaching, I said, is it to be another day off school for Harry and Cissie? When are your mother and father going back to Ireland, do you know? The children are getting behind in their letters and numbers.

Haven't my parents only three months in Australia? he said, his voice gone tight.

It's a wonder your father can stay away from his church so long, I said, not caring if I made him angry.

I heard plenty then. How his father might stay as long as he pleased since he had no church to go back to. Rioters had burned it down when the Parliament in London disestablished the Church of Ireland. But not knowing what disestablishing meant I could only stare at him.

So you see, he said, my father is a disappointed man. Yet you want to add to his troubles by throwing his kindness back in his face. It would drive a fellow wild, the resentment that's in you.

What resentment is that? I said.

Don't think I haven't noticed the disapproving waggle of your backside when you leave the room.

And why wouldn't I be offended when your father went and baptised Ada in my absence? I said. What manners has he showed a mother, may I ask?

Paddy banged his fist on the table that forceful his plate jumped in the air.

How dare you criticise my father!

It's easy for you to talk, I said. Am I not the mother of Ada that should have been with her on her baptismal day? Even if 'twas by a Proddy and herself no better than a heathen at the end of it.

You must know this, he said, soft and steely. I stand for Church and Queen and so will any child who bears my name.

Sure, I said. It's always those who never kneel before God that think themselves best suited to care for others' souls.

And what would you know about it? he flashed out. A bog-Irish woman like yourself.

Ah! I said. You're no better than the rest of your class. Bog-Irish am I? That's a nice word. Better than bum I suppose.

It was an escaped word, he muttered. I wish I could recall it. But if you'd held your tongue I'd never have been driven to using it.

Driven yourself, cried an infuriated voice in my head. I was too cut up to stop now. And another thing, I said. What about Lizzie Doyle? You asked her at the Depot in Townsville. Most likely you don't recall her name, but what was it you wanted? Was it a housekeeper or wife?

He looked at me as if I'd gone stark staring mad.

I was just a convenient female to have your children. If it wasn't me it would've been Lizzie Doyle.

He blinked. What are you talking about?

You! I said fiercely. I'm talking about *you*!

I waited for him to say the words I longed to hear. To deny he'd proposed to Lizzie Doyle.

Believe me, he said, I have no idea who this Lizzie Doyle is that you keep referring to. For all I know you've invented her.

He scraped back his chair and stood up.

I'd better tell Bob to bring in the horses. The children are to go riding today. At least *they* will enjoy themselves.

As soon as he was gone I flung a spoon at the wall and cried. I couldn't stop crying and had to go in the bedroom till the tears stopped.

I am killed trying to do the fine lady for him, I told my tear-streaked face in the mirror. It will never work because I can never be one. And maybe I don't want to.

In the days that followed there was no gab between us. Himself cool out of bed, myself cool in it, is it any wonder distrust lay between us and showed its haughty face when we met? Which happened rarely since he was away with the children at first, and after his parents set sail back to Ireland he was away on other business, for Jackson & McPherson or the Arjaycee, or billiards at the Cri, or judging blood-stock at the Show. Or whatever fancy kept him from the house.

God forgive me but on Paddy's snippety uppity days I consoled myself with thoughts of Dr Royce.

Sometimes when I lay sleepless at night, thinking of Paddy's latest indifference, I wanted to quit *Rookwood*. Take the children and go. Become like Witchety Peg, a manless woman earning my own bread. But when I looked down that road to freedom it was a dark alley leading to poverty. The only work I could hope to obtain was as a servant, and no mistress would ever allow a housemaid to keep her children on the premises. So I cried useless tears but said not a word of my feelings, since Paddy had so few to spare for me. I was in the fury of my life then, with scarce time to know myself, let alone a husband mum in his discontents.

Though not so silent the day Banjo died. The old dog got bit by a snake in the horse-paddock, and never have I seen a man take the death of a dog so hard. Tears running down his face and him cuffing them away, angry to find them there. Fetching a spade and going at the ground like a man demented till he had a hole big enough to bury a small horse. He came back to the house dragging his feet, and I brought tea to him on the back verandah.

He sat in his chair, staring at the stones he had dragged onto Banjo's grave.

Bob knows a man has some good cattledog pups, I said.

He groaned.

He was a good dog, I said, making so bold as to sit beside him. It'll be queer not hearing his tail thump on the verandah.

Ah well, Paddy said, wiping his eyes with the back of his hand. He's in his grave now, under that fig-tree you planted. When it grows he'll be out of the sun. He'd like that, old Banjo.

It will grow a fine shade-tree if Sergeant Lynam is to be believed, I said. And likely is, for just look at those vegetables he gave me the seeds for. They couldn't be more flourishing.

Paddy gazed at the rows of cabbages. You can get rid of them for all I care, he muttered. It only wants a pigsty and turf rack to look like any broken-down tenant farm in Ireland. God knows what Vauncey thinks when he sees your hens in his garden.

He stood up and went inside.

Broken-down tenant farms is it? I thought, watching him go. He knew full well I was a tenant-farmer's daughter. And where do you think your breakfast egg comes from? I felt like shouting after him. I was quite cast down. Well Annie, I told myself, this is what you must expect when you marry a Proddy. A husband who scorns where you come from, and you'd better get used to it.

The Swamp Push

HARRY AND Cissie came late to dinner one night, which was never permitted by their father. Very cranky he was at the head of the table, and his temper no better improved from seeing Ada fretful and pushing away her food. She was three years old and suffering from prickly heat. When she wouldn't take another bite I carried her to her room, slathered her with calamine lotion and put her to bed. The children were dawdling in from the verandah when I came back, and something up, that was easy seen. Harry's sleeve was torn and Cissie's blue eyes bigger than usual. The poor child looked scared half to death.

What have you to say for yourselves? Paddy said from the head of the table, and Cissie began crying at once.

Now then, I won't have you using tears to get out of trouble. Well Harry, speak up!

Sit you down, I said, and they slunk onto their chairs, their eyes fixed on their father.

It was Billy Stapleton, Cissie got out between sobs. He threw a stone at Harry.

That put a halt to Paddy's gallop. A stone! he said. Did he hit you, boy?

He was stealing firewood from our paddock, Daddy.

Now Harry, I ask you a question and you start a new quarry. Tell me now, did that boy hit you? If he did—

He did! He did! wailed Cissie.

Mother of Mercy! I cried, and Paddy banged his fist on the table and Harry gave Cissie a glare.

Little sneak. You promised not to tell.

Where did Billy hit you? I demanded.

Don't worry, Mummy. Big George clouted him and he ran away.

Hah! Paddy said. What was Big George doing there I wonder? Loading his cart with firewood from our paddocks I suppose.

Big George can spit further than anyone, Daddy.

Where did Billy hit you? I repeated.

It was his arm, Mummy, Cissie said, and began crying and hiccupping in earnest.

I knew she would make herself sick if she kept on and I could see Harry wasn't going to die on me, so I sent her to her room and brought her beef jelly soup. By the time I got back Harry was nowhere to be seen and Paddy helping himself to an aftercourse of newspapers.

A bad-minded lot, the larrikins who style themselves the Swamp Push, he said. It's a pity we have to be bothered by them, the way they come up from the Racecourse Road and steal our firewo—

Where's Harry? I said, though it wasn't my habit to interrupt him.

He shot me a look. I sent him to his room. He made a good dinner, don't fret yourself.

I began stacking the plates, meaning to attend to Harry's arm once I got out the door. But he had his eye on me and when I picked up the tray he announced he had news about Mr Jackson. That gentleman was so poorly it seemed, he was obliged to sell his half of the business. I could see Paddy was concerned about Mr Jackson's illness. His dying, though he avoided using that word.

And his family, I said. It'll be hard on them too.

It will. Any rate I'm taking up his offer to buy him out, so that should be a load off his mind.

You could have heard a pin drop when he said that.

Then you have the money for it? I asked. Wondering would we end up the way we did with Mr Praed. I knew from the papers the meatworks was like to close owing to the current drought, and it wasn't a good time to be buying into any business, let alone cattle.

Paddy scowled at me. We'll not find ourselves in the Insolvency Court if that's what you mean.

The children will be glad, I said. They miss you when you're away.

It's only on their account I agreed. I never thought I'd lower myself to become an auctioneer. Never intended going down that road. But Father and Mother needn't know, that's the plus, and I fancy I can make a go of specialising in horses. McPherson's happy with that.

I said nothing but my face must have told my feelings.

Oh for God's sake, why do I bother talking to you?

He snatched up his pipe and went out on the verandah.

I brought the brandy to him but didn't stay to sit. The mood on my man wasn't what you might call inviting. Not that night nor many another. God help us, I thought. He might be a great man in the doss but that's all can be said for him.

He came home with a puppy not long after. A dog about town for a man about town, he told us when he carried the little white terrier into the house. Trixie, he called her and a rare favourite she was with the children, they couldn't get enough of her. And her with a button nose that waffled, wouldn't anyone be soft on her?

Highland terriers were all the rage in the Eighties, no gentleman's outfit was complete without one. But Trixie was more than adornment to Paddy. Such affection he showed the little dog I sometimes felt jealous. As soon as she was old enough she went everywhere with him, following behind his horse in the mornings, curled up beside his chair at night. A one-man dog, Trixie, with eyes for no one but himself.

Not a bad little slut, I would hear him say, casual-like, to his friends when they were playing cards in the drawing-room. But it was a different story after the gentlemen went home. Then Trixie followed him to the bedroom where she had her own bed on the floor. A gentleman's dog may sleep where it pleases, he said when I showed surprise. He was never one to have animals in the house, and got in a terrible rage if he found the hens in the kitchen. She isn't a work dog, he said. You're a house dog, aren't you, Trix?

She set up such a barking one night he couldn't quiet her. Gun shots woke her and us besides. Coming from Murray Lagoon, Paddy guessed. And he was right. Bob Shout heard it from the butcher-man on Racecourse Road next morning—a man out possum-hunting that finding none, killed a black swan instead. Which isn't allowed, of course. They are protected in the colony of Queensland. And rare enough to see them, but we had three on the lagoon below the Botanical Gardens, reared from chicks by Mr Edgar, the head gardener.

Four gun shots woke us that night and put me in mind of the rhyme Ellen and I used to chant when we were small, too young to know what we were singing. *3 for a Wedding and 4 for Death*, is how it ends. It was the four shots ringing out in the darkness put the rhyme in my head, but Trixie might have had it in hers the way she couldn't stop shivering and whining.

In the end Paddy put her by the stove in the kitchen to give us some peace.

I see a new chum was responsible, he said from behind his newspaper next evening. This was the eye of my day, when I sat across from him doing the mending while he read out this and that, giving each item to the air for me to listen to if I wished. And I did wish. I still enjoyed listening to his deep voice and I was all ears when he read out that the man was an abattoir worker, and got fined five pound. A hefty penalty then.

Bad cess to him, I said, plying my needle faster.

What's this? Paddy said, reading again. I see your eccentric friend is in trouble.

Which friend would that be?

The goat-woman, Witchety Peg.

She's not my friend, I said. She has friends of her own I believe, down at the main drain.

He grimaced to show his distaste. Well it'll be a while before they see her again. She's in hospital, beaten up by larrikins.

Magpies were singing outside the window when I tiptoed into the ward. Singing their gladness as if suffering was never invented. Dear God, I thought, staring at the thin bundle hunched under a hospital blanket. Her small head was hid by bandages and what could be seen of her face was grey as a piece of pork after it is soaked in water.

They reckon women that live on their own are witches, and Harry thought so. He was upset when I said I was visiting Witchety Peg, and begged I wouldn't look at her. She's got goat's eyes, Mummy, he said. If you look in her eyes you'll turn into a witch. I had to chivvy him out of his fears.

I pulled up a chair and she opened the eye that wasn't bandaged. It was nothing like a goat's eye and it winked at me.

The wreck of the *Hesperus*, that's me, she said in a hoarse whisper. She chuckled to herself, and had to stop and clutch her side.

Her ribs, I thought. The nurse, the one that showed me in, had told me they were cracked from the kicking she got. Three young men it was who strolled down to her humpy for no better purpose than beating up an old woman.

Bad news travels on hare's feet, she whispered.

It does, yes, Miss Purdy, I said.

For all her woes she was cheerful enough and I soon learned why. It was the whiskey the doctor was giving her for the pain that made her so talkative.

So many visitors I might be the English Queen, she said hoarsely. Mr Milford even, he come this morning and tried to make me lay charges.

She fixed me with her one dark eye. Hand me the bottle, love, she ordered, like she might be Queen Victoria after all.

Love?

I held the flask to her lips and she grasped it with her bony fingers. Heat came from her body like a small furnace. Such a frail birdy creature yet she had an engine-house inside her.

You're like my mother, I thought on a sudden, and knew straight away it was true. The same bright-dark eyes, the same sooty black hair that age cannot grey. The same skinny body dear to memory, and inside, the same quick flame. So that's why I'm here, I realised. I am drawn to you as the sinner is drawn to God.

Ah, she said, settling back. That's better. Water of life, nothing like it for old bones. If only I had my pipe I'd be in Heaven.

And will you? I said. Charge them I mean?

Course not. Why should I? What's in it for me?

But they should be punished.

She had a wheezy laugh to herself. Dunno what you're making such a bobbery about. They'd only get off by saying they was drunk, and cost me good money, and nothing back for it. Not like when I goes after the Inspector of Nuisances. I gets costs then, for my goats. Any road, they is punished already.

Already? I parroted.

She laughed till she had to hold her ribs.

Course they is, she gasped. By being men. God gave them hot blood to balance the affliction of that thing they keep between their legs.

I said nothing to this. The thing between Paddy's legs was no affliction to me, but nor was it of any great interest lately. Instead I made do with a diet of romantic dreams about Dr Royce. He fancied me, and Jack as a fantasy lover suited me better than Paddy in the flesh.

He he he, Witchety Peg laughed. You should of seen the larrikins when my rooster flew at their eyes. And Will Wally, my bonny lavender, he let fly a few kicks. Got one where it hurts. He he he. And my neighbour-man from across the way, he wasn't long coming. They took to the woods as the Yankees say, when they seen the bit of twobefour in Mr Baldock's hands. Nah, I don't need to worry about them riff-raff. They won't be back if they got any sense.

Maybe you should think of moving somewhere safer, I said, remembering the men at Carmel's house when we lived in *South Esk Cottage*. That part of town isn't far from Witchety Peg's humpy at the main drain.

The old woman fixed me with her unbandaged eye. I can't be arranging my life to suit larrikins. I ain't a floating type of female that goes back and forth like a jellyfish. Anyway, I can't leave my goats.

But it's lonesome down there.

Listen here, she said. Her voice was that faint I had to lean in to catch the words. Again I felt the heat coming off her. Was it fever? She hadn't the look of fever. Her one eye was clear, bright as a jet button. It must have been her own engine making the heat. That and the whiskey.

See here, she said. You ain't got much sense that's plain, so here's some to help you. Any place is lonesome without those you care for, but I ain't lonesome. I got my goats and I got good neighbours. A bird without a bush ain't worth tuppence, but I got my bush. I got a house that's paid for, so put that in your pipe and smoke it.

I felt a rush of envy. You own your own home?

She chuckled. A gentleman friend built it for me. We was going to be married once.

What became of him? I said, wondering what age she had on her when she had thoughts of marrying.

Changed my mind, didn't I? I'm more better off with my billy-goats, they are my little husbands. And never knock me about neither.

But they have their own wives, I said.

Wives together, she cackled. The nannies do the needed to make the milk and I do the milking to make the money. That way we stays together.

She was still chuckling and clutching her side when I said goodbye.

I met more people in the hospital corridor that day than I was like to meet in a month of Mondays. First it was Mrs Lynch, the butcher-man's wife, waddling towards me in her dressing gown, for she was just delivered of a son.

We're going to call him Christy, she said. A fine boy he is, Mrs Wilson. A right red bawler. But oh, I declare to my soul, the pains he give me coming out might of made a saint weep.

If only I'd known what havoc Christy would unleash I might have wept too.

Next it was Rhyming Lynam carrying a fistful of daisies, on his way to visit Witchety Peg. That surprised me, I never knew the goat-woman was so popular. Rhyming Lynam was angry on her behalf, like me.

I'd give five pound to the hospital to meet them bastards alone, he said, and he meant business. The old fellow was powerful built and would have done damage if he found the larrikins. Then it was Jessie Philp strolling down the corridor, after visiting her brother Joseph who was laid up with a broken ankle.

Another football injury, she said, rolling her eyes. Come and join me in a smoke, why don't you?

I don't smoke, I said, surprised that she did, but Jessie told me tobacco was a proven disinfectant and I'd better do so if I wanted to ward off infection from the hospital diseases.

I never knew that, I said, impressed.

Out the door we went and had to shoo away a couple of hospital cows so we could stand in the shade of a Moreton Bay fig-tree by the gate. You can't be too careful, Jessie said as we took little puffs on the cigarillo the head nurse had given her, and fell into coughing fits. Then puffed again.

I was a bit light-headed as I went out the gate, and at first I didn't notice the three boys lounging on the footpath.

Lookit the sheila! Lookit the tits on her! one of them said, and I saw it was Billy Stapleton.

Little hooligan, I thought. Only two years ago he was a snivelly kid on the back of his father's woodcart, but now he was taller than me. And neither fish nor fowl. One foot in manhood in his tight bellbottom trousers, but to judge by the slingshot dangling from his pocket, the other one still planted firmly in boyhood.

The Full Fandangle

I N HIS tempers Paddy was never an easy man to live with. Quarter days put him in such a rage over the bills, declaring they would ruin him, I was glad to see the back of him when he went to Duaringa on one of his Racing Association jaunts.

He departed on Sunday and was barely gone an hour when who should present himself at the house than Cabbage Smith. I opened the door to his knock, and before I could tell him to use the back door he thrust a sealed paper at me.

Read it, missus. I'm to bring back your answer direct.

And who is it that wants it? I demanded.

Give over your gabbing will you. Dr Royce is waiting on your answer.

Wait here a moment, I said, and shut the door in his face.

In the hallway I broke the wax seal and scanned the paper. No dear madam or yours sincerely, just a bare string of words.

Can you meet me in the Botanical Gardens at 2?
I have something important to tell you.

What could Jack have to say that was so urgent? He was on the Arjaycee committee with Paddy so he'd be aware my man had left town. I couldn't take in the portent of it all yet never stopped to tussle over the proprieties. Instead I flung open the door.

Tell Dr Royce the answer is yes. I said, my heart banging as if a small animal was trying to escape.

I wish I could say I fought against temptation, but that would be a lie. In the privacy of my imaginings Jack had become my phantom lover and you might say I was starving hungry for more substantial fare. I tore up the note and went over to the hallstand to push the pieces through a long-necked brass vase I kept there.

Who was that at the door, Mrs Wilson?

I swung round and saw Jemima in her blue gingham dress and starched apron, standing in the hallway.

Oh! You startled me, Jemima. It was a … a man delivering church tracts. I sent him away.

I thought it might've been that Cabbage chappie, she said. Thought I recognised his smell.

He was rather like Cabbage in height, I said.

You're quite flushed, Mrs Wilson. Are you feeling alright?

I said I had a headache and would lie down to ease it. Jemima was the lynch-pin of my world and I knew only too well her opinion of immoral women. If she were to suspect me of unseemly behaviour, if I were to lose her regard—the very idea was unthinkable. Yet such were the needs of my pent up heart, such the lust of a woman unloved in her prime, I disregarded these cautions. Knocked them aside before they could take hold, and said, On second thoughts, fresh air will do me good. I think I'll take a stroll, Jemima. That is, if you don't mind giving the children their tea when they come home from school.

You're never going walking in the middle of the day! she said. Surely Dr Callaghan hasn't prescribed such a course?

He has, yes, I said. He's very particular I take exercise.

I got out of her watchful presence as quick as I could. Put on a plain white gown and repinned my hair, but otherwise made no changes to my appearance lest they arouse Jemima's suspicions. Took my parasol and set off along Agnes-street, that snakes its way along the crest of the Range. To distract myself from what I was getting into, I examined the white-painted houses as I passed them, but being so like *Rookwood* in appearance they failed to hold my attention.

Another half hour brought me to the elegant wrought iron gates of the Botanical Gardens, standing open as always, to allow the people of Rockhampton to enter as they please. Only they don't please, most of them. The Gardens are a discouraging distance for working-men on the town flats. But I knew the Gardens well, having brought the children to run about under the trees and feed stale bread to the turtles in the lagoon.

As soon as I stepped through the gateway onto the avenue bordered by hoop pines, my eyes sought and found Jack. He had parked his carriage at the end of the short avenue, and was reclining against the upholstery, smoking a cheroot. He made no move to get down when he saw me. Only puffed on the cheroot, keeping his eyes fixed on me.

I hardly knew where to put mine, though my feet carried me effortlessly toward him.

Mrs Wilson, he said, tipping his hat and showing his white teeth in a smile.

His polished boots descended the mounting step, then he was standing close to me, smelling of smoke and the bay rum he puts on his hair. All my hope and fear was for him to close the gap between us.

He dropped the cheroot and ground it out with his boot.

Fancy a spin in my new barouche? he said. Then we'll have tea at *Richmond House*. Ephie's in Sydney so we'll have the place to ourselves.

The very idea of going to *Richmond House* with Jack sent warning thrills spiking through me. Despite my mad rush to meet him I wasn't prepared for the full fandangle. Paddy's coldness had led to daydreaming about Jack, but I'd never really liked the man. Had always distrusted his devil-may-care airs, even though those airs were part of his attraction.

I can't stay long, I said primly. What was it you wanted to say?

Wanted to see you is all. Isn't that why you're here?

The bald truth spoken out loud. I struggled to return Jack's gaze.

He took my hand and a tremor ran right through me. The hand holding mine had a diamond ring on the middle finger and I stared at it as if mesmerised.

I think I love you, Mrs Wilson, he said. That's the damnable thing.

How could Jack love me when he hardly knew me? I suspected him of lying but even so the corners of my lips crept up in a smile.

If you say so, Dr Royce, I suppose I should believe you.

Can't I entice you? he said. I'm a lonely man and I live in a lonely house.

Nothing he said could persuade me to get into his barouche, the more so since I had just noticed Mrs Dawbridge in the distance, strolling the lawns with another lady. She saw me and put up her lorgnette for a better look.

I shouldn't have come! I exclaimed, pulling my hand from his.

See here, Jack said, I thought we were in this together. I've seen the looks you give me. Ephie's the one at fault, not yours truly. If she wasn't so moody and arty and inclined to give me tongue-lashings I wouldn't be here.

We are alike, I realised.

I started up the slope towards the gates but he took hold of my arm, forcing me to stop.

The thing is, he said, I can't get you out of my mind. God knows, I've tried. Since first I met you … something about you that day at the races … so soft-spoken yet sure of yourself. You're better than other women I know. Apart from my mother that is, and she's dead now—

Please let go of me, I said.

I've done a few things I'm not proud of, but you're the woman to save me. You're my Mary Magdalene and sea-siren wrapped up in one.

Will you let go of my arm?

Go then, he said, dropping his hand.

He tipped back my parasol to send me a brooding stare. You've not seen the last of me, he warned. I'll plague you into loving me yet.

He turned away and I walked quick up the avenue. Had almost reached the gates when I heard his carriage approaching. Saw him touch his whip to the horses as they trotted past. I stood at the big gates, watching the barouche dwindle in size as it rolled along Agnes-street. The oversize wheels seemed to float in the heat haze.

When I glanced back at the Gardens, Mrs Dawbridge was still examining me.

Am I mad or what? I cried in my heart. My treacherous, scarlet heart. The woman's prolonged scrutiny made me feel grubby in a way I had never had occasion to feel before. The shame of it came skulking up to me like a knowing old tomcat.

A Gross Insult to a Little Girl

WHEN I returned to my senses after that bit of madness, I tried harder to be a good wife and forget my husband's high-handed ways. I remembered Billy Stapleton, and when Paddy returned from his trip out west I told him about the boy's rudeness outside the hospital. A forlorn attempt to get his attention, I suppose. And it might be the telling deepened Paddy's suspicions of Billy and caused him to act rash later. I don't know. I hope not. At the time it was only a tiny cloud on the horizon we didn't notice. And why would we with everything else going on? Mr McPherson selling Paddy his share of the business, then buying Paddy's old sheep-station. That was wormwood and gall to my man, and more so when gold was discovered on *Rookwood's* acres. Mr McPherson became a rich man after that.

But Paddy became a big man in his own right through having the business all to himself. He was selling cattle-stations as well as horses now, his auctions well attended for the entertainment they provided. He had the gift of the gab, I heard. Though often as not the men that hung around in the foyer of the Criterion Hotel on auction day outwitted him. They had a way with words too.

Can I bid, Wilson? one of them asked. Certainly, my man, Paddy said from his position halfway up the staircase. Then I bid you good day, the wit said and disappeared into the bar, leaving him to the whistles and laughter.

The papers reported Witchety Peg donated a bag of flour to the hospital, then got herself in trouble for assaulting a man and using language. I couldn't help wondering was he one of the larrikins that went to her humpy. But all wondering was forgot when I read the next item, about the *Kapunda* going down. Friday the thirteenth it foundered, the Devil's day. The single girls locked in their cabin as always, as we had been. Their Matron had the key but could hardly be expected to remember it in her confusion. Any rate she was drowned with the girls.

For a while I couldn't get it out of my head, I was always thinking, remembering. The storm that drowned the sheep in their cages. The dancing we girls enjoyed after they locked us in our cabin at night. We pretended to be fast girls, sticking out our bums, blowing kisses, swaggering about. Laughing, flushed by our daring. If it was a sin we indulged in, there was no one except ourselves to know how our bodies grew warm and desirous, and how pleasurable we found the sensation.

Ah well, it's long gone now, all those memories stuffed in my head like mismatched socks. It was Witchety Peg's words I tried to remember when thoughts of the *Kapunda* filled my head. About having your own bush I mean. That I was fortunate to have a house and children to care for, instead of how it must've been for the girls.

That didn't bear thinking of—the lasses hammering on the locked hatch.

We had good rains that year so I gave Cissie and Ada some seeds to plant, and didn't they mix them up and strew them among the vegetables. You should have seen the colours when they came up, mignonette alongside beans, pumpkins peeping out behind pansies. It was business and pleasure mixed. Cissie was nine and not inclined to keep Ada company, so that was another cause for smiling, seeing their frolics in the garden. She spent most of her time with the Hutton girls up the road and didn't like to have her little sister dragging after her.

Eliza and Nellie Hutton called for her one day. They were going down to see their friend Minnie, they said, that lived on Dawson-road.

Mr Shout will take you in the buggy, I said, perhaps not as firm as I should have.

Oh no, Mrs Wilson, the Hutton girls chorused. We are walking.

I don't think— I said, and Cissie looked at me cross.

We're big girls now, Mummy.

Does your mother know? I asked, and Nellie said she did. She was picking them up in her phaeton and bringing them back at four o'clock.

It's all arranged, she said with that square look she has. A sturdy child with freckles, I always liked her. Eliza also, both sturdy girls with nothing finicky about them, from living most of their life on a cattle-station most likely. They had the sunny air of children brought up outdoors, on the fat of the land.

Well, if your mother knows, I said. But mind you keep to the footpath and don't speak to strangers.

Oh Mummy! Cissie said, raising her eyebrows at Nellie. The little minx, I could have smacked her.

Often I remember my words, trying to find the fault in them. But how was I to know they wouldn't do as promised? It was April, so lovely weather, which was probably why they decided to take a short cut through the Hospital Scrub. Eliza and Nellie's idea most likely, Cissie would never have disobeyed me on her own, I'm sure. Though not a word has she spoke about it since. To this day she is a secret to herself.

Jemima and I were in the kitchen when we heard the knocking. By herrings, Jemima said. That's a queer rat-a-tat. More scrabbling like.

We went out of the kitchen wing into the house, and down the wide hallway to the front door, and there was Nellie with no hat and Eliza beside her making gasping noises. Her eyes round as saucers. I screamed then, before I could stop myself, and Eliza began screaming too.

Where is she? I cried, shaking her to make her stop screaming and tell me. Jemima had to pull me off, I was that beside myself.

Come quick, Nellie cried. Oh please please come quick.

Jemima shouting from the verandah, something about Bob as we ran down the path and out on the street. I remember that. The way Nellie's and Eliza's boots tossed up the hems of their skirts. Black boots, white skirts, black white, black white like some kind of crazy semaphore. The sky giving off silence so hard you could crack it like an egg. We were running in a nightmare and just like a nightmare we hardly seemed to be moving. When the girls darted into the Hospital Scrub it was as if I had known all along—the sight that was waiting. A sight that will live with me forever.

Up against a spindly tree Cissie lay slumped, absolutely still, her eyes staring straight ahead. A bruise on her cheek. The pretty new dress she was so proud of rucked up around her waist. But still. Absolutely still.

A man's cap lying on the ground beside her.

Bob Shout came crashing through the wild raspberry bushes then and ran past us to gather her up. No one said a word, we just turned and began running, back through the bushes and onto the street. Not a soul anywhere to see us and silence pouring out of the sky above. The sky was our only witness.

If the silence had continued it would have been better for Cissie. Though she wouldn't speak, I believe the last thing she wanted was for anyone to know what had happened.

But what had happened?

Dr Callaghan examined her and said she was intact. *Intact with bruising* were the words he used, not looking at Paddy or me when he said it. Paddy came tearing up from town as soon as Bob gave him the news, and could hardly contain himself. Hectoring and questioning me first, then Nellie and Eliza who were sitting cowed on a sofa in the drawing-room. They couldn't offer much, though they were questioned till they cried. Till Mrs Hutton arrived. She was pretty shook up too.

A boy about fifteen years, Nellie said, but she didn't know him. He had jumped out from behind a tree and grabbed Cissie and she and Eliza had run after them. They beat on his back where he was bent over Cissie, until Eliza thought to scream and he ran off. But they couldn't get Cissie to get up so they ran back to the house.

Was it Billy Stapleton? Paddy kept shouting. He was dancing with rage and white as the inside of a flour bin.

We don't know, Mr Wilson, Nellie said with tears in her eyes.

By the Lord Harry! he cried, we'll see about that!

And was gone out the door in a flash.

He came home after dark and wouldn't say what he'd done, but it all came out in the newspapers next day. He was charged with assault and later the court case reported, even the words he spoke:

> I went with a constable to the Racecourse Road to make inquiries into a gross insult that had been offered to my little girl. I called at the house of this young fellow's father, and the constable went inside to make inquiries as Stapleton was then supposed to be concerned in the matter. Young Stapleton came out and before I had said anything, he said to me, 'I know all about it. You said there was a cart loading timber here.' I replied, 'I did not say that,' and he said, 'You did,' in a most impudent manner, so I jumped off my horse and gave him a thrashing with my whip. He gave me the lie direct and interfered when he was not called on, so I beat him.

Paddy was never able to feel hot and think cold. He was ever and always a slave to his heart and ended up paying a good deal of money to Billy Stapleton's father. By then another boy had been charged, but even that didn't satisfy him. About a week after Cissie was attacked the editor of the *Rockhampton Bulletin* printed a notice in the correspondence column:

> Edward Wilson, the well-known horse and cattle dealer, was recently summoned on a charge of assaulting a lad named Stapleton under somewhat peculiar circumstances. Not content with this, Wilson has been writing to

the papers on the subject in a way
which shows still further his temper
is apt to get the better of what little
judgment he may possess.

Cold comfort to Cissie they didn't print his letters. She stayed in her room and was forever washing herself. If you watch a fly when it is doing the same, first you will see it clean its feet, then the wings, and lastly its legs and about the body. But all done in such a humble way with much wringing of thin hands, as if to appease. Cissie was like that. Each time I came in the room she was standing at the marble-topped washstand, dipping a flannel in the basin and scrubbing herself.

I was fit to tear the boy apart with my bare hands if I could get hold of him. Break the bonds of decency in the searing rage of my heart. Oh how I wanted to tear his heart from his breast, and tear out my own heart, for I knew, oh I knew, I had failed to take proper care of my little girl.

Everyone at school is saying Cissie is tampered with, Harry was telling Jemima when I came in the kitchen. What does tampered with mean, Mrs Shout?

A wigwam for a goose's bridle, Jemima said, going on filling the milk jug.

But is it true—

Some things are true and some aren't, I said, and children must ask to be told.

But I did just ask.

Run away, Harry, there's a love, I said, and don't be bothering us.

Jemima said nothing, only poured out tea and handed it to me. She was my comfort in those terrible days, though I didn't agree with everything she said. For one thing, she approved of Paddy rushing off the way he did. Whipping was a gentry habit she reckoned, but in this case it was warranted. Billy Stapleton and his mates were up for anything and Mr Wilson had done right even though he picked the wrong lad.

And what does he get for it? she demanded. The master is miserable as a bandicoot, poor gentleman, and why wouldn't he be? Beastly common scrub bringing him to court. What is the world coming to?

All I could think of was Cissie, her haunted eyes and pinched white face. Though in truth, when I wasn't worrying about Cissie I worried for Paddy. He was listless as a funeral horse, not going out to play billiards, mooning about the house and drinking tea by the gallon. And wanting any amount of sympathy so long as no name was put to it. I was run off my feet tending to him.

Cissie went back to school on Monday. She wanted to, she said, opening her mouth for the first time. Are you sure now? I said.

I have to, she said, her eyes like two pebbles. Otherwise everyone will think it's me who is bad.

Such a sorrowful little girl sitting at her dressing table, her knees pressed together.

And I have to get on with my sewing or Myra will win the sewing prize. And that would be so unfair.

Indeed and it would, love, I said.

How I wish that was the end of it. The boy responsible was found and punished. Another two boys it was that got him nabbed. They heard the screams in the scrub and saw him running down North-street, then a farmer driving a dray stopped and spoke to him. All three picked him out next day among the Salvation Army people he was hiding among, singing hymns with them outside a pub in East-street.

Paddy's horse was standing outside the stables when I returned from a heartfelt talk with Jessie Philp. That was the first warning.

I went inside and found him wearing out the Turkey rug.

Trixie's missing, he said, stopping his pacing. That damned dog, where can she have got to? I thought she'd be here. She wasn't on the footpath at midday, that's never happened before.

It was true. From what I heard tell Trixie was a fixture at the door of his office, the whole town was used to seeing her sitting there. Patiently waiting for her master. Paddy had looked everywhere, asked in all the shops, gone down the lanes and backstreets.

I'd better get back to work, he said, grabbing up his hat. I'll go by the pound and if she's not there I'll drop in at the *Bulletin* and put a notice in the paper.

When he came home in the afternoon I knew from his face Trixie wasn't following. That downcast he was at dinner, the little white dog an absence at his feet.

The notice was in the paper next day:

Lost, in East-street, White Terrier SLUT.
Answers to Trixie. Ten shillings reward.
Edward Wilson & Co.

It brought two callers, Paddy told that evening. A couple of the boys from Swamp Push, they strolled in to claim the reward as he was shutting up.

We know where your dog is, Pat Coogan said.

Good, Paddy said. Have you got her with you?

Give us the money first, Pat said, at which Paddy demanded they produce Trixie at once.

Fat chance, the other boy said. Come down to the Racecourse Road tomorrow with the money and you can have her.

A gunshot woke us that night. One for sorrow, I thought, and so it proved. Paddy went down to the Racecourse Road next morning and found Trixie lying outside the butcher's shop with a bullet hole in her head. And a note writ in pencil driven into her back with a nail:

LAY OFF THE SWAMP PUSH.

In the days that followed Paddy was like a mouse trapped in a wheel. The more he tried to get out of his despair the more it came round to him. What happened to Cissie began it, but Trixie's death broke him in the end. Every night he stayed home and no one calling, till one night he went out to the stables and saddled his horse. To solace himself at the Cri I guessed. And must have found himself welcome for he didn't come home for dinner.

Around three in the morning I was startled awake by knocking on the front door. I went out with a shawl over my nightdress—it was that late I was sure the Vaunces would be asleep and my state of undress go unnoticed—and found Jack Royce standing on the verandah.

Paddy was on the footpath, swaying on his horse in the moonlight.

Ah, Jack said, staring at my nightdress. Mrs Wilson, there you are.

I pulled my shawl closer about me.

Just bringing your man home, as you see, he said. There was only a slight slur to his words.

Now, now! Paddy called. Less not beat about the bush. Tell me the cunshtable dropped the shilly sharge, Jack. All forgotten, eh?

We were in a public place, Jack said in a low, resonant voice.

Shure it was only friends. What's a bit of riding between friends?

Furious Riding, Jack said, sending me a meaning look while Paddy half slid, half fell off his horse. He came staggering up the path towards us.

And yourself? I asked, taking in Jack's crooked tie and flushed face.

As to that, he said, the constable let me off. I wasn't so drunk as your lord and master.

Paddy stumbled up the steps and threw his arms round Jack. Come now, what's a li'l Frurous Riding at two in the morning? No one about to harm, waz there now?

If you remember, Jack said, the constable dropped that charge, seeing it was your first offence. But the other still stands.

Goo' man, goo' man. Paddy tried to slap him on the back. Wha' sharge wazzat now? While we're about it.

Jack's eyes were unreadable in the half light. It's in his pocket, he said. All written out, so nothing to be done about it. You'd best show it to him in the morning.

Bob Shout appeared, shuffling up the driveway in his nightshirt, and led Rebel down to the stables.

Alright, Paddy, we'll help you in, Jack said. You'd be too much for your little lady otherwise.

Between us we got Paddy inside, but even so he managed to knock over the umbrella stand. Shh, I said. You'll wake the children.

Ah, he said. Mushen do that. Cishie mush have her beauty shleep. My li'l girl…

Where to next? Jack said, staggering as Paddy lurched against him. We steered a wavering path up the hallway to the bedroom and Jack dropped Paddy, rather roughly I thought, onto the bed.

I pulled up my shawl which had slipped in the struggle, and drew it around me. Thank you, I said. I can manage now.

Jack stood in the circle of lamplight, his hands dangling.

You'll have to see yourself out, I said, stern as any priest. Take the spare lamp on the dressing table and leave it on the hall table.

Yes, ma'am, certainly ma'am. A lingering look, then he lit the spare lamp and went out. I heard his tread in the hallway.

Trembling all over, I began undressing Paddy.

You're a goo' girl, Annie, he said, looking up at me from the bed.

Let's hope the Vaunces didn't see you come home, I said.

Shorry, shorry, he mumbled. Didden know you cared so mush for Misshus Vaunsh.

Mrs Vaunce takes care of her own same as I do, I said, tugging at his boot.

A faint *tok tok*. A horse's hooves starting up.

My horse! Paddy cried, struggling up from the pillows with a wild look in his eye. Mush see to Rebel thish minute.

And would have got up only I stopped him, saying Bob had already taken Rebel to the stables. I hope you won't forget to apologise to him tomorrow, I said, pushing him back on the bed. Which was easy enough to do.

Poor old fella, he said, looking at me owlish.

It was Rebel he meant, not Bob.

You should have thought of that sooner, I said, knowing what was on his mind. He had told me once that horses know when their owners are drunk, they'd be foaming at the mouth with fear, showing the whites of their eyes.

You're right, you're alwaysh right. Blesh you, Annie, you alwaysh had the true word.

I carried his boots over to the wardrobe.

Ah, come here, darling, he said, following me with his eyes.

I'm just putting your shoes away, I said, but my heart gave a little leap. You'd have thought a frog was trying to jump out of my throat.

So it was still there, the old lure. Standing in the lamplight I felt a sudden surge of, what was it? Power, yes, it was power. It felt good, knowing I was lusted after by two men, even though I only wanted one of them.

I brought Paddy a tumbler of water but he fell asleep before he could drink it. A mug from Mugsville thash me, were the last words he spoke before the snoring started.

171

I went over to his coat and took out the piece of paper Jack had told was there. *Drunk and Disorderly* it said, and he was to appear before the magistrate at ten o'clock in the morning.

What a headache you'll have in court tomorrow, I thought. And him snoring to beat the band, a herd of bullocks driven through the house couldn't have roused him.

When he woke up next morning he was glad to know he wasn't charged with Furious Riding. The shame of it, being put in the same class as the Swamp Push. That lot are well known for their shenanigans, the older lads anyway, forever galloping up and down the streets, making a danger of themselves to others. As for the *Drunk and Disorderly* charge, there's no disgrace in that for the men of this town. It's more like a badge of honour.

So before long Paddy was trotting down the hill on Rebel, a man about town again if no longer with a dog about town.

But the queer thing about it, after all those fears and sorrows tumbling on our heads like rocks till we were reeling, good came out of bad in the end, much like the honey Samson found in the dead lion's belly. It was after that terrible time when the world lost its tune and became a sad racket to Paddy's ears that he turned to me. Seemed to need me. And even when he was charging about again in his rushing way he was never so haughty as before. So we became friends again, you might say, and as for bed, that became sweet territory also.

There were mornings after that in the kitchen, before the house was stirring, when my blood seemed to sing, and I'd catch myself thinking, *How snug you are, Annie.* Don't get too smug, I'd tell myself, and fill the kettle like a woman in a dream.

If I went outside to fetch sugar from the storeroom and felt the morning air soft as baby's breath on my arms, often as not I'd find myself humming the latest ditty. It was the old case of give me today and I'll sell you tomorrow, for I knew my good fortune and gloried in each day, knowing the next could be no better, and might well bring misfortune instead.

And in my ignorance I was right to do so. For troubles did come, but the good days are laid up in memory still. I can take them out any time I like, just to taste their sweetness again.

PART 3

A Fixed Place of Abode

HOW QUICK the girls grew up it seems, though that cannot be. They grew up one day at a time I suppose, and maybe I don't want to remember. It was those days after all, one at a time, that took my girls from me. Took them into a world where mothers cannot follow. For by then they were ashamed of me, or if not *of* me, then for me. They thought I was a drudge, the way I brought in supper for Paddy and his friends on card nights, then hid in the kitchen till it was time to collect the dirty plates. In truth, I hid nowhere, but sat on the wicker chair on the kitchen verandah, enjoying the dark breathing night and thinking my own thoughts.

The girls never said as much but I knew by the way they squirmed when they saw me talking with Mrs Hutton at the grammar school gate, or hurried to get out of the buggy, not to be seen in my company when I took them to the dentist. I didn't talk proper, so who could blame them? Young girls growing up, why would they want their own ma to be a topic of fun among their friends? It cut me just the same.

Cissie disapproved of Sergeant Lynam coming to the house, for he was back in town, living up the road as yardman at Bishop Cani's manse. She said he was a common man and I ought not entertain him.

That was after she came in the kitchen and found us drinking tea. Not a word would she speak to the old fellow, only looked at his boots as if he were some jobber tracking mud in the house.

Please have dinner early tonight, Mother, she said. I'm going out remember?

And tapped out of the kitchen, her nose in the air.

A fine girl your daughter is growing, Sergeant Lynam said in the silence that followed. She has your figure if I may say, Mrs Wilson, though not your manners.

I said he mustn't blame her if she behaved hoity-toity, it was only because she was a lady in her feelings.

A lady is it? he said, rubbing his beard.

But I told him how hard it was for her, not having a mother of her own class, for which I blame myself, for I've never managed to make myself into a lady and it's no use pretending otherwise.

If she knew your worth she'd not speak to you so, Rhyming Lynam said, and gave as his opinion that schooling for girls was against God and nature. Too many books and not enough religion spoiled them, he reckoned.

But if the girls disliked being seen with me, they loved being with their father, Cissie in particular. She couldn't get enough of going with her brother to the races. The fights that went on, the drinking and card-sharpers with their games of Yankee Sweat, she endured it all for the sake of seeing her father's racehorse gallop down the track. The company of black men, she endured that too. For Douglas that used to be Paddy's stockman at Serpentine Water came up to her and Harry in the viewing paddock and made himself known.

My word, he said to Harry, you're big piccaninny now.

How Cissie must have squirmed in her best going-out clothes and himself in castoffs, a clay pipe stuck in his hair. This fella carried you one time, he told Harry, who couldn't remember from being too small.

I was glad to hear jail hadn't destroyed Douglas—there are many native men not so fortunate—and I would catch myself thinking of him as I went about my work. Then one day while preparing dinner I got a great surprise, for wasn't the man himself standing in the kitchen doorway when I turned around. Aborigines never come up to the Range. They know they're not welcome, yet there he was, grinning his bear-hug smile.

Douglas! I said.

Budgery you, he said.

I made him come in and sit down. That was never allowed at Serpentine Water and Jemima wasn't too pleased, judging by the look she threw me. She took herself off with a loud sniff, but I paid her no heed and fetched Douglas a wedge of shepherd's pie and a tumbler of milk.

His eyes lit up. Good tucker, he said. Might be more better stop here.

Yes, stop here awhile, I said, for I had it in mind to sweet-talk Paddy into finding some work for him about the place. Douglas looked a good deal older than last time I saw him, and skinny! Much too skinny for a man his age, that was easy seen under the rags that did for his clothes. And a queer bend to his left wrist, from being broke and not set most likely.

What you been do these days? I asked, for that was how we talked to Aboriginal people back then.

I never been do it wrong thing, Douglas said, pushing out his chest. Look at me now, sing plenty songs at the races. Sing out, *All for Jesus! All for Jesus!* Get plenty sixpence.

You always was a good singer, Douglas.

More better sing, he said. No good cry.

True for you, I said, and true for everyone.

I drink it too much, might be, he said, going shy. Looking at the floor.

Well then, I said, if I give it you money you must promise not spend it on drink.

S'pose I see that bugger drink, Douglas said, I bolt. I run away quick.

I went over to the housekeeping jar and took out the coins in it, wanting to make up for that day in court. That day I gave evidence against an innocent man, innocent by his own law that says you must share. Taking out the money though I knew well enough a drinking man isn't his own master. I was wanting to make myself feel better, I suppose. I gave him the money, little though it was, and said, Stay here and wait, eh? I go talk with Mr Wilson about you.

I was gone awhile owing to everything that had to be said, talking it over with Paddy in the drawing-room. He had finished his second brandy and heard me out, all the while breathing out through his mouth with that faint whistling sound horsemen make. They are used to breathing that way I believe, to please their horses with the rhythm of it and blow the dust from their faces while they're about it.

Really? he said when I told him Douglas was in the kitchen. Have you done now? he said, when I finished. And yawned and stretched himself.

Who'd have thought the old rascal would come calling? I've seen him at the races. Still a dab hand with the horses so there's always someone willing to pay for his services.

I could see he liked the idea of his old riding mate coming up the hill to pay a call.

I'll have a word with him tomorrow. Mind you give him some blankets to take to the stable. He'll need them tonight.

But when I returned to the kitchen Douglas was gone. You eejit, I told myself. And wouldn't he be afraid Paddy would chase him away? Something like that, worse probably. I basted the roast and went back to the drawing-room to tell Paddy about Douglas, but he only grunted behind the pages of his *Practical Horse-keeper*.

I took up my mending and tried not to think about Douglas. Missed chances, wrong turnings, what are they after all? Only the warp that holds fast the weft of our days and gives them the shape God intends. That was what I told myself, and likely would've forgot about Douglas only for what happened next.

A cold wind came scurrying down the chimney and I was getting up to sweep the ashes that flew out of the grate when we heard another noise above the wind's keening. Some kind of barney going on. A good bit of shouting anyway.

A woman's shrill voice rose up, declaring itself among the others. Why, that's Mrs Vaunce, I said.

This I must see, Paddy said, standing up.

It was windy and chill when he opened the door. I followed him out on the front verandah and we peered into the darkness. The gaslights on the Range are spaced far apart and only a horned moon rode the night sky, half hid by scudding clouds, so we could see nothing. But something was afoot. Some sort of bother going on outside Vaunces' house.

Paddy went down the steps and along the path to the gate. Annie, he called. Go in the house will you. Heat the kettle till I get back.

He opened the gate and stepped out into the darkness.

I wasn't having any of that. I was curious as a cat and followed him down the path to lean on the gate. The shape of a horse tethered to the palings of Vaunces' fence was the first thing I saw as the darkness thinned to my eyes. Then the Vaunces themselves, upright on the footpath as a pair of ship bollards. And a constable was it? Yes, a police constable talking to them. And who was that other one with them? A queer thrill went through me when I realised it was Douglas.

I opened the gate and ran along the footpath. Decent folk ... safe in our beds, Mrs Vaunce was saying, and Paddy's deep brogue breaking in, What seems to be the trouble, Vaunce? A babble of voices back at him. The only one not talking was Douglas.

Sneaking in our paddock, Mr Wilson, shrilled Mrs Vaunce. Thieving niggers the lot of them. Have you looked in his pockets, Constable?

Oh yes, and found plenty to be going on with. Three shillings and thruppence no less.

I told you! And he's been here before. Mrs Norris saw him skulking round their house last week. Oh, to think of the danger we were in.

It was myself gave him the money, I said. I was shaking under my shawl and not from the cold.

Coming to decent people's houses and—

I gave him the money.

Paddy turned to peer at me. Well now, he said, that puts a different complexion on the matter.

Is that you, Mrs Wilson? said Mr Vaunce, peering also. No need to be frightened. An unfortunate disturbance but all taken care of now. Constable Lawrie here has been kind enough to—

Did you not hear? I said. *Was he deaf or what?*

Let the gentleman have his say, missus, said the constable.

Yes indeed. Mr Vaunce sounded huffy. A man has a right to say what he pleases on the threshold of his own property.

Look here, old boy, Paddy said, I believe what Mrs Wilson is trying to—

Come now, Wilson, that's all very well, but my wife has received a very great fright. And Mrs Norris likewise. We cannot have ladies afraid for their lives.

Only I'm wondering now, can we be sure this is the same man? As Mrs Norris's one, I mean.

Mr Vaunce let out a short laugh that had no amusement in it. I don't know why you're taking such an interest in the matter, Wilson. You know as well as I do a darky can't be held to have lawful means of support unless he has a master and fixed place of abode. On that ground alone—

Well then, there's little troubling us, Paddy said. This man came up the hill to see me. He used to work for me and I intend employing him again.

That's as may be but he's in my charge now, said the constable.

There was a good deal more spoke and before long it became heated. Nigger-lover was one word bandied about by Mr Vaunce, and Paddy, never one to mince words, told him for two pins he'd knock him down. Meanwhile Douglas and Mrs Vaunce and myself stood by, not saying a word.

Alright, gentlemen, said the constable. We'll leave it there if you don't mind. It's a chilly old night and I've better things to do with my time.

With that he went over to the fence and untied a length of rope from the palings, which was when I saw the other end was fastened round Douglas's wrists. He knotted the rope to his saddle and turned to face Paddy.

I've heard you out, Mr Wilson. You never was bad at going off half-cocked—

Easy now.

But this takes the biscuit if I may say.

The constable mounted his horse and went clip-clopping down the dark road, with Douglas running behind, stumbling in the potholes.

Paddy said he would go to the Magistrate's Court to put in a word for Douglas if they let him. He wasn't a clergyman's son for nothing, and couldn't stand idly by and see a man wronged. I suppose that was so. He always had terrible strong views about right and wrong, but I wonder was regret also troubling him. Was he remembering that time Douglas stood in court, wretched on account of those same notions of his about right and wrong? Not that speaking up for Douglas did any good, for Douglas or for him. Douglas was put in jail for being a vagrant and

Paddy got himself known around town as a Combo. A white man who is too familiar with Aborigines.

Jemima had missed nothing of course. Nothing escaped her sharp eye at the window above the stables. We were in the wash-house when she had her say.

I'd rather it was someone else and not Mr Wilson to be argufying with Mr Vaunce, she said from her place at the tub. And that gentleman dressed up in skirts for the occasion,.

Mr Vaunce was in his dressing gown, I said.

As for that wife of his, she's nothing but an ignorant scold. Anyone with half a brain could see the nigger was only taking a shortcut through the paddock.

But Jemima wasn't happy when she learned Douglas was to sleep below her and Bob in the stables. Is this straight? she said, staring at me. Suds dripping off her hands.

I hope you don't mind, Jemima.

I never thought I'd see the day. Sharing quarters with a nigger! The impudence of him, coming to the house in the first place.

Mr Wilson asked him to, I said, thinking it better to lie.

Is that so? I'll say no more then. Only mark my words, that one will make mischief when our backs are turned.

After Douglas came to live with us she made sure to keep a sharp eye on him. She was up to all his nigger tricks, she said. Douglas always gave her a big flashing smile as he went about his work with the horses, but it did him no good.

Your man has put temptation in the way of yon darky, Jemima warned one day.

Why, what has he done? I asked, and she said nothing as yet but it was only a matter of time.

That's the pity of it, she said. You wouldn't punish a dog for eating a mutton chop would you, if it was yourself left it laying about?

Douglas isn't a dog, I said.

Ah well, it's a temptation for him anyway.

She's going soft on him, I thought. But I was wrong. Ain't nobody learned you whitefella ways? I heard her scolding when she found him cooking up a lizard in the horse-paddock.

Eh, what you shout for? he said, grinning at her. I never been do it wrong thing. You gammon old woman.

I ain't that old, Jemima said, stomping off.

She still had a down on him. I heard her shouting in the backyard one day. Get over here! Let me hear the lies panting in your black throat.

Whatever's the matter? I cried, rushing out from the kitchen, and there was Jemima, arms akimbo among the runner beans, and Douglas grinning at her across the horse-paddock fence.

You'll get a right stropping now, she told him.

What for you always rouse on me? Douglas said. This fella ain't your bloody kid.

I've caught him at last, Mrs Wilson, cried Jemima, red-faced with triumph. Just look at the rogue, bold as brass, dressed up in one of the master's shirts.

Mr Wilson gave it to him, I said. Which was true.

Ah! Give it him, did he? she said with a quick shake of her head. Well, what you astaring at? she said to Douglas. Be off about your work can't you? The master don't pay you to stand idle.

If it hadn't been for Douglas it might have become warfare between them. But he found Jemima comical I believe. Their battles were entertainment to him and he liked coming out victor, as mostly he did. And he had such a beautiful smile it would melt the heart of any woman who was womanly, and Jemima was always that. For all her rough talk she had a good heart.

What has happened to the pumpkin pie? I asked one morning when we were in the pantry.

I give the leftovers to the darky, she said. It'd only of gone bad on the shelf.

Well, I said, it won't go bad in Douglas's belly, that's certain.

I couldn't help smiling at the look she threw me. Cagey and innocent at the same time.

Oh Jemima, I said, trying not to laugh, I do love you so.

She looked at me as if I was a right eejit.

Hail! O Tattersalls

I HAD everything now it seemed. A husband who respected and even loved me, the company of Rhyming Lynam on occasion. Hearing voices in the kitchen one afternoon and thinking to find my old friend, I opened the door and discovered a very different man warming his backside by the stove. The little jockey, Cabbage Smith, with the wart on the end of his nose and a smell about him of damp hay and stale beer. And when I say little, his head reached no higher than mine and I am a little woman myself.

Cabbage! I said.

That's right, he said, pushing out his jaw. I'm Cabbage Smith and I'm here to speak to Mr Wilson on a matter of importance. So it ain't no use hiding him behind your skirts.

Jemima was over by the sink, her work-reddened hands fisted on her hips. I told him the master ain't home, she said, but he won't have it.

No and I won't, said Cabbage, screwing his face in a scowl. I ain't no backslider when it comes to getting me rights. I got an old mother to look after and I must have me rights.

And you're a donkey of importance I suppose, Jemima said. Well you can take your braying elsewhere, you little josser.

Go rinse your mouth in the Fitzroy River, cried Cabbage, giving little jumps like a bantam cock in his agitation. I ain't come here to hear language from an adjectival old tabby like you.

Jemima went red in the face at his words. That's enough of your jaw! she cried. I'll make you go quicker than you came, you pointy-nosed bandicoot.

Quick across the room she darted, took him by the shoulders and marched him through the doorway. And him screeching Murder! all the while.

There! she said, slamming the door and breathing heavy. He'll find he gets the worst of it if he tries any more tricks with me.

Oh dear, I said. We never found out why he wanted to see Mr Wilson.

All I know is his goose is cooked if he comes rampaging here again.

By then her rage was spent, and she began speaking of onions and washing soda and the state of the flour bin. So quick and sudden as a passing squall Jemima's tempers were, over and done with before you knew it. While you still reeled from them.

Paddy got home after dark and a few ales in him when he stepped through the door. I waited till he was sitting down before telling him about Cabbage.

That piece of mischief! he exclaimed. If he thinks he can get around me he's got another think coming. The fellow pulled Headrick's horse, I saw it myself.

I had to listen to a rant about Cabbage. How he was as slippery a customer as you'd find in silks, and should thank his lucky stars the committee had only given him a year. If they'd listened to him the fellow would be out on his ear for life. And so it went on. Men would stop keeping racehorses if such roguery wasn't halted, and so long as he was Chairman no one could say the Arjaycee was more lenient with offenders than Mr Henderson.

For our neighbour up the road who used to be on the Arjaycee committee with Paddy was now Chairman of Tattersalls, a new club set up from Brisbane. And with Paddy made Chairman of the Arjaycee that year you can guess there was a bit of rivalry going on.

I believe Cabbage is worried for his mother, I said. How will he support her if he can't work?

That was another of his lies, apparently. Cabbage's mother lived in Brisbane and had six sons to look after her.

Mr Henderson, the chairman of Tattersalls, him it was whose horse I saw at the front gate when I got home from mass. And found him chuckling with Paddy in the drawing-room.

Lord, that's rich, Paddy was saying. Cabbage'll think twice before writing his hard-luck letters again.

You can bet your sweet life, said Mr Henderson. If he'd paid the fine the committee would never have had occasion to disqualify him.

He's no option now but to leave the district, I suppose.

Ah, Mrs Wilson, said Mr Henderson, noticing me and getting up. I do hope I'm not intruding on your Sabbath.

No need to run away just yet, Paddy said jovially. Come and join us.

He grinned at Mr Henderson who was lifting his coat-tails to sit down again.

I daresay you had a little to do with Tatts' decision, am I right?

You and I have always agreed on discipline, Mr Henderson said. Get rid of the crooked jockeys from both clubs I say, and let the horses run at their natural pace.

Jemima came in with the tea tray and raised an eyebrow at me. To share her surprise at Mr Henderson's visit most likely.

Thank you, Mrs Shout, said Paddy. Will you be Mother, Mrs Wilson?

Oh very smug they looked while I poured out the tea and handed them their cups.

Tell us what you think, Mrs Wilson, said Paddy. Should I take up Henderson's offer and join Tatts' committee?

Seeing my surprise he added, Oh I'll still be chairman of the Arjaycee, that's of course.

They'd feel the want of you if you weren't, said Mr Henderson.

Don't look so worried, Paddy said. It's all above board. Isn't Royce on the two committees, and Headrick and Dawbridge besides?

And they began talking about Paddy's chances of getting a portion of the Reserve in North Rockhampton made over for a racecourse for the Arjaycee—for that was his obsession. What this alderman and that

185

alderman had said about it at the last Council meeting. I'd heard it all before so I made my excuses and left them to it.

I was half pleased and half sorry about Paddy's news, knowing it would be nothing but meetings now, the rare times he wasn't away on other horse business.

Sure enough he became a whirlwind after that, forever rushing out the door with his pudding half eaten on the table till I almost forgot what an Irishman looked like. It was bad as catching eels getting an answer from him as to whether he had time to attend the girls' school concerts, and one morning he slept in till nine.

What the Devil were you thinking of, not waking me? he cried, his hair sticking up every which way. And up he rises and goes rushing off without any breakfast.

All this gallivanting, you'll make yourself ill! I cried, running after him with his hat.

But I don't think he even heard me, he was in such a hurry to be gone.

Look at the rings under your eyes, I said after dinner that night. And him with a face grey as yesterday's porridge while he gathered up his bits of paper to go out again.

Stop your fussing, was all he would say.

But I made sure to speak my mind, and told him he must give up one of his clubs or it would be the death of him.

Don't dictate to me, I'm not a child, he said, stuffing papers in his pocket.

You're morbid from overwork, that's what you are, I said. Always tearing about from one place to another with space for nothing in between. Harry is still waiting for you to look at Lamplighter. He's worried about the swelling on his hock.

Goddammit! he shouted. I'll do it first thing in the morning.

And away with him out the door.

To make matters worse, while all this was going on what does Mr Henderson do but make a hero of himself. The whole town was agog at the news—information made all the more surprising because it was so unexpected. A local wit penned a song about it, set to the tune of *Rule Britannia*. I heard it on the lips of the milkman as he trod up the back steps. *Hail O Tattersalls, Tattersalls rules the nags*, is how the ditty starts. For somehow the man had got hold of a parcel of land to be Tattersalls' new racecourse.

Paddy nearly had a fit when he found out. On the Lion Creek Road the land was, rented to Tattersalls by a business man for the price of a peppercorn. And no surprise in that. The new club were mostly business men themselves and they like to look after their own that way. It was only the old-timers like Dr Callaghan, and Paddy that stuck to the Arjaycee.

Not that I cared two straws for any of their politicking, but I knew what a poke in the eye it must be for my man who had been campaigning for years to get land for the Arjaycee. He ran around even more after that, trying to talk the political men into making over a parcel of acres in North Rockhampton. Nothing I said could make him ease up, till one morning he came over faint as he was getting out of bed and had to lie down.

Bob went for Dr Callaghan and as soon as the Doctor finished his examination he ordered Paddy to take a week's bed rest.

It's only the weather, Paddy said. A cold bath will see me right.

Doctor's orders, old boy. Dr Callaghan took up his Gladstone bag.

Good grief! Paddy said, struggling up from the pillows. I've never spent a day in bed in my life.

Oh come now, Wilson.

Well, except for measles once. A cold bath in the morning has always stood to me and I don't see why—

Because you've run yourself ragged, that's why, Dr Callaghan said. Look at you, man. You're Chair of the Arjaycee, on Tatt's committee, and now I hear you've been put in charge of building their racecourse. And this on top of your own business and CQ Racing Association work.

Someone has to represent the country towns, protested Paddy.

Riding about from one town to another attending meetings, scolded the Doctor. It can't go on. You must pull your horns in and let others take their share of the load.

And out the door with him without waiting for a reply. In the drawing-room he told me to let him know if Paddy gave any trouble taking his medicine.

I will so, I said.

I look to you to keep him in bed, Mrs Wilson. A week's bed-rest will make him like new.

We went down the hallway to the front door, and he said in his gravelly brogue, If only we could get him to give up his work for Tattersalls. As soon as your man's up he'll be like a driven bullock again.

I know it, I said.

We can only hope he takes my advice and cuts back on his committee work.

Such a good kind man, the Doctor, he looked as worried as I was. I was happier now, believing he had done the trick. It only wanted another man to tell Paddy what he wouldn't listen to from me.

And so it proved, though not in the way Dr Callaghan had hoped. A few days later Paddy sent in a letter of resignation right enough, but it wasn't to Tattersalls. It was to his old club, the Arjaycee.

Was he tempted by the racecourse Mr Henderson had got for Tatts? I have often wondered. They do say the Devil comes to an Irishman in the shape of a horse.

All I could know for certain was how offended Dr Callaghan would be. The men in this town have terrible strong loyalties to their racing club, and Dr Callaghan more than most.

Chose Paddy had anyhow, and it wasn't long before his choice came back to bite him. I was awake the night a constable escorted him home. Maybe the boobook owls that play havoc with small creatures in the fig-tree woke me, or else the uneasy feeling in my bones.

Cut me dead the man did, Paddy said next morning. In the billiard room at the Cri. Walked straight past my outstretched hand with every man jack looking on.

Dr Callaghan shouldn't have done so, I said.

I gave him the tumbler of buttermilk I had brought and quit the room, to stop myself speaking words better not uttered. May the Doctor be stuffed in the One O'clock Gun and sent to glory, I thought. He had no business treating my man so.

But Paddy talked himself out of his glooms, bouncing back in the space of a few days. And if he was still cast down by the Doctor's snub you wouldn't know it. A beard is a great advantage to men that way, it makes a sort of hedge for them to hide behind. Not that Paddy had time to dwell on past hurts. He was kept very busy with his own work and Tattersalls' work, and his trips out west for the CQ Racing Association.

Where have you hidden my ties? he shouted the day he was to catch the train to Emerald.

Here you are, I said, making haste to bring him one.

Oh, fiddle! I can't get it to knot! he said, flinging down the necktie. I don't have time for this falderalling. The printers want me to check Tatts' new letterhead and I have to meet the carpenters to talk about the grandstand.

Hold still a minute while I fix your tie, I said. Can't you leave Tattersalls' work alone until your own business is sorted?

Of course I can't! he cried. I'm Trustee aren't I? If the course isn't ready by June we won't have any races, and I'm not going to let that happen. We'll be up and running, and get a good crowd too. The brick-makers and tanners on the Lion Creek Road should swell the numbers coming through the gate.

He checked his tie in the mirror. As for the house and grounds the course is carved from, they're an envy to see. *Lionleigh* is as fine an estate as any in Ireland. I wouldn't mind living there myself, slap-bang next to a racecourse.

He caught my eye in the mirror and grinned. And maybe one day I will.

Tattersalls' new racecourse on Lion Creek Road was all he could think of. Every day something new to be seen to—where to put the totalisator so it didn't block the punters' view, the ladies' luncheon room to be painted—he was happy as a pig in muck. Hell for leather he went at it till everything was ready for Tattersalls' winter races.

The girls were all aflutter in their new dresses when they climbed in the buggy, for their father had told them to buy whatever they needed and charge it to his account.

I own I was surprised. Dresses are the beginning and end of a young girl's life but how should their father know it? Then I remembered the Immigration Depot at Townsville and the dresses he bought for Ellen and me. A man's man, he was always that, yet every now and then he gave thought to the female sex and their vanities. His sisters, I guessed, that was the why of it. He had two of them, both older than him, and himself an only boy in their company in his growing years. They must have seemed a class of gorgeous to him, like my brother Billy was to me.

Won't you go with the girls? Paddy asked the night previous, but I told him there was a deal of work wanting in the garden and it was better so. In truth I had no wish to spoil Cissie and Ada's enjoyment by being seen in their company. Or feel myself crushed by their shame of me neither.

Had I fretted too much over the girls I might be under the sod by now, but each time they scolded me for coming out of the kitchen with my apron on, or looked the other way if they saw me in town, there was always the thought of Harry. He never changed, never noticed the way I talked broad most likely, or not enough to change his idea of me. At eighteen he was taller than his da, and working in town in a big brick building, reckoning up figures for an insurance company. Away out the house he would go each morning, riding down the hill beside Paddy, and most afternoons you'd find them in the paddock, training up one of the horses.

Mad for the horses he was, same as his father, and probably saw the world through a haze of horse dust, his own mother included.

It was Harry who told me Cabbage Smith was back in town. And no sooner back than causing trouble. To begin with he got himself disqualified by Tattersalls and made a great fuss, putting it about he was treated unfair till in the end a deal of bad blood was got up against Tatts. For Cabbage went among the ordinary folk, the wood-carters and hide-tanners and brick-makers, stirring up feeling against the gentlemen on the committees.

And when the newspapers took it up and began saying Paddy was too hard on Cabbage—for by then he was Chairman of Tatts—it became a rare day when he came home without some story to tell of being jeered at or jostled in the street by any passing butcher boy.

One morning he went to work early and surprised a man trying to set fire to the back of his office. He never told me about it, but I read it in the *Rockhampton Bulletin* and went cold all over. The man ran away before Paddy could catch him, but the outrage only made him more stubborn.

We can't haul down the flag, he said. It's beyond joking the way Cabbage and his sort make a scandal of racing.

Jemima had darker thoughts and told me in the kitchen that Cabbage would end up gallows-meat. I thought she painted him worse than he deserved, owing to the time he riled her in the kitchen. Isn't that a mite fanciful? I said. A little fellow the likes of him?

I was smiling as I went out the door.

Horse Politics

I WAS smiling, I remember, when I came in the bedroom one Sunday, on account of St Joseph's Cathedral was finished at last, and ready for business. Such an important occasion and cause for celebration I had put off wearing my bombazine and chose the black silk instead. Paddy was still among the bedclothes when I came rustling in. Fatigued out and out the man was from all his running around, but it was never in him to stop still. I went over to the mirror and saw him following me with his eyes.

You'll do, he said, yawning.

I looked at him in the mirror while I pinned on my hat. I wish you'd get a tonic from Dr Callaghan.

I'll not have that man in the house, he said, or should I say snapped it out, so I left off speaking. I was living with him long enough to know when to change the subject.

I'll light a candle for you then, I said, and he gave me a pasted-on grin to show what he thought of such superstitious nonsense.

Bob took me down the hill and as soon as I went inside the cathedral I made sure to light a candle and say a prayer to St Jude on Paddy's behalf—for isn't he the patron saint of hopeless cases? Then the hymns began and such a wonderful swelling up our voices made in the height and space of the great building I would have been carried away, only for the woman next to me. She sang like a crow and I wanted to put a sod in her mouth.

But the priests that came from Brisbane to help with the mass looked so grand in their robes and Cardinal Moran said the Latin that solemn and beautiful you knew he must be speaking holy words.

When I came outside into the sunshine Mrs Lynch was looking out for me. The mother of Christy Lynch, though I had no cause to fear him then. No reason not to have a gab with his ma

Mrs Wilson, Mrs Wilson, she called, for there was a very great crowd and she had to squeeze through to have a yarn with me. She had her youngest with her and the poor child looked fazed from being among so many people.

Hello, Lizzie, I said, but she just gawked at me.

Did you ever see such an altar? Mrs Lynch said. That little one I mean, in the side chapel. All green marble it is, brought out from Ireland. I never seen the like before. Did you ever yourself, dear?

I did not, I said and gave as my opinion it was very pretty.

Isn't it? Different altogether. Do you know what I think, Mrs Wilson? It's a pity they didn't make the big one the same while they were at it. Oh leave off will you, she said, giving her little girl a push. Get your paws off of me new dress before you spoil it entirely. Don't it beat Banagher? she said. Them Proddies won't know where to put their faces now, such a wee place they have for themselves down the road. It's nothing to ours.

All the while she was looking about, not to miss anyone and know what they were wearing. And to think, she said, they had Cardinal Moran all the way up from Sydney. Quite the big shebang.

Here! Don't you know Our Lady blushes when she sees such a thing? she called to Lizzie, who had gone over to stand against a hitching-post and stroke a horse's muzzle.

What, Ma? Lizzie said, gawking at her, and I couldn't blame the child. I had no idea myself.

Did you ever see the like, Mrs Wilson? Shaming me before everyone.

What, Ma? wailed Lizzie.

I'll give you what, miss. You have your ankles crossed, that's the what of it. It's all them fast Australian girls she's copying, Mrs Lynch said, apologetic.

And how are you keeping, dear? she said next. Still on top I hope, after that business in town.

What business was that, Mrs Lynch?

Why, your man. Ah well, wouldn't he keep it from you I suppose. He could of been killed only for the good Lord taking care of him.

Dear to God! I said.

Oh yes, near killed entirely. Did you know nothing then?

I did not, Mrs Lynch. But what was it?

I'll tell you, she said. A horse and dray it was. They went on a rampage and didn't they smash against Mr Wilson's office in their madness? Only for your man stepping quick inside the door he'd of been in the way of it.

Never! I said. My knees were shaking.

It's what I tell you. Big George the firewood man, he seen it. He was coming behind in his cart and seen the whole thing.

But the poor driver?

Jumped off without never a scratch. Right as rain, Big George said. Whistling even, while he fetched back his horse.

She took another squiz at me. Oh dear, I wouldn't like to be the one to tell you, only how was I to know you hadn't heard? But no bones broken so all's well that ends well, isn't that right, dear?

And she began talking about the new idea of giving votes to women. Tell me now, she said, what would you think of that, women voting? I said I hadn't thought about it, liar that I was, and stood like a stunned ox while she gabbed on, about why would anyone want to vote for a lot of old windbags in waistcoats.

As soon as she paused for breath I made my farewells. Her words were going in one ear and out the other till I felt like nothing so much as a cracked cup that can't hold water. I'm a foolish woman maybe, but I couldn't get the picture out of my mind of a great cart-horse and dray bearing down on Paddy. And wondering if Cabbage Smith had a hand in it. If he was a friend of the whistling milkman.

I feared Paddy's haughty manner would provoke Cabbage to further outrage, but beyond what Mrs Lynch chose to tell me and

194

what I could learn from the newspapers there was no way of knowing his affairs. Ladies might have been living in harems in the Nineties for all they could know of the outside world. A servant-woman though, she could go where she liked without fear or favour, and keep her ears open while about it.

If I may say, Jemima said one morning, your man is down in the mouth lately.

She was sitting on the sugar bin, for we were in the storeroom in the back garden. We liked to chat among the scents of that place, the tea and molasses and raisins. Crickets thrumming in the grass, sunlight slanting through the doorway to pour dusty gold among the grain bins, it was an agreeable place to have a yarn and not be overheard.

The tick plague left us with a deal of money worries, I reminded Jemima.

Wouldn't you know it? The prices butchers are charging these days for any old bit of stewing steak. But what I was saying, about the master—

He won't see Dr Callaghan, I said, but I wish he'd get a tonic from the hospital.

Never that! Jemima exclaimed. Begging your pardon, Mrs Wilson, but the day you go through them doors that's the end of you. What it is, it's them racing folk he's pally with.

Oh that's all sorted, I said but she cut me short.

I think you oughta know, she said. Your man takes his life in his hands when he goes among roughs the likes of Cabbage Smith. As for them racing gents, they're nothing but a lot of silly children. Mr Henderson took the Chair off the master just to have it himself.

No, Jemima, I said. I must put you right there. Mr Wilson resigned. He missed some meetings through having to go to Duaringa and Baralaba for the Racing Association, and felt obliged to write a letter stepping down from being Chairman.

Not to put a tooth in it, Jemima said, he was pushed. Dr Royce and Mr Headrick have given up their membership over it, they're that indignant.

Paddy hadn't said a word of any of this to me, but experience told me to trust Jemima. I liked Jack Royce better now, after hearing her words. Then glory to goodness, doesn't the man put himself out further for Paddy, riding up the hill with a bottle of claret to talk him out of his glooms.

When I came in the drawing-room with the sandwich tray they were playing some game. Jack had hold of Paddy's walking stick and was swiping at a ball of crumpled paper.

Hole in one! he shouted, knocking the ball into the wastepaper basket. Paddy was laughing when he turned and saw me. Golf, he explained.

Jack stood with his legs apart, swinging the walking stick. Could you do as well, Mrs Wilson? he said, laughing.

I put the tray on the table. Likely I can, I said, but you will never know.

Don't be annoyed, dear lady. We're celebrating. Your man has agreed to rejoin the fold.

I looked at them, not understanding, until Paddy explained that Jack had brought a letter from the Arjaycee committee.

It seems the committee wants me back.

Every curmudgeonly one of them, Jack added, and they roared laughing.

I was very glad to hear it, and thanked Jack in my heart as I left the room. Likely Paddy would make up his differences with Dr Callaghan now. Any rate, next thing you know he was back in the Arjaycee and no longer on Tattersalls' committee. Yet I never could have guessed there would soon be another reason to like Jack, for it was himself who came up with a plan for Cissie.

She had left school and become a teacher, but was that peaky of late, ever since the education people took her away from the Central Girls School and sent her to teach at Central Boys.

I can't abide it, Mother, she said. All those horrid boys who never bath. She was quite beside herself.

I knew it was another lad she was thinking of, the one in the Hospital Scrub. It was him she saw when she looked at the rows of sweaty schoolboys in front of her, I was sure of it. She became a shadow of herself, not chattering anymore, keeping to her room like the other time, till I was worried out of my mind. One morning she couldn't bring herself to go to school and said she would never go again. That was music to my ears but not to Paddy's. If she gave up teaching, he said, she wouldn't find another situation. There was next to no work in town for men right now, and never had been for ladies, except teaching.

I fretted then, knowing Cissie would have no money to buy pretty dresses to go about in, like Ada—for by now Ada was working as a pupil-teacher—and she couldn't look to her father to supply the want. He hadn't the money either, thanks to the tick plague laying waste to horses and cattle.

It was then Jack came up with his idea.

The other gentlemen had gone home, the playing cards were put away, but Jack stayed on and was in his usual spot propping up the mantelpiece when I came in.

Nothing for it, old boy, he was saying. Cissie must come to *Richmond House*. She can keep my accounts and show in the patients.

Paddy agreed at once. A respectable situation in a doctor's surgery, and his best friend to keep an eye on her, why would he refuse? I listened to him thank Jack while I stacked the plates in the sideboard.

So all settled then, Jack said. I suppose you're happy with that, Mrs Wilson?

I am, thank you, I said. Bless you for your kind heart.

Jack chuckled. I see you keep your wife in better order than I do mine, Paddy. A woman with a soft tongue is something of a rarity these days. I rather envy you your home life, if you want to know.

I suppose you do, Paddy said thoughtfully.

Cissie was delighted when her father told her. Oh yes, she said. Oh thank you, Father.

It's Dr Royce you must thank, he said, though later he told me Jack was a lucky man to have such an excellent bookkeeper as his little girl. She was hardly a week in her new job before Paddy told her at dinner he had heard she was making herself useful at *Richmond House*.

Dr Royce is very pleased with you, pet.

Cissie blushed. He's such a nice man, Father. He lets me go out at lunchtime to look in the shops.

And Mrs Royce, is she nice too? I asked. I was curious to know more about Ephie after hearing Mrs Lynch's story about her blackened eyes.

I don't know, Mother. She never comes in the surgery. But she paints pictures of flowers, I know that. Dr Royce has named his new racehorse after one of them.

That's right, Paddy said from the head of the table. Sunflower, not a bad little filly. We should see some good running once she's trained.

He has a man to do that, Father, and live in the stables to look after her. A trainer called Smith.

Paddy frowned. Is Jack still employing Cabbage? Well, I suppose he knows what he's doing.

But perhaps he didn't, for it wasn't long before Cissie told us the little man was gone, sent away from the stables. Dr Royce was angry with him, she said, though she had no idea why, except a man was found in the stables with him. But what could be wrong with that? I thought Cabbage might be angry in the bargain. He wasn't one to take setbacks, and losing a situation with regular wages would be a blow to any man. Jemima gave her usual warnings, saying Jack Royce would rue the day he sent the little jockey-man packing, but for once she was wrong. It was others rued the day.

Walking About With Guns

IT ALL started the day Mr Henderson got set upon and beaten up in East-strect. Not by Cabbage, he was too small for the job. Another man did it on his behalf. For feeling ran high against Tattersalls on account of they had disqualified Cabbage yet again, and being the new chairman Mr Henderson got the brunt of it. I was glad now that he'd taken the Chair off Paddy. He had saved my man the beating he would have received. But I worried Paddy might get attacked anyway. It would be easy for people to become confused and think he was still in Tatts, and besides, he was well known as a fierce man for sending jockeys out.

I took my tea out to join him on the verandah one evening. He was in great good humour that day, having won the Corinthian at a country race meet. And not by a nose either, he was saying when a shot rang out.

The frogs in the lagoons ceased their croaking. Every breathing creature held itself still.

That was a mite too close for comfort, Paddy said, and stood up, saying he would take a look.

By the time he had lifted his Winchester from its place above the mantelpiece, Bob was up from the stables, and they went outside to satisfy their curiosity. Gunshots are a great frighter of nerves when you first hear them but they're common enough in this town, and after my heart stopped skittering I wasn't worried. Ada and Cissie were staying at Emu Park with the Huttons, and Harry had gone down to join them for the weekend, so I had no fear as to their whereabouts. I was closing the curtains in the drawing-room when Paddy got back.

He came through the door in a rush. It's Henderson! he cried, staring at me. He's been shot!

I could only stare back. Such a thing wasn't possible, not on the Athelstane Range.

In the stomach! God, what a mess! Callaghan's been sent for, and the police, but they'll have their work cut out finding the bastard.

The hairs stood up on the back of my neck. But who—

Cabbage! Who else? He came up the hill in a horse-cab and told the driver to wait. The driver heard a shot, saw Cabbage run across the road into the Hospital Scrub. Now look, you must lock the doors—No, wait! Bob's bringing Jemima up from the stables. You must both stay tight and don't answer the door to anyone.

But you're not going out again?

Of course I am. We have to find him before he kills someone else.

But surely ... you're not saying ... you don't mean ... is Mr Henderson dead?

Not yet but he soon will be by the look of him.

Oh please don't go. Ah no, Paddy, please, stay here will you, for the love of God.

Stop agitating, he said. Uh, here's Bob with Jemima! Douglas is coming with us. Now remember, fasten all the windows, not just the doors.

Before I could say another word he and Bob were tramping down the hallway with their guns, stern in the face as any judge under a black cap.

Jemima and I flew to the doors and windows to lock them, and when we were satisfied the house was shut fast we returned to the drawing-room.

What did I tell you? Jemima said, breathing through her nose a bit raspy. Didn't I say that one would make gallows-meat?

I could see she was as shook up as myself. You did, Jemima, I said. But sit down now, sit in this chair.

Did you ever hear the like? Giving out he'll shoot every man on the committee.

Which committee? I said, scarce able to get the words past the lump in my throat.

Oh not your man's, don't worry. It's Tatts, Bob reckons, but madness whichever it is.

We both fell silent, thinking about what was afoot, out there beyond the curtained windows, in the plentiful dark of the paddocks and Hospital Scrub. A murdering villain let loose among the gum trees. I was in a fever of fear for Paddy, and Jemima no better over Bob. It was easy seen she loved him, despite she gave him the sharp end of her tongue when it suited her, for that night she was no better than me in her agitation. We couldn't stop picturing our men in the darkness, and frightening ourselves by our imaginings.

Hours we sat in the drawing-room, murmuring while we knitted. It seemed like eternity, but the clock of the heart never takes its time from ones made of brass.

Jemima pushed off thought with the sound of her own voice, but even so I was precious glad of her company in those dragging hours. The little shifts and easings of the night, a bough scraping against the guttering, a waterhen crying its alarm on the flats, a possum growling in the fig-tree—every familiar sound made us start up and stare at one another, as if the answer to our question lay in the other's eyes.

We were just settling from hearing some noise when Jemima said she'd often wondered why people called my man the Irish Earl.

I used to wonder that too, I said, and told her the story I'd heard from Paddy, about his grandparents Thomas and Eliza Cuffe who had owned a country pub in Ireland.

I held Jemima's gaze in the easy way of yarners.

There was this Englishman you see, called Lord Townshend. A terrible drinker and turnip-eater in his day, and by coincidence the most important man in Ireland. The Lord Lieutenant no less. What happened was this, Jemima. His lordship was travelling one night with a party of friends when the axle on his carriage broke. It was a freezing winter's night, did I mention that?

You did not, Jemima said.

201

Bitterly cold, I confirmed. So Lord Townshend and his party were obliged to put up in Cuffes' humble pub which they would otherwise have scorned to enter. Mr Wilson's grandfather was a genial man and he made his guests comfortable, showed them into a private sitting-room with a fire crackling in the hearth, and set about organising the repair of his lordship's axle. Meanwhile his wife Eliza served the gentlemen roast venison and steamed river fish with lashings of buttery mashed turnips, and was kept very busy tallying up the drinks. By midnight Lord Townshend was so cheerful from the amount of venison and fine Kilbeggan whiskey he was putting away, he became infatuated with the idea of knighting his host.

Is this true? demanded Jemima.

You can read about it in *Freeman's Journal* if you doubt me, I said. So as I was saying, Thomas was summoned from the kitchen. He presented himself in the sitting-room, no doubt still buttoning his waistcoat, and was informed of the honour about to be bestowed on him. It's not known if Thomas thought it was a joke, but what's certain is the ceremony took place. Witnesses attest to that.

Jemima burst out laughing. I bet the old pisspot changed his mind next morning.

He did. He tried to take back the title as you'd expect. The turnip-lover was sober by then and suffering from an almighty hangover. He sent for Thomas and told him to forget the incident entirely and on no account mention it to anyone. Thomas was agreeable, but not Eliza. She had spent half the night running her legs off tending to Lord Townshend's party and she wasn't averse to the idea of being addressed as Lady Cuffe.

Mr Wilson's grandmother was right acourse, said Jemima, wiping her eyes. She had laughed very hearty.

She was, I agreed.

Jemima stretched herself. Isn't it a pity we can't heat the kettle? she said. I'd give my right arm for a cup of tea. What d'you think, Mrs Wilson, will I go in the kitchen?

Indeed and you won't, I said. I'll not have you risking yourself on the verandah.

Around midnight we went down the hall and fetched blankets from the linen press to cover ourselves, and sat on into the night, wrapped to our chins. I remember I was thinking what a terrible snorer Jemima was when I must have fallen into a doze. For next thing you know the sky outside the window was like a kitchen fire and birds giving out their morning song.

He hasn't come home! was all my thought.

I got up quick and unlocked the verandah door, and soon as I opened it there he was, fast asleep in his squatters chair. The Winchester lying across his knees.

Mr Henderson didn't die, thank the Lord, but he was a long time healing. They couldn't get the bullet out of him that was the trouble. It was himself came out of Tattersalls' committee meeting to tell Cabbage he was disqualified, so 'twas himself received the bullet. And meantime the police scouring the Hospital Scrub every night, and Paddy and Bob and Douglas patrolling the paddocks. And others besides, Mr Vaunce, Mr Dawbridge, Mr Headrick, Mr Pennycuick: all our neighbour-men were out there in the dark, walking about with guns. Jack Royce, he rode up the hill each night to join the men on their patrol.

What are you doing here? I hissed when I opened the door to him the first night. I was trembling with the surprise of finding him there when it wasn't a card night.

He tossed his hat onto the hallstand and sauntered towards me, smelling of alcohol.

I'm here to help my mate.

I'd rather you didn't come to the house so often, I said.

Jack's eyes glinted in the gaslight.

I'm buttered and sugared if I listen to your strictures. Why should I? I get no joy from you.

His hand on my arm. Don't touch me, I said sharply, stepping away, and we looked at each other like two people who have betrayed one another. Paddy's in his office, I said, and stood back to let him walk ahead.

But for all the searching and patrolling Jack and the other men did, Cabbage might have crawled under a rock. They found him at last in Urandangie, way down on the South Australian border. Months it took to bring him back, on a Cobb & Co coach to Winton, then a train to Townsville and from there by steamship to Rockhampton.

In the fearful days after the shooting we weren't to know any of that. All we knew was he'd bought fifty cartridges and a revolver at the gunsmiths, and told a lot of people he would shoot every man jack on the committee. Or it was two revolvers he bought, I should say, for Jack Royce took the first one off him. And told the story often enough, after Cabbage was safely behind bars.

Here's the way of it, he'd be saying from his place by the mantelpiece when I came in to set the supper dishes on the sideboard.

Here's how it was if I tell a lie and damn me if I don't. Dawbridge and yours truly were strolling down Denham-street don't you know, about five o'clock it must've been, when who should come up to us just as we were about to turn into the Rose and Crown but the little toe-ragger himself. Fairly hopping with rage and says to Dawbridge, Are you going to remove my disqualification or not? Well, Dawbridge wouldn't answer of course—you know how he gets—so Cabbage follows us into the bar. Have you seen Henderson? he says, and that's when I noticed something odd about him. The way he was holding his right arm under his coat, d'you see? What's wrong with your arm? I say, and doesn't he take it out and show us the revolver. One of the new pin-firing jobs no less. What are you planning on doing with that, my man? I say, and he says, Shoot Henderson and the rest of the flaming committee if you want to know. Look here, I say very cool, why don't you hand it over, there's a good chap.

And what was Dawbridge doing in all this? Paddy would likely say, to egg Jack on.

Oh Dawbridge, he was green about the gills and why wouldn't he be? He's on Tatts' committee. Anyway next thing you know Cabbage starts throwing a fit, jumping up and down, shouting, I don't want to shoot you but I will if you try and take it from me. So up I step and simply take the revolver from his hand.

That's not what the papers reckon, another gentleman would say. They reckon Dawbridge put his finger in the trigger.

Well he may have done I suppose, I don't remember. Anyhow, as I was saying, I took the revolver off Cabbage and went over to the bar and gave it to old Birchy there for safe-keeping. And didn't the little freak turn the air blue? He was ropeable of course.

The gentlemen laughing and settling to their sandwiches while they talked about Mr Dawbridge, and whatever had possessed him to act so cool. And who would have thought he had it in him?

A Beautiful Corpse

ICOULDN'T take in at first what Mrs Lynch told me after mass. Am I not telling you? she said. Sergeant Lynam is dead entirely, took away by the pneumonia.

Old proverbs and lines from hymns began running through my head—*We sport with our years likes toys*—bits and pieces like that, jumbled together.

Them big-chested men is always the worst for the cough, Mrs Lynch said, and told me the wake would be at the Bishop's dwelling-place. Up on nob's hill where you live, Mrs Wilson.

In the manse? I said, the words coming out as if spoke by someone else.

Sure and it will not, 'twill be in Sergeant Lynam's dwelling-place out the back.

She told me the time, two o'clock, and asked was I bringing scones or what. Yes, scones and ham, I said, and made some excuse to get away to the buggy. I felt that queer in myself, as if nothing was real.

Next day, walking down the carriageway past the Bishop's grand manse, it became real enough. A black crepe bow was the first thing I saw in the backyard, tied to the door knob of a small cottage. Rhyming

Lynam's house, I realised, and tears ran down my cheeks. They were real too, and somehow their warmth made me feel a bit better.

Mrs Lynch came up to me as soon as I stepped through the doorway and led me over to the iron cot where he was laid out.

Don't he make a beautiful corpse? she said, but I didn't think so.

How cold and grey his dear face looked, stern and reproachful as it never was in life. I made myself keep looking but he was gone alright. Fled away to a better place with only the husk of him left behind.

Come away, dear, Mrs Lynch said. You've turned a queer colour yourself.

She led me away and I was glad to go. She stayed to help unload my basket at the table. I believe that's Miss Purdy over there, I said.

It is, yes. If you'd come to me, dear, she said, busy unwrapping the ham, I could of sold you a smaller leg.

I know it, Mrs Lynch, but the Lion Creek Road is out of Bob's way when he's doing the messages.

I looked over at Witchety Peg where she was standing against the wall with some others. She did look like my mother in a raffish way. I knew I must go over.

I wonder where Sergeant Lynam met her? I said.

There's not many come out on ships didn't know Sergeant Lynam, Mrs Lynch said, and leaned across the table to whisper, Besides, wasn't he the one that built her humpy?

So *he* was the one she was going to marry! My head was whirling as we took ourselves over to a form to listen to the music.

The fiddles and tin whistles made a grand lament, and the slow air that followed brought moisture to many an eye. Who are they? I thought, looking round the room. All these people, hunched or upright, dressed up smart with gold watchchains draped across their waistcoats, or down-at-heel in flannel shirts and patched breeches, sharing memories in the spaces between the music. Immigrants mostly, if Mrs Lynch was to be believed, come to remember the man that took them to safety along the wharf.

Keep together, girls! Quick march now. We'll have you out of here in no time.

In my head I heard Rhyming Lynam's rumbly voice speaking the same words the wardsman in Townsville had used while swinging his heavy stick. All these people crowded in the room, they were come to farewell their old wardsman. As for Witchety Peg over there with her skirt dragging down at the back, he would have been kind to her when she was a lonely girl sent out from England for being an orphan.

She wasn't young anymore but lively still, her little head with its cap of black hair nodding along to the tune. Her sharp eyes fixed on the singer. When the song ended I went over to her. You again, she said.

It was Sergeant Lynam built your humpy for you, I said.

She narrowed her eyes. What of it?

Only, I mean, he was a good friend to me too. A good man.

Not a bad man as men go.

Yet you wouldn't marry him?

Why should I? she snapped back. It would only of been, Do this, do that, this's no good for you, that's no good for you. I couldn't stand it the length of a day. Anyway, he weren't fond of my goats.

He never liked goats, I agreed. They got in his vegetable patch.

We would of been at each other's throats in no time. I ain't such a fool as that.

True for you, I thought. She was no fool, but I don't suppose old maids can afford to be.

I ain't like you, she said, fixing me with her bright-dark eyes. You got the married-all-over look you have, and won't never be a widow-woman neither.

Pray to God I won't.

Your man is the one will do the burying, she said. There's not much I don't know about you. Your games now, carrying on behind your man's back.

What are you saying? I exclaimed.

At the Botanical Gardens, she said, cackling. I wouldn't like to tell the end that's in store for you.

Ah now, I said, suddenly afraid, though I was careful not to show it. It's none of your business what I do, but for your information I was taking a constitutional. Not carrying on, as you claim. As for the end that's in store for me there is no saying what anyone's end will be. Only God can know and decide.

The old woman tapped her temple. Three times she tapped it.

Didn't nobody tell you I have the Knowledge?

I got goosebumps then. We have Traveller women like her in Ireland. I couldn't think what to say, what answer to give, and was glad to hear the fiddles starting up, so I could to back and sit with Mrs Lynch.

Jack's Downfall

WITCHETY PEG died the same week the colonies became the Commonwealth of Australia. Perverse to the end, she departed this world at a time of grand celebrations, none of which were for her. They buried her in the graveyard down on Dawson-road, in the Protestant section she must have been, still apart from Rhyming Lynam that once she had thoughts of marrying. He was in the Catholic section, his sturdy set of bones awash in the loam there, dreaming of his potato crops it may be. She would have liked that, being on her own, not stuck alongside him as an afterthought, her name carved under his. She never was one to be obliged to any man, for his name or a space in his grave.

I went to visit her grave, walking between the headstones decked out with plaster wreaths, and couldn't find where they put her. An unmarked grave, that would be it. An immigrant like myself, laid to rest far from home under the great sky of Australia, as I must be one day.

I am twenty-five years landed in this country, I thought, and how I long to see Ireland again. Then another thought followed:

I will never go back.

White cockatoos screeched overhead, making for their roosting place in the hoop pines that border the eastern end of the cemetery.

Goodbye Witchety Peg, I said in my heart. You're in good company here where the birds take their rest, for you was always a little birdy creature yourself.

As for her goats, I hoped someone was looking after them now she was no longer able, for precious little feed grew in the paddocks. The wispy grasses between the graves were yellow and shrivelled, and made me think how different this country is from Ireland. At home the moisture gets in your thoughts till you grow sodden with it, till you long for a sunny day just to dry out your rain-steeped brain. But Australia is immoderate in its own way, driving its inhabitants to the outermost weathers of the sun, leathering skin and brain till they grow tough as old boots. Like Witchety Peg learned to be, for she was obstinate as any native-born, never crying and falling about, only cadging potatoes to feed her goats while she waited for better times.

Better times were become a matter for prayer by 1901. The worst drought anyone could remember, the country on its knees and business gone to rack. Oh how we yearned for rain, the whole town was united in longing for it. Such a dearth of rain clouds, even the old-timers reckoned they'd never seen the like. And another two years to come, though we didn't know it.

Tattersalls was only a memory, closed down because the drought had given it such a degree of debt. But the Arjaycee struggled on, and there are many in town would say it was thanks to my man, as I believe. He was made Chairman again and nothing could stop him dreaming up schemes, whatever was needed to keep horse-racing going. In gratitude the club made him a life member, and Dr Callaghan the same, the first men in club history ever to have that honour. They were that pleased you'd have thought they had discovered gold.

And Jack Royce near as glad. He rode up the hill with bottles of champagne in his saddlebags to mark the occasion, and a rare time they had of it, roaring out songs and breaking a few glasses.

Not Dr Callaghan of course, being a teetotaller, and around ten o'clock they went back to their horse-and-stirrup talk and were still at it when I came in to clear the dishes.

How's this for an idea? Jack was saying. I'm going down to Sydney for the Commonwealth illuminations, so why don't I have a word with some of the racing men?

Dr Callaghan said it was a capital idea and Paddy gave Jack the names of some men he might try. Make sure you see John Browne at Randwick, he said. Tell him if he brings up some gallopers we'll throw a levee for him at the Cri. He was scribbling names on a piece of paper as I went out the door.

Now I don't know if Jack succeeded in getting horses up or not—I no longer had any interest in his doings—but I do know he received a nasty surprise in Sydney, when he discovered Ephie in intimate relations with Mr Timms.

Jemima hinted, and Mrs Lynch knew 'for a fact', the news spread like bushfire. The whole town was gabbing about it before ever the newspapers condescended to print a word, and no wonder. William Despardieu Royce, the well known doctor and racehorse owner, had brought a divorce claim against his wife, Euphemia Jane Royce. The first divorce case in Rockhampton, such a topic for scandal that when the lawyers foregathered in court to fight it out the newspapers printed every sordid word.

I was all agog at the news, and why wouldn't I want to learn more about the man I had once desired? Jessie Philp knew Ephie from their ladies' painting group so she was agog too. The courthouse was packed out every day with inquisitive townsfolk, but Jessie and I had only to open the newspapers each morning to be shocked by fresh revelations.

Reading the newspaper the first day led to a disagreement with Paddy, for I was much amazed by what I learned and told him so.

You can't believe that jade, he said, pushing off the bedsheets. It was a terrible hot night, so torrid and airless he was in his underpants.

Then it's not true? I asked, raising on an elbow to look at him. About Jack using marked cards and loading his dice?

Lucky with dice, unlucky with his wife I'd say.

But who is to know the truth of it? It's her word against his.

Depend on it, the jury won't think so, he murmured, trailing his fingers up my arm. Always a sign.

But Jessie Philp reckons Mrs Royce is a decent woman, I persisted. She knows her from their painting group.

Women always stick up for their own sex, he said. His hand on my waist now.

But the Jezebels? I was determined to make my point. They reckon Jack visits them regular.

Paddy left off caressing me. No! he said loudly. I won't have that! You're better off not reading that rubbish. Jack's a hard drinker that's all. He likes to knock about in pubs it's true, but the rest is all lies as the jury will find.

I couldn't see why that should be when there were six Jezebels and only one of him. I was worried for Cissie's reputation, to be employed by such a man, and told Paddy the newspapers wrote that the barmaids Jack Royce knocked about with in pubs did double duty as ladies of the night.

Then the papers know more than I do, Paddy said, resuming his finger-walk. I can't speak for the ones at the Rose and Crown but they keep a decent type of girl at the Cri. Young Lily is fresh as a daisy and always obliging.

Is that so? I thought, in a green rage to know what ways she was obliging, and turned on my side. But while I was settling to sleep he began dropping kisses on my neck. And so it went on further, and a bit further still until there was no stopping him. Not that I wanted him to.

Afterwards, when Paddy fell asleep, I thought about Ephie, wondering if her stories about Jack were true. They had the ring of truth. I remembered what she said in court, how she came third or fourth on the list with her man. He should never have called any woman wife, she reckoned, because it wasn't in his nature to think of anyone but himself and his everlasting sport and horses. In the end, when I did fall asleep, I dreamed Jack was chasing Cissie around the surgery while Ephie sat in the doctor's chair, ticking off lists.

Next morning, opening the newspaper for more news, I received a great shock. Mr Feez, Ephie's barrister, was reported as asking Jack if he had ever visited *Paris Villa*, a house of ill fame owned by a man named Leonard Bignal.

A cold, sinking sensation came in my stomach. Bignal? A *whoremaster*? And to think I had danced with him at *Richmond House*. For a horrible split second I was back in the man's arms, being whirled about.

Jack denied visiting *Paris Villa*, but Mr Feez countered by saying there were witnesses to testify otherwise, and he believed Jack had once entertained Bignal in his own home.

You heard that, did you? Jack said. Then you heard no more than the truth. Bignal is an acquaintance of mine, an independent sporting gentleman. He potted a couple of ducks—or was it hares? I don't remember—so I challenged him to cook them up at *Richmond House*.

Mother of God, what next? Sweat was running off me. I was in mortal dread Mr Feez would ask who else was present during the whoremaster's visit, and if so, what Jack would choose to say. Would he name me? I knew he hadn't forgiven me for throwing him over.

But by the greatest good luck Mr Feez veered off on another topic. Had the plaintiff, before he married, been a travelling salesman who went by the name of Rorty Jack?

I used to own a horse called Jack Rorty, Jack replied. Someone must've mixed up the names.

Isn't it true, pursued Mr Feez, that the girls at *Paris Villa* know you as Rorty Jack?

Jack said that was all nonsense.

Paddy refused to read the newspapers and stayed loyal to Jack, though he wasn't so far gone as to want his daughter working for a man whose private life had become a scandal.

But we needn't have worried, as Jack closed down *Richmond House* for the duration.

The jury men couldn't agree on a verdict, though they were locked up for five nights in a very hot room. In the end the circuit judge made the ruling himself. The marriage must stand, he said, because both parties were proven adulterers. I never understood the logic behind that.

Jack upped sticks and went to live in Brisbane and Ephie fled there too. A dentist bought *Richmond House*, an old fellow who asked Cissie to stay on and keep his books. Which she agreed to do. Secretly, I felt nothing but relief to see the back of Royce, though I couldn't help wondering how he and Ephie would manage, still yoked together in marriage.

But as Jack had left town in a hurry, without leaving a forwarding address, it was unlikely we'd ever know.

Lionleigh

THE ROYCES might have departed but the Big Drought lingered on like a despised guest, and what drove Paddy more than anything else was how to keep horse-racing going.

On the nights when Dr Callaghan called I would come in the drawing-room and find the Doctor puffing on his pipe while Paddy paced the floor, giving out his latest scheme.

Smaller prizes, that's the answer, he was saying one evening.

We haven't the money, Dr Callaghan said, handing me his plate. Quite delicious, Mrs Wilson, thank you. You're a dab hand with the puftaloons.

Paddy stopped his trot to look at his friend.

We have to give horse-owners something, otherwise they'll drop their membership. What do you say, Callaghan? A winter meeting?

How can we get up a race when half the committee have resigned? the Doctor replied. Tell me that if you can.

Why, hunt up new men of course! Paddy fired back. If we don't the owners will take their horses elsewhere. They've little enough encouragement as it is, the class of jockeys we have to put up with.

And off he galloped on his hobby-horse, complaining about the boys that pull horses. Dr Callaghan's face took on the secretive air of a man biding his time. He'd heard it all before and likely was remembering what happened to Mr Henderson. I know I was.

We're as tough on jockeys as anyone else, the Doctor said when Paddy paused for breath. What it is, Wilson, though you seem intent on ignoring facts, is that people ... don't ... have ... any ... money.

For God's sake! Paddy cried. I tell you the club will go under if we don't get up some races. I've never known such a block to take place in all the bad times in the last thirty years!

And still arguing his case as I left the room. I heard him from the kitchen, begging Dr Callaghan to agree, to anything, any style of racing, just so long as it was racing.

But if he was never a fly man with money, or even very strong on common sense, by the same token Paddy wasn't one to take setbacks neither, and next thing you know he was out all hours, trotting up and down on his town hack, giving out his fulsome blarney to the men on the Range and the racehorse-mad publicans in town. Till in the end he got his way.

And became something of a hero in town, for in the fizz and pop of his passion he had got together a new committee, and money besides. Enough to have the winter races put on in Show Week, which would have been a very poor affair without them.

The races proved a great success, so Harry and the girls told when they came home. 300 free tickets for the ladies and cheap ones for the men, they came through the gate in droves to forget the hard times and distract themselves with a little pleasure. In the upshot the Arjaycee put 145 pound through the totalisator and they had music from the Foresters Band and refreshments brought in from a hotel. A raffle for the Distressed Jockeys Fund. And with Harry coming first in the gentlemen's handicap we weren't short on smiles at dinner that night.

But listen now, Paddy said. I must tell you we made a loss.

The grins dropped off our faces.

On the other hand, he said, if we hadn't held the races we'd have had no subscriptions, so therefore the club's better off to the tune of fifty pound.

He meant fifty pound less of debt, but no one was in the mood to think about that, so we clapped and hallooed, and Paddy looked at me and said he wished I had come with the girls. He could have shown me *Lionleigh*.

Maybe it was memories of chasing foxes with his sisters, popping their horses over hedges on his uncle's demesne, that fed an old dream, for he never stopped talking about the big house on Lion Creek. Green for it he was, to be a landed gentleman like his Uncle Thomas Cuffe in Ireland.

Fetch your hat! he said one day, coming through the door in a rush.

Whatever for? I said. What crotchet have you got in your head now?

Leave that mending. I'm taking you down to the Lion Creek Road to show you *Lionleigh*.

Grinning as if all his birthdays had come at once, for he'd just learned that the gentleman who owned *Lionleigh* had died, and the house and land were put up for sale.

But Paddy, I said, we're happy here. And it would be such a long journey for Ada and Cissie to travel to work.

Up with you, old girl! The buggy is waiting and at your disposal.

I pinned on my hat and we set off down the hill. It was another cloudless day, no good for my garden but a fine one for excursioning. We turned off Wandal Road and went along the Lion Creek Road, passing a brickworks first, then a stinky tannery. Next a hotel with horses tethered outside. A great class of loafers on the upstairs verandah, leaning on the railing to spit their tobacco juice in the dirt. A couple of men outside a blacksmith's shed, sweating as they forced a metal hoop onto a cartwheel. A butcher shop with children squabbling under the iron awning.

I was watching them when Mrs Lynch came through the doorway and handed out a smack to the biggest one.

That must be Mr Lynch's butcher shop, I said, and gave her a smile and wave as we went by. And didn't she look surprised.

We rattled across the tight-packed logs of Lion Creek bridge and I peered down at the scummy water-holes that were all that remained of the creek. Dead gums reared their leafless branches along the banks, ghostly white and hung with flying foxes. It wasn't what I'd expected, though I should have known the drought would make the creek a poor remnant of itself.

Tattersalls' abandoned racecourse hove into view, stretching away into the distance. From my seat in the buggy I had a good squiz at the work Paddy had supervised: a cluster of white-painted buildings near the gate, a covered grandstand overlooking the finishing line, a judge's stand. But I hardly had time to take everything in before Paddy turned into bushland, and in another few minutes was pulling up under a tree.

It is queer the way silence settles on the bush when you come to a stop. The crack of a twig only makes it more complete. So still it is you feel yourself no more than a speck in the vastness.

There's a fine pair of gates for you, Paddy said, pointing with his whip.

A lady was sitting on a folding-stool in front of the big gates, painting a picture of them on a little easel she had there.

But where's the house? I asked.

You must go down the driveway and then you'll see it. But the wrought iron gates, don't they remind you of home?

I suppose, I said. They weren't like any I remembered around Ballyconnell, that were wooden things with rickety hinges. But the ones with iron spikes at Reverend Venables' big house, sure. They did look alike.

Paddy tipped his hat to the lady, who had turned to look at us, and started up the horses. Back we clattered across the bridge and this time I avoided looking at the creek. We trotted past Mr Lynch's butcher shop but when we drew abreast of the hotel we were both shocked by what we saw. A young man getting off his horse, it's sides running with blood. He stood shouting curses at the distressed animal until he swung off and went lurching up the hotel steps.

See that? Paddy said as we watched him stumble on a tread. The bastard's broken one of his spurs on the stallion. I'd go after him if you weren't in the buggy. Filthy bounder, I always knew him for a cur.

Who is he? I said, crossing myself.

Christy Lynch. Drunk as a boiled owl as usual. I'll drop in at the police station when we get back to town and have a constable sent out.

Mrs Lynch's son got charged for his cruelty right enough, but the magistrate in his wisdom let him off. So that's her fine son, I thought. I didn't like to think we would have Christy as a neighbour if Paddy had his way. But by the grace of God he did not. He didn't have the money they were asking and nor did anyone else. *Lionleigh* was rented out a good few years before the letter came from Ireland that sent us to live on the Lion Creek Road.

217

With all the time at her disposal while *Richmond House* was closed, Cissie had begun visiting her old schoolfriends, and she kept up the habit when she was working again. She never seemed taken with the idea of marrying, and gave all her suitors the run around so far as I could see.

I shall never chance my name with a common shopkeeper, I heard her tell Ada once, which didn't surprise me. She was always fastidious in her nature. Not that there was any shortage of more gentlemanly friends to take her to concerts and tennis parties. Such a pretty girl with her wavy brown hair and blue-brown eyes like her father's, and her new man seemed quite to dote on her.

You missed Jimmy Sherwin, I told her when she came home from one of her tea parties. Bun fights she calls them.

Mother, she said, I hope you didn't entertain him in the kitchen.

Certainly I didn't, I said, though I knew Jimmy liked nothing better than being fed scones straight from the oven. Pray to God she will stick with this one, I thought, though I don't suppose she will. And as if to prove my fears what does she say next, but—I'm glad I missed Jimmy. He's tiresome.

To hear you talk, I said. Such a strapping young man and thinks the world of you. And thought to myself, Only three days ago you were making eyes at him in the drawing-room.

Of late she and Ada had taken up dancing the Cake Walk, which made Paddy no more than grumbling angry. He wasn't the same man who used to dance and swear in his rages, and didn't get in a temper when the government gave women the vote.

If working men can have it, he said, gentlemen's wives certainly must.

And took a deal of trouble to explain the political men, and which ones the girls and I must vote for. Ada disagreed with him, for she had taken up a little socialism through attending lectures at her school-teachers' union.

Paddy laughed and said socialism was as likely to work as a horse riding its owner, and was that easy in his gab he had Ada laughing.

But then it came, the fateful day. I heard him shouting before ever he came through the door.

Fetch the Bordeaux claret, Annie! It's time to open it! The best news ever, you won't believe!

Oh he was mighty pleased. Whatever is it? I said.

We're rich! he cried, and pulled a letter from his pocket. Uncle Tom's died and left all his money to me. I knew he'd give me something but I never expected—I was struck in a heap. Milford was grinning. Jumping Jemima! I said. Three thousand pounds? Read it yourself, says Milford, it's all in black and white. Holy Harry! I said. And what do you think I did next, Annie? Straight away I asked Milford to put in a bid for *Lionleigh*.

But shouldn't you ... wouldn't it be better to wait till you have the money in your pocket?

He burst out laughing. Be damned to that! We're moving, old girl, we're moving. You'll be lady of the manor now.

So there it was, come at last, the prospect of living on the Lion Creek Road, which I had hoped would never be. Knowing something in my bones maybe. *Three for a wedding* the old chant goes, and it was three right enough. First *Rookwood* on the Isaacs River, then Serpentine Water, and now *Lionleigh* to be the acres of Paddy's estate. And as it turned out we did have a wedding.

I grieved leaving my garden. It had grown very fine with the flowering bushes I planted, but I was more sorrowful by far when Jemima said she wouldn't come with us. We were in the spare room sorting the linen when she broke the news.

I'm getting old, she said. I can't see myself living by water, Mrs Wilson, not with me rheumatics.

Oh Jemima, I said, trying to keep the face on me. What will you do?

Bob and me have money put by. We're buying ourselves a bit of land out at Kabra. Bob always had a hankering to go back to farming, and myself no different. We was born at Kabra so it's in our blood acourse.

We looked at each other. I hadn't even known Jemima came from Kabra. She never talked about herself.

I shall miss you, I said.

No more than I'll miss you, she said.

She turned away, to hide the tear in her eye it might be, and I was glad of it. I couldn't keep a few from mine.

But that was only the beginning. When we set out in the buggy for *Lionleigh* there were only four of us. Douglas was away on one of his hunting trips and Harry had gone to Maryborough to be under-manager for his insurance company.

Put that in your pocket, Paddy said the day of his departure, but Harry told him he was his own industry. That's of course, Paddy said, but keep it in case of drought.

I clung to Harry when it was my turn to say goodbye. Write soon, I said. Watch out for snakes now, keep safe and come home safe. Promise me, love.

And he did promise, and shook his father's hand before he boarded the train. Such a fine young man, I scarce could see him for tears.

A tear bleared my eye from remembering as we clip-clopped along the Lion Creek Road.

Father, what's that funny smell? Cissie asked.

The horsefeed, pet.

For goodness sake, Father, why bring *that* along? Ada demanded.

Why wouldn't I bring it? Paddy fired back. If you want good horses you must feed them the best. And there's no better diet than the correct ratio of corn, oats and milkfeed. That and uniform kindness are the only way to raise an even-tempered mount.

Yes, Father, she murmured.

You must treat your horse kindly from the start. Feed her high, work her reasonably and handle her as gently as you would a child.

He looked over his glasses at Ada. And keep the stable ventilated and remove the manure daily.

Yes, Father, you've told me before.

When we arrived at the tall iron gates Cissie jumped down and unlocked them and then it was another world we entered. A winding gravel carriageway bordered both sides by hoop pines, and beyond them a great class of flowerbeds set among lawns. Summertime blooms, red and orange and yellow in colour—so geraniums, hibiscus, gladiola, tiger lilies and allamanda. A mango grove making a dark pool of shade, and more orchards, orange and lemon trees, guava and grapefruit, enough to feed the tribes of Israel it might be. And when we rounded a bend in the driveway we got another surprise, for there was Lion Creek, and much like Serpentine Water in its seeming, with waterlilies and all manner of waterfowl paddling about.

Why, it looks like a lake, I said, and Paddy said it was in a way, for the creek was dammed further up to give a better outlook from the house.

It's like Heaven must be, I said. And thought how foolish I had been not to want to live in such a beautiful place.

The girls were excited. When Paddy pulled up outside the house they cried out at its grandness and jumped down to peer through the windows. Do hurry, Father! Ada said. She was skipping in her eagerness to get through the door.

It proved just as grand inside. Five big bedrooms, cedar panelling and parquetry floors throughout. Chandeliers in all the living rooms, another big room Paddy said must be his library. A room off the pantry made of brick, fitted out to be a butter-room, with a cellar let in the floor. A permanent well in the kitchen garden. And so roomy and airy with modern windows everywhere a king might be happy to stay the night, if only there were curtains.

Well, Mrs Wilson, Paddy said, do the reception rooms meet with your approval?

They're very grand, I said, but how are we to fill them? We haven't half enough furniture.

You must make a list of whatever's needed.

And so many windows, I'll be sewing for months.

Have the curtains made up, he said, and took me by the waist and waltzed me across the dusty floor.

Stop it will you, I said, laughing.

Fal-de-lal-tum-tum-tiddle-i-ay, he sang.

Father! Ada said, coming into the room with Cissie. Anyone would think you were a young man.

And so I feel at this moment, he flung back as he waltzed me about. I believe you and I must go to the Mayor's Winter Ball, Annie. Trip the light fantastic with the good burghers of Rockhampton.

But Father ... Cissie said. Ada and I ... and anyway, Mother doesn't have a ball gown.

Ball gown? I said, seeing a way out of the girls' difficulties. I pulled out of Paddy's arms to stop his cavorting, and announced I had no such gown.

Then you must get whatever's needed, Paddy said. Have a seamstress make it up.

It takes weeks to stitch an evening dress, Ada said, stealing a glance at Cissie. How sad, Cissie said with a laugh. Mother won't be able to come with us.

What is so amusing? Paddy wanted to know. Wipe that smile off your face, miss. It's no wonder the world's going to the dogs when young people forget their manners. Your mother is coming with me and that's final. Even if she has to buy a ready-made dress. Go down to Stewart & Lucas tomorrow, Annie, and order the best.

I felt a skittering in my heart, knowing he cared enough to take my part against Cissie.

To be sure I will, I said, smiling.

But later, when he was asleep and dreaming of I know not what, horses I suppose, I lay on my side of the bed in the unfamiliar room, listening to the unfamiliar sounds. The great house that had echoed all day with our voices and footsteps was silent, but outside was another world. The timber blinds on the verandah creaked, and when the wind got up they banged against the verandah posts. Somewhere in the paddocks pigs were squealing—what were pigs doing there?—and a bird in the garden began an eerie wailing call.

A curlew, I realised. The first one I had heard since Ellen died.

I slipped out of bed and tiptoed across to the window. Something huge and black and faintly gleaming loomed at me through the glass, and I jumped back in fright. Heart in mouth, I crept forward to peer again, and saw it was the water in the damned up creek.

A few hundred yards away, on the other side of Lion Creek Bridge, late night riders were still trotting along the Lion Creek Road, their way well lit by street lights, but *Lionleigh* and its grounds were sunk in darkness. No gaslights made fuzzy balls of light through the intervening trees. No soft beams revealed the whereabouts of neighbouring houses, for there were none. Only our house and the bleached remains of Tattersalls' abandoned racecourse broke the monotony of the surrounding bush. Except for the homeless men who slept in Tatts' empty luncheon rooms, no one but us lived this side of the bridge.

We were hardly settled a day but two before Paddy began hiring carpenters. Building a new milking shed, fixing the outbuildings, new shelves for the storeroom, the aviaries taken down. It was nothing but hammering and men going back and forth for weeks. And himself riding out each morning to inspect the paddocks, for he meant to make *Lionleigh* another Serpentine Water with horse and cattle-breeding, to give himself an income in retirement. That hale and quick he was for a man in his seventies, though of late he was growing forgetful.

He didn't neglect to find help for me. A brickmaker's daughter he hired to come in each day for the char work. Minnie she was called, and able enough I suppose, but I couldn't take to her. A pert miss, always slipping off in the afternoons without so much as a by-your-leave. But that was the way of it in 1909. Girls like their freedom and who can blame them? We were lucky to have her and her brother at all.

Young Charley did the yard work and milking, with a bit of help now and then from Big George. For it turned out our old firewood-man lived with an Aboriginal woman in a humpy down by the creek. Lived there illegally since it was our land, as Paddy pointed out to me. Though never to George.

The two men got on well from the start, and more so when Paddy learned the mare pulling George's wood-cart was a great-grand-daughter of Dainty Davie. I liked Big George too, from remembering the time he stopped Billy Stapleton throwing stones at Harry.

Minnie now, she didn't like him at all. She looked aside if she passed him on her way to the well, on account of he was a Combo. He got a gin living with him, she said, sliding her eyes at me.

Whatever will she do if Douglas turns up? I wondered. She'll be out the door before you would notice.

Christmas came and went in a swelter of heat and by February Paddy had racehorses up from Sydney, and stud bulls to graze on the creek pastures. If it hadn't been for Christy Lynch's pigs getting under the fences he'd have been in horse-heaven.

It's cattle now, he said at dinner one night. I found six of his steers in the top paddock. If he does it again I'll have them impounded.

Sure and you won't, love? I said.

Confound it, I will! That's valuable pasture he's making free of. Fattening his beasts on the cheap.

Lord knows, I worked hard to talk him out of it. The last thing I wanted was bad blood between Paddy and Christy Lynch. If the man passed me on his horse when I was walking to his father's butcher shop, he would tip his hat the way he needn't have bothered. And his face that red and angry and puffy, he looked like a Devil in man's flesh.

Three For a Wedding

SO PRETTY, Mother. Mr Coates will like them, I'm sure, Cissie said when she found me arranging my first crop of roses in a vase.

Two summers had slipped by with one beau following another, but this one had her in a dream. Her thoughts became beads on a string, it was nothing but Mr Coates this and Mr Coates that, till I knew well enough what was in the air.

Her new man was an Englishman and correct in his manners, though I liked him better for his jokes. They would go a long way to lightening Cissie's strictness I hoped. And he had land of his own so that was a mark in his favour with Paddy. A man with a farm is always an attractive notion to an Irishman, and Mr Coates had one called *Harveston*, situated not so far from us on the banks of the Fitzroy River.

Only to think how they met. Mr Coates went to see the dentist at *Richmond House* about a toothache that was plaguing him, and Cissie was the one who showed him into the surgery. He must have been taken with her from the start because in no time he was paying calls. Being made to write in the girls' confession albums—what colour eyes he liked best, his favourite girls' names. A better excuse for flirting was never invented.

And fortunate that Paddy liked him, for one day he paid us a visit to ask for Cissie's hand in marriage.

Well then, my sweet, you couldn't ask for a sounder man, Paddy told her after Mr Coates had departed. A deal better than some of the unlicked cubs you've brought home in the past.

Cissie went pink knowing her father was pleased. I don't believe Mr Coates' visit took her by surprise, girls know when such things are in the wind. She looked that rosy and dimpling you could tell how happy she was. It was a day for rejoicing, and more so since they planned to wed at once.

Never let moss grow on the path of love, I said, hearing my mother speak through my mouth.

God knows, none grew on Ellen's path. But I couldn't think of Ellen, it was Cissie's day and so it should be. She had happiness coming to her that was overdue. She was thirty-three years old.

I wish I could say nothing came to spoil her happiness, but misfortunately life goes by its own rules. It's all slides and roundabouts and no way of knowing when the next plunge begins. It began soon enough. We had hardly finished getting Cissie's trousseau ready when Paddy gave out his terrible news. The money had finally come from his uncle's will in Ireland, but for one reason or another it was a good deal less than promised, and he was facing the Insolvency Court again.

He was demented with rage, and cursed the grubby lawyers for stealing his inheritance. After he exhausted himself shouting and swearing, and was sitting slumped in his chair, he said sadly,

And no way of fighting them. That's the damnable part.

I was bewildered. I knew *Lionleigh* had cost £900 and Paddy had spent hundreds more on improvements and furnishings, so where was the rest of the money?

Surely that leaves us £1500 at least, I said.

Oh for— Paddy looked around, as if seeking aid. What's the point discussing it with you? Isn't it enough we're in a bloody great pickle?

Only I don't understand.

If you must know, he said, a cousin contested the will and got a share in it. The legal fees for that business alone amounted to £300. All I got in the end was £600 and half that went into Harry's account.

Harry's *account?* I said.

Didn't I tell you? he said. I thought I had. The boy's engaged now and needs to buy a house. I told Milford to see to it.

And see to having our furniture carried out by bailiffs, I thought. I was bitter, knowing how upset Cissie would be. Her wedding would be a poor affair now, if we could afford one at all.

Paddy didn't have the wherewithal to pay off the bank, or the bills he had run up stocking the paddocks and making improvements. To satisfy his creditors the racehorses and cattle had to be sold, along with the workhorses and buggy horses, the new phaeton, buggy and spring cart and anything else the insolvency people could get their hands on. In the end we had a huge mortgage, a half-furnished house and no cattle to bring in an income.

Not long after this shambles Paddy went to Blackwater for a Racing Association meeting, and later that night Cissie tiptoed into my room. On account of Ada's snoring she said. A likely story since they slept in separate bedrooms, but I was half awake and let her slide under the covers.

She's like a foghorn, Cissie said in my ear. And another thing, Mother, I wish you would manage Father better.

Mm? I mumbled.

You know! The way he made a show of himself in court. It was written up in the papers, every word he said.

Mmm...

Mr Wilson said this, Mr Wilson said that. My friends reckon he's a freak.

Then they're fools, I muttered.

She sighed. I see Father in a different light now. His recklessness, his impertuniousness.

Impetuousness, I corrected her. Go to sleep, dear.

She was that shamed by her father's disgrace—that was how she saw it—she wouldn't see her man for weeks. If it hadn't been for Mr Coates' good sense, and better still his good heart, I doubt there had been a wedding at all. But he surprised her one day when she was coming through the big gates in the old pony trap that was all Paddy could save from the creditors, and what he said to her I don't know, but it was all smiles after that and the wedding to go ahead.

Not the grand affair Paddy had planned, though I liked it better for being homely. Eliza Hutton loaned Cissie her orange-flower wreath to set off the wedding gown—cream-striped crystalline over glacé muslin it was, with sleeves of silk-embroidered net. When she came in the drawing-room on her wedding day the lady guests oohed and ah-ed, and why wouldn't they? She looked that lovely, all shimmery like a Fairy that shines with its own light. And up-to-the-minute modern besides, for her gown was in the new tunic style and had silk medallions on the train at the back.

The minister took her aside to speak in her ear, then a knock on the door and Paddy went out to bring in the last of the guests.

Last but not least and doubly welcome, he said, leading Jimmy Sherwin and his parents into the room.

I was tying up a flower spray that had fallen sideways on the bamboo archway, and straight away Mrs Sherwin came over to me, though I had never met her before.

Quite charming, Mrs Wilson, she said. Maidenhair fern and white begonias. So very fresh and bridal.

It was myself made it, I said. I didn't mention Paddy was in despair how to pay for the wedding and hadn't the money to give his own gift. Mr Coates' wedding cheque had proved a Godsend, it had paid for Cissie's and Ada's gowns, and the bouquets and wedding cake besides.

I always say, Mrs Sherwin said, putting up her lorgnette to watch her son find a space on the sideboard for his gift, I always think, don't you, Mrs Wilson, that May weddings are wise. You can depend on the weather being agreeable.

What has Mother been telling you? Cissie said, coming up to us and smiling.

Cissie, my dear, said Mrs Sherwin, your mother was just saying she made the archway herself. I suppose you were happy with that.

Mother knows everything there is to know about flowers, Cissie said. You couldn't get a prettier archway if you ordered one from a florist.

That is my own opinion exactly, said Mrs Sherwin.

Jimmy had a hangdog look when he joined us. Cissie stood in her flowing silken gown, thanking him for his gift—a handsome set of china plate it turned out—then Reverend Lewin cleared his throat and said it was time to begin.

Cissie and Mr Coates took their place under the flowery archway and the minister spoke his words. Do you take this woman to be your lawfully wedded wife? he asked Mr Coates at the end of it.

I do, Mr Coates said loudly, grinning at Cissie. The bold young man.

I do, Cissie said when it came her turn, so low we could hardly hear.

That pretty and gladsome our girl looked under the white begonias, blushing and turning the gold band on her finger as she fluttered her lashes at Mr Coates. Small wonder I shed more tears than Ada thought proper. I was a bit wrought from doing all the cleaning and cooking for the wedding, I suppose. It wasn't only Cissie I cried happy tears for. It was memories of standing with Paddy in St Joseph's church, exchanging our own vows.

After the wedding lunch we went out on the lawn to kiss and hug and speed the newlyweds on their journey. Cissie broke down and shed tears in my arms. Mother, was all she could say till she whispered in my ear, I'm sorry I haven't always been a good daughter to you.

Mr Coates stood watching, and afterwards bestowed his own peck. Don't cry, Mrs Wilson, he said. I'll take good care of Cissie, you have my word on it.

He helped her into his carriage, and away they went to start their honeymoon. Way down in New South Wales in the Blue Mountains, we found out later.

It was queer not having Cissie come home afternoons. I think Paddy felt it most. And queerer still knowing Harry was married too. Obstinate bachelor though he was, he had beat Cissie to the post and found himself a bride in Maryborough called Mary Hyde. Ada went down for the wedding—that was all we could stretch to—and came back full of stories. Mary was a proper lady, she said, and pretty besides.

They're in Cairns now, Mother. Harry got promoted to manager, that's why he proposed to her. He's quite besotted with her but perhaps he should wait until the honeymoon's over.

Why wouldn't they be happy? I said a bit sharp.

In truth I didn't think any woman good enough for Harry, and wondered about Ada. Would she ever find a man *she* thought good enough? It's useless telling her there is no such article as a perfect man.

She has it fixed in her heart there is one such miraculous creature waiting for her. Young men invite her to tennis parties and it's a sorry business when you have beaus on all sides and can't find one of them the juicy apple of your eye. Ellen would have been amazed to see the manners of modern Australian girls.

But I worried more for Paddy. He had meant to wind up his business before the wedding. He was seventy-six and ready for it. But after the insolvency he had to work in town another two years, to re-stock the paddocks and replace his lost horses. The new ones made up for it, he reckoned when they arrived. How he loved fussing over them, Chieftain in particular. As fine a black stallion as ever was born, if Paddy was to be believed. And he was a free man at last, glad to be out in the paddocks all day instead of only after work.

He came in the kitchen one morning and glared at me.

That mongrel Lynch, he said. He just dodges about telling one lie after another. God almighty couldn't make the fellow straight.

Which Lynch do you mean?

Christy! Who else? I put his cattle in the holding paddock but after lunch I'm turning them out on the road.

Where did you find them? I asked. Was it in the paddock Mr Robinson rents off you?

What the dickens has that got to do with it? Christy hasn't got permission from Robinson.

He has a key to the small gate, I said. I saw him use it one time.

Does he indeed? Paddy snatched up his hat.

Don't be rushing off hasty, I said. Let me have a yarn with his mother. She'll take the key off him most likely if I ask nice.

That old biddy! I doubt she can get out of her own way, the size she has on her.

Wait now, I said. I'll slip down the road and have a word with her. Sure and it's for the best and no trouble. Christy is bound to obey the mother of his own flesh.

I left off topping and tailing the beans and took up my shawl. Such a hulking fellow Christy Lynch is, who knows what he would do if his temper was up. So there I was trudging along the Lion Creek Road, and in being so nigh to the butcher shop another ten minutes had me walking through the door. And saw at once I was in luck. Mrs Lynch was the one behind the counter.

Grand day to you, Mrs Wilson, she shouted, for there was a terrible screaming out the back, enough to make your blood run cold. Some creature in its death throes, a badly pithed ox by the sound of it. I told my errand as best I could over the desperate roaring, and when I finished Mrs Lynch looked at me doubtful.

I don't know I can ask him about it now, she shouted back. He's butchering out the back with a terrible headache. He was screwed last night. It's that wife of his drives him to it.

We must do something, I was shouting, when the screaming died down to a blubbering moan.

Mr Wilson is quite upset, I said, lowering my voice. Christy's beasts have got in his paddocks again.

Isn't that the great pity, she said, creasing her face in a smile. It is torn in himself Christy is to know his pigs did go bothering your gentleman last week. And that's true as a prayer, dear.

I don't know it's just pigs, Mrs Lynch. It is cattle today.

Wait a minute till I think, it was going astray on me. I remember now. It was this way, Mrs Wilson, wait till I tell you, dear. Christy let them out for a roam on the road and must of forgot to put them back. I'm always telling him. Why do you let them out, I say, if you can't remember to put them back? Well never matter, dear, I'll tell him your man is vexed, so I will.

But the key to the gate, Mrs Lynch, I said, wishing I could take out my handkerchief without causing offence. Such a stench there is in Lynch's butcher shop and not only from the offal. The lavender oil they keep in bowls to cover it makes a bad marriage I believe. Any rate, the two smells mixed together never failed to turn my stomach.

I'll speak with him I will, dear, said Mrs Lynch. Your man is such a gentleman we wouldn't want our few beasts bothering him.

She rambled on till it was all I could do to get away in good conscience. I heard a clatter of hooves behind me as I hurried up the road, and looked round to see who was riding so fast.

Christy Lynch. And never gave so much as a nod as he galloped past. Fine boy you are, I thought. Better the back of you than the front.

But when I came through the big gates who do I see but Christy again? In the holding paddock with Paddy. The two of them astride their horses, facing each other. Lynchs' cattle pressed against the rails, watching on with their big gentle eyes.

You tarling villain, I thought. You came in by the small gate and rode over my flowerbeds.

What are you doing with our steers? I heard him say. Are you going to impound them?

I am not, Paddy said, the haughty way he has. I'm turning them out.

If looks could kill Christy would have been meat that minute.

You can't do that! he cried. Them beasts are my father's.

I don't give a damn who they belong to, Paddy said. They've no right to be here.

They must of walked in from the road!

Oh they walked alright. They walked nice and easy, out of your yard into mine, but how they got here is the mystery. They don't have a key.

You needn't get magging with me. We can't help if the cattle wanders.

That's a lie and you know it.

Christy wheeled his horse. You got plenty feed here! he shouted. Leave them be or I'll kick your brains out!

Is that so? Paddy's voice was dangerous polite. If you say another word of impudence you'll get more than you bargained for.

If you turn them cattle out, yelled Christy, it's *you* will get lacerated!

Chieftain took a quick side-step, his flanks quivering.

I've every right to do so, Paddy said, stroking the stallion's neck. But since you're here, why don't you take them yourself?

Oh hoity toity. Fucking bastard, I'll smash you!

Come and smash me now! Paddy shouted.

Christy stood up in the stirrups, slashing the air with his whip. I was all but paralysed by fear.

Stop! I cried, and he looked over and saw me. Such a scowl distorted his face, then for whatever reason he turned his horse and came galloping across the carriageway, that close I had to step back or be knocked down. And away with him across the flowerbeds.

Paddy rode over to me. Did you get the key?

Mrs Lynch is talking to her man, I said. I was shaking.

We went down the carriageway together, myself walking alongside Chieftain.

I'll leave the steers in the yard another while yet, Paddy said. But if that milcher from Munster doesn't take them today I'm driving them to the pound tomorrow.

Ah no, you shouldn't, love. It will only cause more trouble.

You saw the fellow's behaviour. I can't let him bully me.

When we reached the house Paddy kept going. The horses had to be fed, but I had a bad feeling as I watched him trot off. I tried to get on with my work but not long after I heard a great hammering on the back door.

When I opened it Christy Lynch was standing on the top step, sucking the knob on his whip-handle.

A Winter's Night

I WANT to see your old man, Christy said. Go and tell him.

Mr Wilson's not here, I said. But go down to the holding yard why don't you? Aren't the steers waiting for you, the patient creatures, and the gate left unlocked for them.

Is it? he said.

He mounted his horse and cantered off in the direction of the holding yard. I breathed a deal easier from seeing the direction he took.

Minnie didn't come on Fridays so I was kept busy after that. Christy Lynch and his shenanigans had put me behind. When the roast was in the oven I went out to the store-room to get flour for the pudding, and met Big George coming round the side of the house, on the way to his humpy.

Art'noon, missus, he said, keeping on with his walk, and I gave him a nod and smile but no more. Such a big man he is, yet grown shy over the years and doesn't care to gab.

Paddy came in at dusk with another temper on him, and who could blame him? Christy hadn't taken the steers. What he did instead was leave the big gates open and turn our calf out of its pen. For a time it was nothing but curses while I tried to get on with peeling the vegetables.

May the Devil fly away with him, Paddy ranted. Such a knave and fool I am cursed with for a neighbour! And went on with a good deal more, how Christy Lynch was short of a shingle as everyone knew, such a misbegotten cur as would provoke a saint.

But a hot meal on a winter's night does wonders and we were going over to *Harveston* in the morning to visit Cissie and John—I was calling Mr Coates that by now—so what with talking about our new granddaughter, and a good roast dinner it wasn't long before Paddy was himself again.

Ada and I went in the kitchen to make the pudding and he followed us in. A new habit of his, such a thing he would never have done in the old days. But being several miles out of town he had little company to distract himself of an evening, and he liked to yarn with us while warming his backside at the stove. Any rate, there he was with his back to the stove, hands in pockets, coat-tails hanging over his arms, when Ada looked up from setting out the bowls.

Father, she said, I met Christy Lynch on the road on the way home and he said—now what was it? To tell you to lay off him, I believe were his words.

That's rich coming from him, Paddy said with a sour laugh.

Ada, I said, can you fetch me a cup of sugar? I forgot it.

She took up the kitchen lamp and went out to the storeroom.

A sweet-tempered girl, our Ada, Paddy said, rocking on his feet. What's it to be tonight by the way? Golden Pudding?

Ada came back without the sugar. There's someone outside, she said. I think it's two people. They're standing on the lawn and they seem to be looking in the kitchen window.

A strange time to call, Paddy said. He went out on the verandah, Ada and myself following, and we peered into the darkness. There was no moon that night, and no sound. Not a hint of a breeze to rustle the leaves in the chilly air. A few moths flittering in the light from the kitchen window, that was all.

Who's there? Paddy called.

We heard Mr Lynch's voice saying, Are you in, Mr Wilson?

Then the man himself stepped out of the darkness into the light thrown down by the window. Queerer still, who should waddle from the shadows to stand beside him but Mrs Lynch. We looked at them from the verandah and they looked up at us, and nothing was said for a moment.

Is that you, Lynch? Paddy said.

Yes, Lynch is here, he said. Come about my cattle. What's this I hear about you impounding them?

A night-bird shrieked in the darkness. Paddy had to wait till it stopped before he could speak.

Your boy's got it garbled as usual. I told him no such thing.

There! Mrs Lynch said to her man. Didn't I say it was a lie?

Next we heard rustling in the bushes, and out into the light crept the youngest Lynch children, Katie, Joe and Patrick. They huddled round their mother, staring at us with solemn eyes.

Who told you to follow me? Mrs Lynch scolded them. Be jabers, you kids, I'll tan your hides later.

And what if I *was* going to impound them? Paddy said. That cur of a son of yours is everlastingly tormenting me. He's been here after your steers and left the big gate open and turned my calf out of its pen.

Now isn't that the lie for you, said Mr Lynch softly.

A lie is it? Paddy got furious immediately. If you say lies again I'll have your liver. You'd better leave before you say more.

The whinny of a horse in the bushes—what was a horse doing there? The sound of branches crashing and out of the darkness rushes Christy Lynch.

I'll smash him! he yells, staggering in the square of light on the grass. I'll take the gab out of the nigger-lover!

As on a signal, up the steps runs Mr Lynch, shouting, *Bastard!* Christy not far behind. The stink of alcohol on him, he might have been a brewery.

I'm at him! he yells. I have him!

Mr Lynch catches Paddy by the coat and Christy's fist flies out like a snake striking. The blow smashes against my man's cheek. His head rattles from the impact.

Ada and I jump forward screaming, tearing at Christy like hounds at a fox, and in my fury don't I rip the shirt off his back. It's in my hands anyway. Mrs Lynch is with us. I never saw her come up the steps but she must have done for she's at our feet and sometimes under them, her fat arms holding fast to Christy's leg, clasping it from her seat on the floorboards.

Christy snarling like a madman, flailing at us, Ada and I go down like ninepins. My head banging, with blood it feels like, but up I jump and go at him again because he's still hitting Paddy. I spring at him and pull and tear and hear Ada screaming *Help*! *Murder*! as she runs down the steps and out into the dark shales of the night.

Paddy's face is cut dreadful and Christy still landing grievous blows, and more blood coming. But then he leaves off, swaying and snorting like a spent horse.

Mr Lynch hasn't laid a blow the whole time, but now he goes up to Paddy and shakes him as if he would shake the life out of his body. He puts his face up close to Paddy's till there are only inches between them.

You called my son a cur, he hisses.

He wrenches Paddy by the collar and pulls him over on his back. Mrs Lynch and I grab hold of her man who is dragging mine along the verandah, his head bumping on the boards. We scream at Mr Lynch like the Furies of Hell until he stops.

Paddy gets to his feet slowly. He's dazed and tottery. I dart forward and half drag, half lead him into the kitchen. And *bang*! *clank*! slam the door and shoot home the bolt. I sit him down at the table, he's trembling as in an ague fit, blood running down his face. I'm cleaning it off when a fist comes through the window. Christy shouting, Fucking bastard, I'll kill you!

Splinters of glass flying everywhere. Plates tumbling off the window shelf. The kerosene-lamp toppling, landing sideways on the floor.

I run to pick it up to stop the fuel catching from the kitchen fire, and hear a queer thump, a wheezy gasp. More thumps. The Lynch children screaming.

Something heavy falling.

I peer through the shards of glass and see—dear heaven, Big George! And was never so thankful in my life to see his weatherbeaten face. Sure it was himself and no other saved my man's life and that's true as daily bread. For there he stands, legs apart, and isn't the murdering villain lying at his feet, splayed out like a frog on the verandah floorboards.

Don't hit him again! scream the children in the darkness.

Friend, George, friend! gasps Christy from the floor.

You break a man's window, Big George says, his hands fisted and knotty.

Another voice from the darkness. Yeah, Christy, you done the wrong thing, mate. You shouldn't of hit the old gentleman.

It's a man, standing a little way off. Mr Wickham, another butcher-man that lives on the Lion Creek Road. But who's that in his arms? Ada! Fainted black out.

Out the door I run but she's on her feet by the time I get there, though still needing support from Mr Wickham. We bring her in the kitchen and she's that scratched and cut about the legs I tell her to go in the bathroom and tend herself. It's all I can do, I have enough on my hands caring for Paddy.

I'll see Christy off, Mr Wickham says. I'll see him home, Mrs Wilson. He's cut pretty bad from the window. Needs stitches most likely.

And my man also, I say tartly. Thank you kindly, Mr Wickham, but I wonder could you send for Dr Callaghan while you're about it.

You're bleeding yourself, missus. Your old man don't look too flash neither.

He melts into the darkness.

All is silent. The Lynchs have gone, slunk away like foxes to their lair. As for Big George, he has disappeared as suddenly as he arrived.

Dr Callaghan turned up a few hours later. He was retired like Paddy but kept a few of his old patients, and never minded getting on his horse. Day or night, it was no matter to him.

He seems confused, he said after he had put stitches in Paddy's face and cleaned Ada's and my wounds.

What do you mean? I asked.

We'll see. Best keep an eye on him tonight. Shine a lamp in his eyes now and then to see how they look.

How should they look?

Well, normal, not dilated. Just a precaution. A good night's rest should see him right.

After the Doctor had mounted his horse and trotted off into the night, I went back to the drawing-room and stood there, dazed. Staring at Paddy's empty armchair and the pictures of horses on the walls. Everything was the same, yet nothing was the same, and I knew as well as I have ever known anything it never would be again.

Rookwood

PADDY GOT up in the morning much as he always did. I couldn't stop him, no one could ever stop him when he had a mind to it. I had to find his walking stick because he had trouble walking, and after breakfast, his face and head half-hid by plasters and bandages, he hobbled off to the stables.

Mrs Lynch came down the carriageway next, limping too. From her high jinks the night previous it must be. Now isn't that a great impudence in you to come back, I thought, watching her struggle along the gravel.

Mrs Wilson, Mrs Wilson, she called, waving and hobbling faster. I turned on my heel and went inside.

There wasn't much starch left in her by the time she poked her head round the door, but even so she managed to get down on her knees and kiss my hands.

I'll give you ten pound, she kept saying, crying into her handkerchief. Only please will you stop Mr Wilson from taking out a summons.

I don't want your money, Mrs Lynch.

Ah now, will you not take twenty pound to pay for the window?

No thank you.

I'll give you forty for the breakages, dear. I have it in the Savings Bank, I can draw it out without my right hand knowing.

I said I would see to the breakages myself and after heaving sighs and making sorrowful eyes at me, she went away. I watched from the doorway and saw her greet Paddy who came trotting down the carriageway on Chieftain.

Here is poor Mrs Lynch broken-hearted! she cried out to him. Try to do all you can for her, Mr Wilson. Her heart is quite broke.

I would have done the same for my menfolk, I suppose, but I had no mercy for her and no more did Paddy. He took out the summons and we went to Court as was only right. You would hardly believe the class of lies the Lynchs told. They swore black was white and Christy the brazenest of all. Mrs Lynch now, I never thought she would take such liberties with the truth. She couldn't look me in the eye when she stepped out of the box.

Mr Pattison, their lawyer-man, he lied too. Tried to explain Paddy's and Ada's injuries away by saying they'd been thrown out of the buggy. Sure and who would believe that? So when that didn't work Mr Pattison said, Did your wife and daughter not give you a hiding with sticks?

They have never struck me in their lives, Paddy said, but I wish *you* would do so, Pattison. By the Lord Harry, I'd give it to you then.

The courtroom broke up in laughter.

Did you not get a hiding from your wife and daughter for visiting the woman down by the creek? Mr Pattison asked.

I suppose he meant Big George's Aboriginal woman.

That question is like yourself, utterly contemptible, Paddy said, and turned to the Magistrate. Is this sort of thing allowed? he asked. I have never been so insulted.

This caused further merriment. It was well known he wasn't a ladies' man, it was horses he loved, and the crowd enjoyed his discomfort. Nigger-lover, someone shouted and others yelled, Combo! until the Magistrate called for silence.

Mr Lynch was put in the box next, and said it wasn't true, he had never grabbed Paddy by the back of his coat and pulled him down. He had known the Irish earl for thirty-one years and would never do such a thing.

Earl? said the Magistrate. Is Wilson a titled man? He peered at Paddy.

It's what people call him, your Honour, said Mr Milford. My client isn't an earl, I assure you. Then why call him one? demanded the Magistrate.

I believe the nickname may have started when he inherited money from an uncle in Ireland.

I'll tell you why we call him the Earl, spat out Mr Lynch. It's because he is one, as everyone knows.

That's nonsense, your Honour, Paddy said. I'm no lord and never have been. What Lynch is referring to was a grace and favour title given to my grandfather for his services to the Crown.

Mr Lynch's face contorted as he stared at Paddy. The curse of Cromwell be upon you and your grandpa, he hissed. We know what those services were that you speak of. Bayoneting the Irish is the long and short of what your precious ancestor got up to. We come to this country to escape the likes of you.

Witness will refrain from addressing the plaintiff, ordered the Magistrate.

Mr Lynch's words might have been Dada's. The same hatred born of the same ancient wrongs, except I was on the other side now, and I doubt even Ellen would have rebuked me. The Lynchs were the ones at fault here, as the Magistrate found. There were too many witnesses to do otherwise. He fined Christy and his father five shillings each plus two guineas costs, three shillings costs of court and ten shillings witnesses' expenses. I was in a rage at such paltry punishment but Paddy seemed unbothered. Which was strange coming from a man known with good reason as Mad Paddy.

Only when we got home did he become irritable. Where are my glasses? he asked. I said they were on his nose, and when he found them there he went over to the bookcase to take out his *Practical Horse-keeper*. But he had trouble reading it and polished his glasses, and when that didn't work he took the book outside to read it on the verandah.

Ada and I were in dread for his life. *Lionleigh*'s fancy gates with their sharp spikes had done us no service. They had all avoided the gates: Christy using Robinson's key to unlock the small gate; the other Lynchs walking in by the same route; Mr Wickham jumping the hedge when he heard Ada screaming inside it, desperate to get through and find help. The gates meant nothing to any of them.

Ada was in a terrible flap coming and going to work along the Lion Creek Road, and myself not much better in the house. We both wanted to quit *Lionleigh* and any time we judged a good moment we would beg Paddy to sell the place.

We had chances aplenty. The old fire was going out of him and when he wasn't in the paddocks you'd likely find him in the house. I couldn't count the times I came in the drawing-room and saw him staring into space. A feather carried in the air couldn't have looked more aimless. But it was the best time to catch him and it might be constant dropping wore the stone, or the bank was making difficulties and wanting more payments, but it wasn't long before he agreed, and *Lionleigh* was put up for sale.

Dr Callaghan said Paddy would fare better in familiar surrounds, so then we were at a loss until Ada heard *Rookwood* was advertised for rent. A great piece of luck altogether, and didn't she arrange for us to take it. Even so, coming back to the Athelstane Range would be a bitter exile from my man's dream, and I feared it might cast him into further gloom.

Yet when we drove through the gateway all he said was, Look at that! Bob has forgotten to shut the stable door.

Ada and I looked at each other but said nothing, and after he had fastened the stable door he went in the house as if it was every day.

Time for my brandy, he said, dropping his stick and sitting down. Not noticing he was sitting on a packing crate.

When I came in the kitchen after fetching his brandy, Ada was sitting knees up on the bench by the stove, cradling a tin cup in her hands.

The tea's still hot, she said, nodding at the flask we had brought with us. Sit down, Mother, you look exhausted. I'll get it for you.

Up she jumped and poured a cup, and handed it to me where I had sunk down on a packing box.

It's so lovely being home, she said. I never wanted to leave *Rookwood*, and now we've come back.

I sipped the tea, grateful for its heat and sweetness. *Rookwood* had always been home for Ada, it was where she was born and grew up. The metal cup felt good, warm between my hands, and a thought crept into my tired brain that maybe *Rookwood* was my home too.

The place where I had grown up as well, where I went astray and lost myself, then found my way home. Jack Royce had a hand in that bit of mischief, though in Ireland it might be the Fairies, or searching for a lost calf, or walking over the grave of an unbaptised baby that makes you lose direction. It can happen to anyone and in Ireland no blame is attached, but either way, Australia or Ireland, the trick is to find your way home.

And somehow, all unknowing, in my love for Paddy and with Ada's help I had done just that.

I couldn't have managed without Ada. Paddy wasn't fit enough to go out on his own, so it was Ada who put a notice in the paper for a girl to do the char work. Two days a week was all we could afford; Paddy's debts had swallowed most of the money from the sale of *Lionleigh*.

Ada was that worried for her father she brought home some pills from the chemist, which she said I must make him take.

They're for nervous disability, Mother. Father isn't himself and it's no use pretending otherwise. He told me this morning Dr Royce was slow in calling. How could he forget he lives in Brisbane?

It may have slipped his mind, I said.

Stop putting your head in the sand, Ada said. She got quite upset and went off in a huff.

I don't know why I said that. I knew Paddy's mind was going astray. I didn't like hearing it said outright I suppose, not with the unwelcome stranger we had in the house. I was loath to give the creature countenance and encourage it to further boldness. A foolish notion maybe, but that's how it seemed to me, not having the benefit of Ada's book-learning. A stranger had got loose in Paddy's head while he wasn't on his guard and was unravelling the thread of his thoughts. For by now he was forgetting things regular and giving way to misplaced angers. The worst of it was when he began to mistake us.

Is that you, Meg? he'll say if hears me in the hallway. Or, Harry! he'll call, and a few minutes later, Harry! again, and bang his stick on the floor. Where is the boy? he'll say when I come in the room. Is he in the bush with Billy Stapleton?

But mornings and evenings he's out in the paddock with the horses, which puts him in better heart. And for a time Dr Callaghan rode up the hill on Mondays to sit with him and talk racing. Such a good man the Doctor, himself failing in health, and that busy with his charities and committee work, yet still made time for Paddy. And once they were seated you wouldn't know anything was different.

Paddy became lively then, going over the stories of their palmy days in the Arjaycee, and often as not remembering better than Dr Callaghan as to what horse won which race, or what age it had on it, or who the sire was.

But the Doctor is dead these past twelve weeks—took quite sudden and unexpected by his heart, God bless the dear man—and without his company Paddy grows morose. He keeps forgetting his friend has gone to a better place, and in bed such a turmoil of despair comes over him, at first I had no idea what to do. But then I thought to sing him lullabies, the ones I sang to the children. The same ones Mam sang to Ellen and me. God must have given me that idea for those songs proved very soothing.

You never were bad at singing, he said when I came to the end of one. But watch out for snakes now. They like music and might creep under your gown.

An old bushman's fancy, he had told me about it once. I smiled and began another slow air till I saw his eyes close and his breathing deepen.

Are you sleeping? I whispered.

He opened his eyes. I am not. I'm worrying now.

Why would that be?

The children, he said. They're spending too much time with the Stapleton boy. You must put a stop to it.

Sure and I will, I said, and took up the lullaby again. He was asleep before I finished.

I quenched the lamp and lay beside him, the two of us stretched out in the bed that once was the raft of our loving. Such seas we have sailed in this bed, crying out and holding each other till the storm of our passion abated. Words cannot tell the grand journeys we made in this bed and it breaks my heart to see him the way he is now. Ah the poor man, the poor darling man, he is the chapter of my verse, there is no saying otherwise.

One morning in the wash-house I sensed someone behind me and when I turned round Douglas was standing in the doorway.

Glory to goodness, I said. Is it you, Douglas?

Where you been go, missus? he said, flashing his huge smile. This fella been look out for you. You go walkabout I think.

'Twas yourself went walkabout, I said, grinning back. But come up to the house, Douglas. Come with me now. Mr Wilson will be that glad to see you.

Paddy got excited, I knew he would. Where the bushfire have you been? he said, his eyes lighting up and the grin on him like an imp's.

I been look down that road, my dream road, Douglas said.

Curious words. I wonder what he meant by them. But you can never know what is in a black man's head? They have their own religion and don't like to talk about it to us whites.

It warms my heart when I look up from staking the beans and see Paddy and Douglas in the horse-paddock. My man has none of his old diversions, billiards or the races or judging blood-stock. He hasn't wits enough, but with Douglas he can talk horses and laugh. Douglas always made Paddy laugh, he's a laughing man himself and has a great store of comical capers and jokes. I hear them cracking up when I'm in the garden.

The flower beds have been let go to rack, and the weather being pleasant-warm I spend a few hours most days setting the beds to rights. And see again the lagoons glinting on the flats. The ducks will be coming in to settle for the night while I carry armfuls of wattle blossom to the house. Being winter, the trees are heavy laden with the sweet-smelling tossy-balls and to put your nose among their soft gold is to know a bee's heaven. I can never resist picking them though I know they'll only drop pollen on the table.

I came in from the garden one afternoon and found Ada waiting for me. Mother, she said, I didn't like to tell you before but I wrote to Harry and told him about Father.

Ah love, you shouldn't have. He has his own family to worry about.

Someone must be worried, she said. And since you're not it must be Harry. Here's his reply, it's addressed to you.

With that she put an envelope in my hand and waited while I opened it.

Dear Mum,
Ada says Dad isn't too good so Mary and I have talked it over and decided to come down for a visit. Milly is four and Meg two but Mary says they are able for the voyage so we'll see you in September. Don't bother coming to the wharf. Cissie and her husband will meet us and bring us up the hill. I had a good day at the races on Saturday you will be pleased to hear. I won the gentlemen's hack race by a good yard.

Your loving son Harry.

Oh the blessed day. I hugged Ada and kissed her and she said, Calm down, Mother, and took the letter to read. I got it back after and went in the bedroom to pore over it again. Then folded the paper and put it in the biscuit tin with Ellen's letters.

I'm in such a dither of joy. Harry is coming home and Mary and the children with him. And he's well and hopes I am too. In deed and in truth I'm not all that good. The worry over Paddy maybe, but of late I've been getting pains in my chest and have to sit down. Real fierce they are sometimes and leave me feeble, but what matter. At my age you must expect a few pains. All that matters is Harry's coming home and I will meet my grandchildren.

And Harry will know what to do, what's best for Paddy, and we'll all be together. No wonder I'm all of a flutter.

Such a drear sight my man is, hunched under his blanket, though it's not cold now that spring has come. Ada is seeing to dinner tonight so I can keep an eye on Paddy, and we're on the back verandah as usual, watching Douglas put Chieftain through his paces. No brandy to warm him tonight. He has no taste for it anymore.

I wonder is he thinking of Harry? He keeps forgetting our boy is coming up the hill tomorrow. Each time I tell him he gets excited as if he never heard it before.

That sup of rain we had yesterday has put new tongues on the bushes I see, and freshened the flowers wonderful. The box-tree might be a bride the way it is clothed in white. But September is always the most beautiful month in Australia, the air that sweet with blossom, birds everywhere, supping from the flowers. I always like watching them. Butcher-birds giving out their evening song, that tuneful in their callings you forget their horrible butchering ways. They'll be asleep soon anyway, bedded down for the night.

In Ireland it won't be butcher-birds, 'twill be corncrakes giving out their lonesome calls among the corn. The fields should be ready for harvest now, or is it August? Sure, it's a long time ago and I've forgot. It does flit through my dreams sometimes, the old farm at Ballyconnell, the sweet loamy smell of the grasses in particular. Ellen and myself among them, running about blowing dandelions. The queer thing is, *Rookwood* is like the old house the way it's set in a broad surround, with paddocks beyond and lakes below. The bats and swallows even, they're much like the ones at home.

Like a centaur, Paddy says on a sudden, making me start. It's not often he says anything these days. He's watching Douglas on the stallion so he must be talking about him, but I don't know what a centaur is.

When they turn it's the one animal, he says. If Douglas was a gentleman or a jockey he'd soon show the rest of us up.

Like Conan, I say.

Paddy's eyes are fixed on Douglas. Never heard of him. A jockey is he?

A king, I say. Yourself and Douglas, remember, at Serpentine Water. Like kings you two were, riding round the paddocks.

He's not listening. Just look at the seat the man has, he says, and gets up with the help of his stick and goes down the steps. He is going out to the paddock, still wrapped in his blanket, and Douglas getting off the black stallion to bring it to the gate.

Talking now. Paddy stooping to run his hand over Chieftain's front leg. The grass flowers under his feet yellow as pats of butter.

Douglas leads Chieftain a little way off, to check the way he walks most likely. Coo-up, coo-up! Paddy calls.

But what's this sudden darkening overhead?

Birds! Flying fast, hiding the sun. Not geese, thank the Lord. When the wild geese come to the lagoons Douglas will go away to hunt them, and not a bit of use asking him to stay.

Oh what will Paddy do then?

We have pulled together well, not counting a few missteps, just as he said we would. So long ago he said that, I scarce can remember who I was then. A stranger it seems to me now, though she still lurks inside my wrinkled skin. I hear her whispering sometimes, telling over the sweet joys of her youth, myself listening, yearning or smiling as the fancy takes me. So many years fled away and so many people gone with them. Was it Burns said man was made to mourn? I suppose he meant women too, for I mourn for Paddy I do, for the affliction that is taking him from me. And I fear for him, that it will steal his dignity and leave him a sad remnant of himself. Sorrow the day when that happens. The sun will come up over the Berserker Mountains but I won't care to see it.

It is slipping below the horizon now, the sun. The trees have lost their fire but the men are still yarning, and there's just enough light to see Douglas waving his arms as he tells one of his stories. Already the bushes look like sleeping beasts but I sit in the gathering dusk, watching my man. Pain stabs my chest but I ignore its clutch because suddenly fireflies are among the jasmine on the verandah posts. Fairy lights they might be, the way they tempt you, but I must get up and close the doors. If they come in the house, and they surely will, the foolish creatures, the little lightsome things are done for.

ACKNOWLEDGMENTS

My mother Elsie had the gift of the gab and it was her anecdotes about her grandmother Annie Callaghan that sparked my interest in Annie's story. Elsie had heard from her mother Cissie that Annie was 'bog-Irish', kept to the kitchen when her husband's friends came to call, and had big feet. Peasant feet, my mother said. As I have big feet this drew me to my great-grandmother and made me wonder what thoughts Annie had entertained while hiding in the kitchen. Years later, when nearing the end of her life, my Aunt Shirley confided to me a carefully guarded family secret: our ancestress Annie Callaghan, a dirt-poor Catholic girl, had on arrival in Australia accepted an unknown gentleman's proposal and married him 'off the boat'.

This struck me as romantic—heaven knows why, since it was clearly the opposite—and inspired me to research Annie's history and give her the voice she wasn't allowed to have in life. From Shirley I also learned that Paddy's parents undertook the arduous sea voyage to Australia to meet their grandchildren, but refused to meet their daughter-in-law.

So many people have helped in the creation of this book, but special thanks must go to Isabel D'Avila Winter who from the beginning inspired me to keep writing Annie's story. The close reading and spot-on advice given by Ali Sinclair, Alex Nahlous, Lesley Chase and Jessica White were equally invaluable. Teresa Dunne of Kilbeggan alerted me to the fact that the family belief that Edward Wilson came from an aristocratic family was incorrect, and the truth was far more interesting.

Literary agent Sophie Hamly, and Clem Cairns of Fish Publishing generously offered their time and professional advice, while Sarah McKenzie of *Hindsight* gave me hope by believing in Annie's story. Special thanks go to Ian Wilson and his mother Helen, for the pleasure of knowing them, if only electronically, and learning more about our shared family history. A big thank-you to my goddaughter Kim Dixon; as my imagined reader you kept me on the straight and narrow.

Grateful thanks to Kathy Panton, Athol Chase, Marcus Hockings, Kathleen Hastings, Ted Reithmuller, Helene Young, Ruth MacDonald, Margaret Kennedy, Denise Traynor, Lynne and Peter Priem, Ann Neville, Stephen Little, Cheryl Rickard, Dawson River man Ross Watson, Concepta McGovern, Kevin Kearney, John Fletcher, and the ever helpful staff at the Queensland State Library and Mitchell Library. Thanks also to the Queensland Literary Awards for their gift of a mentorship award with novelist Pamela Rushby.

I particularly want to thank the voluntary workers who continue to make the treasures of Trove available to the public. My great-grandfather Edward Wilson was a well known racing identity in his time, and the ups and downs of his impetuous career were regularly recorded in Rockhampton's colonial newspapers—information now easily accessible through Trove. These wonderfully informative broadsheets were three in number: the *Capricornian*, *Northern Argus*, and *Rockhampton Bulletin*, and proved a rich resource for which I can never be sufficiently grateful.

As in everything else, my greatest thanks go to Peter Kearney for his unfailing support and encouragement.

www.ingramcontent.com/pod-product-compliance
Lightning Source LLC
Chambersburg PA
CBHW022010010726
47494CB00003B/972